Whiskey Lullaby

Keren Hughes

ISBN 978-1-912768-97-4

Published 2020

Published by Black Velvet Seductions Publishing

Dedication

This book is for you, nan. You gave me my love of music from a very young age, and though I have eclectic tastes, I am a country girl at heart. You taught me to love Garth Brooks right from when I knew what music was. You told me he was the 'King of Country' and I'd have to agree with you.

Acknowledgements

To my nan; thank you for always being my inspiration. I love you from the bottom of my heart. It feels strange living in a world where you're no longer here. Your passing hit me hard and I didn't want to read, let alone write. But then after a while, I realised you wouldn't want me to give up, so I poured myself into my work and now I've written fourteen books. Can you believe it? Actually, you would believe it. You never doubted me.

Thank you for always being my biggest cheerleader. I owe so much to you. A debt I'll never be able to repay. You were my mum, my rock, my everything. I still feel your love surrounding me every day. You are my North Star. I love you. <3

To my son, Calum; thank you for always being you. You're funny, witty, smart and I love the bones of you. You are the very best part of me. Being your mum is the best thing I could ever do. Thank you for cheering me on in my writing all the time. I am humbled every time you say you're proud of me. Love you, kiddo. <3

To Jodie, the daughter I never had; thank you for being my best friend, my sounding board, the Coraline to my Other Mother. You're beautiful, funny, intelligent and sassy. I love your sarcasm and that it seems to be our second language. Whether we're talking in *Friends* quotes, or you're sending me memes—as seems to be your hobby—I'm always happy when I'm talking to you. Thank you for being my BETA reader, my constant companion and my moral support. I love you. <3

To my BETA girls: Anne, Melinda, Kara & Shawna; thank you for reading and loving this book. Your support means the world to me. In a world where I am sometimes unsure what I am doing, your love for my work is what keeps me sane. <3

To Ric, my boss-man; thank you for always taking a chance on my writing. For every contract I've signed with you. I've not only gained a publisher; I've gained a friend. Thank you for everything.

To Jessica, my cover designer; thank you, as always, for another amazing cover.

To readers, bloggers and everyone else; thank you for choosing to read my books. Without amazing readers, authors wouldn't be able to do what we love most. We'd have stories in our heads but no-one to tell them to.

Thank you for your continued support. It means the world to me every time someone takes a chance on my books. It means the world to get reviews that talk about what you guys loved. I am humbled by every review—both positive and negative, because without the negative ones, how would I grow as an author? I wouldn't!

Whether you've been here since my journey began in 2013 or only just picked up a book by me, thank you for everything. You rock!

I hope you all enjoy Caleigh and Brent as much as I enjoyed creating them. <3

Keren xoxo

Love is like playing music;
First you must learn to play by the rules,
Then you must forget the rules
And play from your heart.
~Unknown~

Prologue

Once upon a time a girl met a boy, looked at him and BAM! She instantly fell in love. Isn't that how all fairy tales start? Well not mine. Let me tell you my story. It goes a little like this…

I'm sitting in the airport, and because of my obsessive need to be early for just about everything I am far too early to board my flight. I'm obviously less obsessive about my need to charge my Kindle because that darn thing won't turn on, so I know I'll have to wait a long-ass time to finish reading my deliciously dirty new obsession.

I am so bored it's untrue. I'd go to the gift shop and look for a book, but if the weight of my luggage is anything to judge by, it would only take one tiny book to make me incur excess-weight charges. No thank you. I paid enough for this darn flight as it is. I'm not paying one penny more. Especially not for a cheap book.

My mum always tells me I'm too tight. Her favourite thing to do is tell me I have short arms and long pockets, aka I'm a penny pincher. But I have to be on the meagre wages I earn as part-time barmaid. That's one of the reasons I flew here in the first place—I've had an interview for a new job. Lord knows whether it went well or not. I'll just have to hope.

Anyway, I digress. Back to my unending boredom.

I pick up my phone to look at my social media, and as I do, Tinder sits there looking at me, daring me to finally swipe right.

I open the app and swipe left so many times I fear I might actually get RSI. Suddenly a voice pipes up from behind me.

"Ouch. That's a hard no for that guy then?!"

I don't answer right away, so he speaks again, sending shivers through me with the sound of his gravelly voice.

"Seriously, what was it about that dude that made you swipe left so hard?"

"Nothing in particular, I just—"

And that's when I turn around to get a good look at who I'm talking to.

My heart feels like it's going to fall out of my ass. I didn't take a very good look at the guy on the screen, but now I'm staring at the guy behind me, I just know it's the same guy I just swiped past.

"I-I … I just don't swipe right," I finish awkwardly.

I feel my skin flush profusely. I don't know what else to say, so I'm sure I look like a goldfish as my mouth opens and closes.

"Then may I inquire as to the point of being on such a dating site?" he asks, a puzzled look crossing his face.

"Oh, umm … well … my mother. She constantly moans at me about finding a nice guy. But I hate internet dating. It doesn't give you much of an impression of the guys. They umm … well, they mostly just want to hook up and I'm not *that* kind of girl."

I'm babbling and I know it, but he's got me flustered and that expression on his face tells me he knows as much.

Suddenly the tannoy booms with a boarding call for a flight. I have no idea where it's going, but wherever it is, that's where I'm going too.

"Oh, umm … if you'll excuse me, that's my flight," I say as I hastily grab my bag and slide my phone into my pocket.

"No worries," he says with a smile.

My palms are sweaty as I race to get away from him. The annoying click-clack of my heels rings in my ears as I rush towards the door of the ladies' room.

Once I'm in the stall, I close the door and sit on the lid of the toilet. Normally I would hesitate to use public toilets—just the thought of them normally makes me shudder—but right now, I need somewhere to hide.

I pull my phone out and close the dating app. Pulling up my best friend's number, I hit call and wait for her to pick up. At the message on her answerphone, I hang up and shoot her a text instead, telling her I was only calling to say I'd made the journey to the airport safely and would call her when I get home.

Looking at the time on my phone, I see I still have over ninety minutes left to wait until I can board my plane. The question is what to do in the meantime. I can't very well walk back out and risk him still being there. Instead I decide not to move an inch. I just sit up straighter and pull up the Kindle app on my phone, which is what I should have done in the first place. If I had just done that, I wouldn't be in this mess.

When I finish the book, I check the time again. Thank goodness I didn't miss my flight due to the highly combustible book I was engrossed in. Seriously, any hotter and it would have melted my phone.

Walking out of the ladies' room with my head held high, I race to the lounge. Thankfully, there's no sign of Mr. Tinder.

Breathing easily, I take a seat and wait for the tannoy to announce it's time to board.

Chapter One

Caleigh

I can't believe my rotten bloody luck. I'm stuck in a window seat. That's what you get for waiting until last minute to book a ticket. You get the shitty seat next to the guy with overpowering body odour. But at least there's nobody sitting next to me yet, so I inhale the clean smelling air while I can.

I really wish I could ask the flight attendant for a whiskey to calm my nerves. I hate flying. I hate being shoved into ridiculously tight spaces like I am crammed into right now. And it's only set to get a lot worse when someone sits down next to me.

There's never enough room in these seats.

I close the blind on the window, not wanting to look out when we eventually take off. I know, statistically speaking, I'm actually safer on a plane than in a car, but right now I'd give anything to be in my little red Miata, or better yet, home in bed. The job, if I get it, isn't even far from home, but their headquarters is a couple of hours away by plane, longer by car. Though I did almost convince myself to drive instead of being stuck in a flying tin can. The only reason I didn't is because I hate long journeys in the car. I feel almost claustrophobic. That might sound silly to others, but I've always been a person who needs space and fresh air.

Flying was the lesser of two evils only because it was faster. So here I am, like it or not.

We've been waiting what seems like forever for all the passengers to get on board, but in reality, it's probably only been minutes. I keep looking at my watch, but you know what they say about a watched pot never boiling. So, I sit back and try to get comfortable. I pull my sleep mask out of my bag, wriggle it over my eyes and focus on my breathing.

In for three seconds, out for three seconds, just like I was taught to try and combat my anxiety. When that doesn't work, I try tapping it out. It doesn't work for everybody, but it seems to do the trick for me. However, I'm not at the point of needing that. Not right now.

"Your seat is just there, sir," the bubbly flight attendant says from somewhere close.

I almost take my mask off to take a peek, but I can't find the energy. I'm trying my best to be chilled here, after all.

"Excuse me, miss," a voice says. "Your bag seems to be on my seat."

Wait one gosh-darned minute. I know that gravelly voice.

No, no, no. A thousand times no. It can't be him. It just can't.

Pulling my mask off, I move to grab my bag from the seat next to me and look up right into the chocolate brown eyes of Mr. Tinder. Well, knock me down with a feather. What in the ever-loving fuck is he doing on my flight?

"Oh," he says as he stares at me. "It's you. I thought you caught a flight to Barcelona?"

A mischievous smile lights up his features. Features that I am now noticing to be rather handsome. Why did I swipe left on him again? I can't fathom how I'd do that to someone with such enticing eyes and that chiselled jaw covered with a scruffy but sexy beard.

"I ... umm ... I ..." I can't think of a convincing lie.

Someone shoot me. Shoot me now. Please, someone have mercy on me. I can't think what to say, and he knows he has me cornered. His eyes twinkle with mirth as he takes his seat next to me.

Oh my god, he's so close. And to think I was worried about a man with overpowering body odour. I should have been worried about a man with come-to-bed eyes and a delicious smell of rich aftershave. Something woodsy. I can't put my finger on what.

"Go on," he urges with a playful smile.

"Well ... look, I-I won't lie. Well, not again, anyway." I try to stifle a giggle as he laughs at me, knowingly. "I just ... Oh, I'm not making much sense."

"Would you like to start again?"

"Yeah, okay. Umm ... truth is, I was just flustered earlier. I shouldn't have lied, but you caught me swiping left on you. What else was I supposed to do? I'm sorry. I actually should have just told you the truth. But the truth is, I just don't know what I would have said."

"I meant would you like to start again as in start over from meeting, like, you know, start a clean slate. But thanks for the apology."

"Oh."

My voice squeaks out high-pitched and almost painful.

Mr. Tinder bursts out laughing, and I can't help but join in with him.

***

The rest of the journey is spent making idle chit-chat. He introduces himself as Rhett. Yes, after Rhett Butler in *Gone with The Wind*. It was his mum's favourite film, and their surname is Butler, so he has—in his opinion—a rather clichéd name.

He tells me about his siblings—two brothers and a sister. He says Eliza has always been like his shadow, always choosing to follow her eldest brother around as a kid. It makes me laugh when he says that she's a feisty young thing, which in his opinion is just like me.

I know I'm feisty. I won't lie. But I guess I've had to be. I've grown up fighting my own battles. No siblings to protect me. I had to grow a thick skin and wear it as my armour every time someone had a problem with me. Which in high school was pretty often.

I guess I come off as feisty to people that don't know me very well, much like Rhett, because I have long pink hair, tattoos on my arms and multiple piercings, including the most recent addition of something called an Ashley—a piercing in the middle of my lower lip. I look … different to most people, always choosing to have my own style rather than being a sheep who follows the latest trends. I'm not a goth, but a lot of my wardrobe is black. I dress for comfort over style.

People that spend time with me know that I'm a big softie at heart. I think I keep most people at arm's length and act like a bitch because that way I don't get used.

I've always been the type to wear my heart on my sleeve, but all that's ever earned me is heartache and pain. So I've learned to disguise that about myself.

Rhett keeps me entertained with stories of his siblings and what it was like to grow up being the eldest of four. He seems sweet and genuine. I realise somewhere along the way that I shouldn't have swiped left on him, but his Tinder pic and bio didn't give much insight into who he is. I wasn't to know he was actually pretty cute under that rugged beard, as well as funny and down to earth. Just goes to show my mother was right when she said never to judge a book by its cover.

He buys me a much-needed whiskey and I relish the slow burn as it travels down my throat. It also calms my nerves about flying. Or is that more to do with Rhett himself?

As I hail a taxi outside the airport, Rhett helps me wheel my bags and loads them into the boot of the car. Who said chivalry was dead? It almost has me swooning. Almost. I'm not some dewy-eyed teenager after all.

My taxi pulls away from the kerb and I'm left wondering who Rhett is and what he's doing in River's Edge. It's a quiet little town, not some suburban concrete jungle, the likes of which I imagine he's used to. When I say little, I mean remote and with not much to do.

We have a population of only a couple of hundred people. There's a post office, a small school and a corner shop. For food, we have to either survive on what the shop has in stock or go further afield for a supermarket. There's also a pub, Da Vinci's Lock. Or as the locals call it, The Lock. It was so named because Leonardo Da Vinci invented the locks we see on rivers and canals today. That ends my knowledge on the subject. I only know that much because I work there part-time. Then there's the bed and breakfast and that's about it really.

I love it here. The people are friendly and the rent is reasonable. Yes, everyone knows everyone's business, but it's not like we're a bunch of gossips or anything. It's just hard not to know everything about everyone when you're so tight knit.

I ponder what Rhett could be here for. A holiday? Maybe, but we're hardly a tourist trap.

As we pull up outside my little cottage, the front door opens, and Hardin runs down the garden path and pulls my door open. I smile as my baby hugs me so tightly you'd think I'd been gone for a month, not a couple of days.

Managing to move to the boot of the car with a small human being clinging to me is a feat in itself. I grab my bags and pay the driver before wheeling my case up the path to the front door where my mum is waiting for me.

"Caleigh, darling, you're home," she says with a pearly white grin. "Did you have a good flight?"

"As good as flying in a tin can gets, I suppose."

I choose not to tell her about Rhett. She'd only read too much into it.

"It's so good to see you, Mummy. Did you get me a present?"

I look down into the most beautiful green eyes I've ever seen and feel a genuine smile grace my face.

"Oooh, I can't remember," I lie as I rub a hand over my chin, pretending to be lost in thought. "Did I buy a present for the most gorgeous person in the world? Hmm."

"You did, Mummy, you did. You promised me you would, and you *never* break a promise."

I open my carry-on bag and pull out the gift-wrapped parcel. Hardin's eyes light up like it's Christmas. I hand it to him, and he runs into the house to open it.

"Here darling, let me help you with those," my mum says as she grabs my bag.

I wheel my case in behind her and crane my head around to look at Hardin as he pulls the last of the gift-wrap off his present.

My little angel is five and he's due to start school this autumn. I can't believe where the time has gone. One minute he's swaddled in a blanket, held tightly against me, smelling the way only a new baby does, and the next he's starting school.

It's hard being a single mum, but my mum and dad have been a godsend in that respect. Sadly, Hardin's father passed away when he was only two years old, leaving me a widow at the age of thirty-one, and Hardin had to grow up without him. We have pictures on the mantel and pretty much every wall in the house. He knows how much his daddy loved him until he took his last breath. I often tell him bedtime stories about Angelo, about the things we got up to and who he was. He was a good man, taken way too soon. But that's something we have to live with.

"Mummy, you told me that this game hadn't even come out yet," he pipes up as I walk into the living room.

I don't often buy him video games. I prefer to take walks with him, go on day trips, pack a picnic and go to the beach—even if it's an hour's train journey away. A lot of children spend too much time with gadgets these days. That's something I never did as a child and I had a happy childhood, so I want the same for my boy.

"I know, baby. Mummy wanted to surprise you."

He runs up and tackle hugs me, which in turn ends up in a tickle fight that has me landing on my ass with a hard bump.

There's nothing more I like than being a mum. Hardin has made me a better person these last five years. Being a mother can do that to you.

Chapter Two

Brent

I lied because it's easier than explaining who I really am. But lying to Caleigh felt like it physically hurt me. I wanted her to like me for me, not for the fame and fortune. But thinking back on it, she didn't really strike me as the materialistic type. I probably could have told her who I am, and she wouldn't have batted an eyelid. But I didn't, and now, if I bump into her—which there's rather a large chance in a town as small as this—I'll have to keep up the pretence. Rhett Butler. How fucking stupid am I? Of course she's seen *Gone with The Wind*, and when I introduced myself as Rhett, she asked if my mum had been a fan of the film. Which, of course, she really is. But then I ended up adding to the lie that our surname was Butler and that's why Mum had chosen my name.

Realistically, it was the only name I could think of when Caleigh had asked. Now it'll have to be my name for as long as I'm here—however long that may be.

I mean, I needed to use a pseudonym anyway, but why one so clichéd? *Damn Brent, you're an idiot of the highest order*, I think to myself as I scrub a hand over my face.

I feel the stupid beard that I hate so much and wish I didn't have to be in disguise. But I can't have anyone finding out I'm here. All it would take is one teenager to ask for a selfie and post it online, then all and sundry could find out exactly where I am and descend like the vultures they are.

I don't mean that our fans are vultures. I mean the paparazzi. They'd give their right arm to get a picture of me to sell to the tabloids. And that is the last thing I want right now. I came here for peace and quiet.

My head spins with an oncoming migraine as I check into the bed and breakfast. Audrey, the proprietor, leads me to my room and tells me just to pick up the phone if I need anything. I won't, not for a while anyway. I intend to take a nap to try and stave off the incoming migraine.

"Dinner will be served at five-thirty, Mr. Butler. But don't hesitate to ask if there's anything you need before then," she says with a smile.

"Thank you, Audrey. I'll be sure to let you know."

"I hope you enjoy your stay."

Me too, I think as she closes the door behind her.

I strip to my boxers and slide underneath the duvet. The warm material cocoons me and lulls me to sleep.

***

I wake and look at the clock on the bedside table. It's five o'clock. How on earth did I sleep so late? I lie still and close my eyes for a second, feeling no sign of the migraine from earlier. Thank goodness for that.

I get up, pull fresh clothing from my suitcase and head for a quick shower in the en suite before heading down to dinner. There's a towel hanging on the radiator, so I grab it and throw it over the glass door of the shower.

Standing under the hot jets, I allow the water to soothe my aching muscles, relieving all the tension in my shoulders. As I begin to relax, I grab the little bottle of shower gel from the shelf and chastise myself for not grabbing my own from my case. This will have to do for one shower.

Closing my eyes, I lather up the soap in my hair—having also forgotten to grab my shampoo—and let the water wash it away. Behind my eyelids, I picture a beautiful pink-haired woman with stunning green eyes. She's the epitome of sassy, spunky, feisty and fun. All the things I need to stay away from, but am drawn to, nonetheless.

On the plane, we'd been in such close proximity that I could smell her perfume, see the ink adorning her arms in all its resplendent glory …

I can just picture those soft, full pink lips. Especially the bottom one with the way it was pierced in the centre. I wonder what it would be like to kiss someone with that kind of piercing. But such temptations lead me to a place I cannot go. I'd only end up hurting her, and that's the last thing I want to do.

I didn't come here to get tangled up in something romantic. Nothing good could ever come of it. Nobody ever realises what they're letting themselves in for when they open up their world the way I have mine.

Even I didn't realise at first. That's one of the reasons for my hiatus from the band.

Tired of fame, fortune, and women throwing themselves at my feet. Tired of being in the press for my "assignations" as my mum calls them. Tired of them printing lie after lie about me. I'm just so bone tired of it all.

The boys didn't understand when I said I needed a break from the headlines. Ash said there's no such thing as bad publicity, but that's bullshit.

There was never going to be a good time for me to take a break, but right in the middle of the tour might just have been the worst. Our manager, Gordon, was outraged when he heard I was gone. He insisted—to my voicemail because I refused to answer the phone—that I "get my ass back right now or find myself in breach of contract and at risk of being forced out of the band".

It's not that I don't care. I do. It's just that nobody understands how much I need to get away. For my sanity as much as anything.

I shake those thoughts from my mind and step out of the shower. I wrap the towel around me and wipe the condensation from the mirrored cabinet over the sink. As I look at my reflection, I don't recognise the man I see. His hair is grown out to almost shoulder length and his beard is shaggy. The chestnut colour of it is the polar opposite of the blond it used to be, until a few days ago.

I walk back into the bedroom to grab my toothbrush and toothpaste, then head back to the sink to brush my teeth. I mull over what I'm really doing before returning to the room to get dressed.

I make it downstairs at five-thirty on the dot, and Audrey compliments me on being punctual, which makes me smile. I always pride myself on being on time.

She shows me to a table by the window and I look out to see the river. It's beautiful as the evening light reflects off the water. Maybe I'll take a walk after eating. I literally don't have much else to do.

After eating a delicious medium well steak with homemade chips, I am full to bursting. Hats off to the chef; it was the best home-cooked meal I've had in what feels like forever. I miss my mum's cooking. But if I'd gone back to hers to get some rest, the paparazzi would have caught wind and I didn't want to bring a media storm to my mum and dad's door. My brothers and sister have all grown up and moved out, but they still don't need that shit on their doorstep. The thing is, as private as you wish things were, people always have a way of finding out where you live and setting up camp. So it's not like I could go off-grid if I went home or to stay with any of my family.

The wind whips up around me as I walk along the edge of the river. I find a stone and skim it across the water, something I always did with my siblings at the beach. It sinks and I carry on, moving wherever my feet take me.

Audrey suggested going to The Lock to grab a drink and relax. She said I'd find it if I followed the river. So I guess that's what I'm doing, stopping every now and then to gaze out across the water and wonder what my family and friends are up to right now. What would they think if they could see me now?

I wonder if they've heard about me going MIA. Nobody has called me, so I'm guessing that Gordon hasn't called them raging about their asshole son.

I can see a building at the bottom of the hill, which I assume is The Lock. I guess a whiskey couldn't hurt. It would sure warm me up from this biting wind. Audrey warned me that the evenings get pretty chilly around here. I should have listened and gone to my room to retrieve a warmer jacket, but I'm a stubborn mule, so I just left in my turtleneck jumper, jeans and all-important cowboy boots. It seems no matter what else I wear—unless it's a suit—I'm always in my favourite black leather boots.

I find myself humming as I stroll down the hill. I always looked up to the singer as the god of the genre as I was growing up. Pop music never really appealed to me. I can appreciate a good song, no matter the singer or the genre, but country is the music of my soul, and Garth Brooks writes songs that speak to my heart.

I sing along to the all-too-familiar melody, but quietly so as not to draw attention to myself. I don't want locals thinking I'm some kind of weirdo.

At the front door of the pub, I quit my singing and walk into a warm and seemingly friendly atmosphere. The bartender serves me a whiskey, neat. No sane person dilutes it, not in my book.

I find a table in the corner; it suits me because it's a little darker back here. I always fear recognition everywhere I go these days. I used to live for the fame, the fortune, the women who threw themselves at us everywhere we went. I used to love the limelight and to sign autographs for fans. Nowadays, I pull on a baseball cap and sunglasses, pull my coat up around me and walk as fast as I can, trying to outrun everything that comes with being a member of Whiskey Lullaby.

I slip my phone out of my pocket and do a quick Google search for the band. Articles pop up with headlines such as "Where's Brent Gone and When Will He Return?", "Brent Flakes on Band Members Mid-Tour", "Ryder Leaves Whiskey Lullaby: Is It Permanent?" and "Brent Ryder: Is He Sick or Sick of The Band?"

The one that makes me click it though is titled "Fans Are Furious at Brent Ryder for His Wanderlust."

I knew I'd hurt people—family, friends, fans—but the article says that fans are outraged that they paid to see the band and only got to see the other three. They're furious at me, as lead singer, for leaving without warning. Gordon is going to be batshit crazy when I finally stop ignoring his calls, sending him to voicemail without hesitation.

I never meant to piss off so many people. I never intended to hurt the fans. We've worked too long and too hard to get to where we are for fans to start dropping.

"Can I get you another?" a familiar voice asks, startling me so much I drop my phone.

I look up and see a flash of pink hair paired with emerald colour eyes. Oh boy. My cock twitches and I'm suddenly very grateful I chose to sit in a dark corner.

"Umm, that would be great, thanks."

Handing her my glass, I feel a tingling sensation as her warm hand brushes against mine.

"Jameson neat, right?" Caleigh asks with a smile.

"Right."

Great, so she's reduced me to being a man of very few words.

"I'll be right back."

I watch her denim-clad ass as she walks back to the bar. She's perky and upbeat, one of the things I like most about what I know of her so far.

Picking up my phone, I close the browser and slip it back into my pocket. I don't need to be reading all the articles slamming me for my sudden disappearance from planet earth.

Caleigh heads back in my direction and I watch as her perky breasts bounce softly with her stride. She's dressed in skin-tight jeans with a purple tank top, and I can see the ink adorning her arms. Remembering admiring the patterns on the plane, I inhale as she gets closer, committing the scent of her to memory. What I wouldn't give to trace the patterns on her arms with my fingers … or my tongue …

"There you go," she says with a megawatt grin as she hands me my glass.

"Thanks."

I set it down on a napkin and smile at her. I pull my wallet from my pocket and pay her for the drink, telling her to keep the change. She beams at me in appreciation before setting off, and I watch as she changes a bottle out on the optics before wiping down the bar.

She really is beautiful. But I'm not here for that. And if I really need to satiate my needs, that's what I use Tinder for. Although I'm sure in a town this small, they probably don't have many women on there for me to choose from.

Chapter Three

Caleigh

He watches my every move, and I don't know whether to feel complimented or creeped out. Having spent a couple of hours on a plane in a very confined space with the guy, I didn't get the feeling he was a creep, so I'll give him a pass for now.

I almost didn't recognise him in the dark corner of the pub, but nobody comes in here that I don't know. It's where all the locals hang out on a Friday night unless they venture further out of town. Plus, I kind of expected to see him in here at some point. I heard on the grapevine that he's staying at Audrey's B&B. There aren't many places to go around here, and I can't see him venturing out of town on his first night.

"He keeps his eyes fixed firmly on you, you know?!" Deb asks as she pours a pint of Guinness for a customer. "And he's cute too."

"Cute? Aren't *babies* cute?" I ask with a chuckle.

"Okay, he's hot as, but I'm a married woman so …" she trails off.

"You can look but you can't touch."

"Yeah, but *you* can touch, girl. And by the looks of it, he wouldn't mind if you did. In fact, he'd actively encourage it."

"Settle down, Deb. I'm not looking for anything with anyone, you know that."

She knows how broken I've been since I lost Angelo. He was the love of my life. We were two stupid kids when we got together, but young, dumb and infatuated blossomed into real love. A love so real that it took my heart and left me irreparably damaged when he died. The only thing that really keeps me going is our little boy, the one piece of Angelo I have left. He's the keeper of my heart now.

"Girl, you have to live a little sometimes. You have to get out of your own head. I know you're not looking for anything meaningful, but he's probably not here for very long—out-of-towners never stay long—so you should use that to your advantage. It's not like you could sleep with someone from here without it being the talk of the town, but—"

"Deb, seriously," I chide as I whip her with the bar towel.

"I give up," she quips as she throws her hands in the air.

"Good. Now get back to your job."

"Looking out for you is *my* job."

"Okay, get back to the job that pays."

She shrugs and goes to serve Dennis, the nicest guy you could wish to meet. He's about sixty-five and a widower. Dotty was his world until she passed away last year. Since then, he's been in here propping the bar up every night. Even if it's only for one drink. He enjoys the company more than the beer.

I'd like to say I don't know how he feels, but I know it all too well. I quit my job out of town to look after Angelo, and when I lost him, I didn't want to work. All I wanted was to hide out from the world or drown my sorrows. That's one of the reasons I ended up working here, because Damien was sick of seeing me propping up the bar with Dennis, so he offered me a job.

A customer shakes me out of my own head, so I get back to my job. When there's a lull in service, I take another Jameson over to the table for one.

"Thanks Caleigh."

"It's a pleasure." I go to turn away but stop at the last second. "So, staying at Audrey's, huh?"

"That's right. How did you know? Oh." He pauses momentarily. "Small town."

"Some say small, I say quaint. But yeah, town grapevine and all that."

"I didn't know you worked here. It's a nice place."

"Yeah, it used to be a bit more popular, but then Denny's opened on the outskirts of town. We lose out to them on a weekend now, but I don't mind when it's quieter like this."

"I'd say I'll check it out, but you might hate me."

"Of course I wouldn't. How long are you here for?"

"Oh, I don't know. I haven't made my mind up yet."

He looks almost pained as he speaks. It's not my business, but I'd say he's got something on his mind that he's trying to outrun. I know the look all too well, having seen it reflected back at me in the bathroom mirror every day for the first couple of years after Angelo died.

I still see it every now and again, but less frequently these days.

"Well it's not like it's the biggest town, but if you need a tour guide …"

"I might just take you up on that," he replies with a smile.

"Well, you know where to find me," I say with a wink, which I regret immediately, so I rush back to the bar. I was in such a rush, I forgot to take his money, but I'm too mortified to go back over there now.

"Who's the new guy?" Damien asks, startling me.

"Jeez, way to give a girl a heart attack, boss," I say with a palm to my chest.

"Oh, get over it already. So?"

"So, what?"

"New guy."

"Oh, umm … his name is Rhett."

"He just passing through or here to stay?"

"How the heck should I know?" I ask a little too defensively.

"Isn't it a barmaid's job to make small talk? You know, a bit like a hairdresser asks you where you're going on holiday."

"All I know is he's staying at Audrey's, so I'd assume he's passing through."

"Well crack open a bottle of the good stuff and he might be persuaded to drink here instead of Denny's."

"The good stuff?"

Damien hands me a bottle of Johnnie Walker and grabs a glass from under the bar.

"In fact, I may go over and introduce myself. Rhett, you said?"

"Yeah."

Damien pours two decent measures of JW and walks off in the direction of our guest.

I wipe down the bar and head to the washer to grab more clean glasses. After restocking the shelf with more mixers, I look up and see that Deb needs a hand. It seems the evening crowd are about to descend.

***

After a long evening, I'm wiped. Getting home to complete silence, I realise how much I missed Hardin while I was away. He stays with Mum whenever I have to work a night shift, but I really wish that wasn't the case tonight, having spent the last couple of days away from him. I guess I'll have to make it up to him tomorrow when I take him out for burgers and shakes at his favourite place, The Roadhouse, over in Pedmore.

Deciding I need to relax, I head up to run myself a bath. I pour in my favourite scented bubble bath, before stripping and testing the temperature with my toes.

As it warms up nicely, I slide down under the bubbles, grab a flannel and soak it before folding it and putting it over my eyes as I rest my head back.

The only thing that could make this bath complete would be a glass of wine. Oh, and maybe some nice chilled out music.

As the water cools, I pull the plug and wrap myself in a towel. My thoughts turn to next weekend's live music and how I can get the night off work. Nothing gives me more of a headache than the bands Damien books. What would it take for him to book somebody who plays something more than indie rock? I mean, it's no wonder we're losing custom to Denny's. This town is probably sick of the same old songs rehashed by different bands. I don't mind indie rock, but when it's all I hear two weekends out of every month, I get fed up.

I pull a fresh pair of pyjamas from the drawer and make sure my phone is on charge on the nightstand. Seeing a text from mum, I open it.

>Hardin was in bed by 8pm. Hope you didn't work too hard tonight. See you in the morning. Love you. Mum xx

I decide not to text her back because it's too late, but I'm glad to know Hardin is okay.

It's time I went to bed myself, so I slip under the duvet and turn off the bedside lamp.

Chapter Four

Brent

A brisk morning walk shakes off the cobwebs from last night. Having Damien's company last night meant drinking more than I'd intended. He's a cool guy. He told me if I'm still around that I should drop in next weekend to hear some local band play. I won't lie, it would be cool to hear live music again, even if it isn't my own. In fact, *especially* since it isn't my own.

Finding a place to sit at the edge of the river, I sit and listen to the birds in the trees. Music comes so naturally to them, which reminds me how much of a struggle it's been for me recently.

I slip my phone out of my pocket and dare to turn it back on. Too many missed phone calls and unread texts taunt me, plus that little red icon that says I have a voicemail, probably tons of them left by Gordon. I turn it back off immediately and put it back in my pocket.

A voice interrupts my internal thoughts about what comes next.

"Beautiful isn't it?"

I turn to look at the person and realise it's Damien from the pub.

"It is. So tranquil. I could sit here all day."

"How are you enjoying your stay so far?"

"Great, yeah. It's a lovely little town you have here."

"I bet it's not what you're used to at home, hey?" he asks with a chuckle.

"Yeah, you could say that. It's nice to have a bit of quiet time every now and then."

"If you are after a bit more life than you find here, Pedmore is a few miles that way," he says as he points in the general direction. "Do you have a car?"

"No. I didn't think to rent one at the airport."

"Well, I'm off into town this afternoon to go to the wholesalers, so if you want a lift, come by the pub around twelve."

"That would be great, thank you."

He offers me a smile and a nod before turning to walk in the opposite direction. He waves backwards over his shoulder and then leaves me to the peace and quiet.

I might as well take him up on his offer. It might have been better if I'd rented a car at the airport, but I couldn't risk using my driver's licence and credit card under my real name, and of course you can't pay by cash.

While I'm in town, I can see if there's somewhere to grab a pay-as-you-go SIM card for my phone. I'll text the boys in the band my number but ask them not to give it to Gordon. I know I'll have to talk to him eventually, but I'm not ready. I don't want to hear his speech about breach of contract or letting down the band and the fans, not to mention the pound signs in his eyes which is his main concern. He's losing money. But I can't help him with that, not right now. Maybe I never will again. I just don't know.

***

Damien drops me off in the town centre, telling me to text him when I'm ready to leave and he'll see if he's around to take me back. I try telling him I'll call a taxi, but he won't hear of it.

I'm wondering around aimlessly, just window shopping. It beats sitting in my room at the B&B, and there's only so much to see in River's Edge.

There's a newsagent advertising the sale of SIM cards in the window, so I slip my baseball cap a little further down over my eyes and head in. After grabbing one and topping it up, I head back out into the sun and take a seat on a low wall around a statue in the middle of the town.

I slip my phone out of my pocket and message the boys, using a group chat on WhatsApp. Of course, their first response is a flood of *Where the hell are you?* and *What are you doing?*, along with *How long until you come back?*. Then Jude brings up the topic of Gordon.

I reply, trying to evade the Gordon subject.

>I can't tell you where I am or how long until I come back. As for what I'm doing, you all know I've burned myself out lately, so I'm taking a hiatus.

Jude asks:
>And just what do we tell Gordon?

>I don't know. Tell him whatever you like, but you are not to give him my temporary phone number if I give it to you. You have to promise me.

Ash responds:
>New number? Dude, WTF?

>Just trying to dodge unanswered calls, texts and voicemails. Plus, he's probably got a bloody tracker on my phone, knowing Gordon.

>You're probably right, but you should call your mum, she's been going out of her mind.

>She knows all about it actually. If she's going crazy, it's for all of you and Gordon's benefit.

>Good to know you're still a mama's boy :P

>I called her before I left and again when my plane landed.

>Plane? Dude, you've left the country?

Ash is clearly as perceptive as ever.
It's not like Evan to be quiet, I guess he's either not around or he's just reading the conversation. One thing Evan Winslow is, is calculating. He's always playing the long game.
>Thank fuck Evan isn't here telling me to get my ass back on a plane this instant. I type, trying to bait him.

Ash replies:
>He's probably trying to figure out how to find out which plane you got on and where it was going. He'll jump on the next plane and drag you back home by your ear.

Evan chimes in at long last:
>I'm here, fuckers. I'm just waiting to see what's said. I'm also trying not to rip Brent a new one.

Jude replies:
>Look at you being mature for once.

He's the joker of the pack. He's always in trouble with Evan for something.

Evan is the 'daddy' of the band because he's a good five years older than the rest of us. Me, Jude and Ash were in the same year at school, but Evan was already in college by the time we started high school.

He's a great guy, don't get me wrong, but he's so stern and stoic. I like to think it's because he's not getting laid enough.

>Fuck you, Jude. Where are you, Brent? You'd better come up with an answer for Gordon soon you know.

>All in good time. I need some time and space. So, if you can't give me that, I'll give the boys my number privately and ask them not to give it to you.

>Jeez, calm your titties, Brenda. It's all good. I won't ring you constantly and I won't tattletale to Gordon. I'm not all bad, you know?! I do have a heart.

Jude replies:
>Yeah, you bleed compassion buddy.

Evan tells him to fuck off before he beats the crap out of him, and once they stop bickering back and forth, I give them my temporary number.

I turn my mobile data off so that I'm not interrupted by notifications. I won't even bother logging into social media while I'm here. And it's not like Tinder will show many fish in this particular pond.

Walking around a little while longer, I spot a guitar shop and stop to admire the Stratocaster in the window. It makes me miss the cherry red one I left at home. This one is sleek and black. It's beautiful.

The guy in the shop notices me, so before I can draw attention to myself, I set off at a brisk pace.

Once I'm safely away from the beautiful guitar, I stop to take stock of where I am. Not that I can get my bearings in an unfamiliar town, but because I'm thinking of calling Damien. I see a little bookstore, an independent place rather than a big chain kind of place. As if by some gravitational force, I find myself drawn towards the front door.

There's a tinkling sound as I open the door and the person behind the till looks up.

"Good afternoon," he says, his tone friendly and bright.

"Good afternoon," I reply with a small nod.

"Is there anything I can help you with?"

"I just thought I'd come and browse until something takes my attention, if that's okay?"

He smiles and nods at me and goes back to his book on the counter.

I wander around and look for the fantasy section. Once I find it, I pull out a copy of *The Hobbit* and admire its cover. It's an older edition and I find myself lifting it to my nose to inhale the scent. There's just something about the smell of a book.

I don't have much free time these days, and when I do, I don't spend it reading. I used to, before the band really took off. But these days, I'm busy writing songs and practising with the guys.

Slipping the book back into place, I look around for something to take back to the B&B with me. I spot a copy of *The Last Wish*, so I pick it up and take it to the guy at the till.

"Ah, good choice. Have you watched the Netflix series?"

"Not yet, I just haven't found the time. Too busy with the day job."

"Well, you know what they say about all work and no play," he jests.

I laugh, and he rings up my purchase before slipping it into a paper bag.

"Yeah, I'm owed some downtime. I doubt I can get Netflix at the B&B though, so I'll settle for reading it instead."

"I didn't think you were a local. Where are you from?"

"Leeds." The lie rolls off my tongue before I can stop it.

"You don't have much of an accent, if you don't mind me saying so."

I guess it's too late if I do mind, but I know he's just being friendly. I'm so used to lying to people about where I come from, not wanting fans to know where they can find me.

"I guess I don't," I reply, with a smile to let him know I'm not offended. "I moved around a lot as a kid and I travel for work, so ..."

"Oh, I see. Are you staying in town long?"

"I'm not actually sure yet. I'm staying in the next town over, but not sure whether it's a long break or not."

"River's Edge? Nice little place to take a break. Quiet, but then that's ideal for people who want to get away from the hustle and bustle of city life."

"It's a change of pace, for sure. Nice little place though."

"My niece works in The Lock. Beautiful lass with long pink hair by the name of Caleigh."

"Ah yes, we've met. Met on the plane actually, then again in the pub."

"Lovely lass. Her son is my only great-nephew. Handsome boy. Got his mother's looks, that's for sure."

I didn't know Caleigh had a kid. But then we haven't really talked much apart from small talk. And there were many things I omitted to tell her, so I can hardly blame her for not telling me her life story. I'm many things, but I'm not a hypocrite.

"I can't say as I've had the pleasure of meeting him yet."

"Oh, well if you do, please tell him hello from Uncle Ted."

"I will."

"Actually, would you mind giving Caleigh a message if you see her?" he asks as I turn on my heel, about to leave.

"Sure."

"Just tell her that Miriam is away for another week or so at her mother's."

"No problem, I'll be sure to tell her."

"Thank you. My wife's mother had a fall, you see, so she's been called to her side to look after her. She's already been gone for three weeks."

"Oh, that's terrible, I'm sorry to hear that, Ted. You must miss your wife."

"Boy do I? She's a far better cook than I am," he replies with a wink.

A chuckle escapes me. It feels good to talk to someone who hasn't got the foggiest idea who I am. Refreshing.

"I'll be back for book two in the series if I finish this one while I'm here."

"Sure thing. We're open six days a week. If I'm not here, it'll be my assistant, JoAnn."

"See you soon, Ted. I'll let you know if I manage to watch *The Witcher*."

"Aye, good lad. Have a good day."

"You too, Ted."

I offer him a wave before turning and making my way back out into the sunshine. Damn, I really should have bought a bookmark. Guess I'll have to use the receipt. I refuse to dog-ear the pages.

I pull my phone from my pocket, find Damien's number and press call.

"Hello?"

"Hey Damien, it's Rhett."

"Hey buddy, still in town?"

"Yeah, just left One More Chapter. Was going to call a taxi but realised I don't know the number for a local one."

"I'd rip you a new one if you called one when I'm still around anyway," he says with a laugh. "I'm just leaving the wholesaler. Give me ten minutes and I can meet you where I dropped you off."

"Thanks, buddy."

"Not a problem. See you in a few."

I bid him goodbye and slip my phone back into my pocket as I head off in the direction I came from.

Passing by Strings and Things again, a feeling of melancholy runs through me. I wish I'd brought my Stratocaster from home. I mean, I came here to get away from all that, hence why I left it on purpose. But there's just something about it that makes me long for some fresh song inspiration.

That's part of the problem. I seem to be completely burned out. I spend my days and nights writing, then scrapping and rewriting lyrics. Nothing seems good enough anymore. It was easier when it was just the boys and no record label.

Vox Records had our demo from Gordon, which got us a deal with them. That was six years ago now. Six years of being lead singer and guitarist. Six years of writing most of our songs. Of course, now they have to appeal to the public, not just to us lads anymore. So there was a slight shift in gearing our music to a larger audience. Not that we did badly before, just needed a few tweaks here and there. But having sold multi-platinum singles and albums worldwide in that time, it all seems like it's been done before nowadays.

We've done some covers in our time. "Friends in Low Places" was an obvious choice. It really suited Evan's voice and it's such a well-known song. "Peaceful Easy Feeling" was another track we covered, but only on the album, not as a single. Then there was the song we took our band name from, though why we chose such a morose song to name ourselves after, I don't know. "Whiskey Lullaby". Again, it was an album track. Gordon will only let us release original songs as singles.

Hearing a horn beep, I look up to see Damien's truck. He smiles and waves, so I run around to jump in the passenger side.

"Buy anything nice?" he asks as I buckle up.

"Just a book."

"Anything I would have heard of?"

"*The Last Wish* by Andrzej Sapkowski."

"Oh, that's a good one. The Netflix series is a *must*-watch."

"So Ted told me."

"You haven't seen it?" he asks with a small gasp.

"Not yet. Too busy working."

"Then we must remedy that. You won't get Netflix at Audrey's, but that's okay. I'll grab some beers from the pub, and we'll watch it back at mine. You free tonight?"

"As a bird. There's really no need though, you're a busy man."

"Nah dude, it's my night off. Deb's covering cos she wants next weekend off."

"I don't want to be too much trouble."

"You won't be. Meet me at The Lock at six?"

"Sure. Thanks, man."

"No worries. It's nice to have some company, especially when you don't know anyone in town. Although, I don't want to impose," he rushes to add. "It's just that there isn't much to do in town, so you might get fed up."

"You're not imposing, man. I can either spend the evening in my room reading, or I can open a few cold ones with you and chill."

"That's settled then."

We settle back and listen to the radio on the drive back to River's Edge.

"You got a good voice, man," Damien says as he switches the engine off.

Shit, I hadn't realised I was singing along. Give me good music and I just can't help it though.

"You should come along to karaoke night while you're here."

"Oh god, no. I don't like being the centre of attention," I say, rushing my words out.

"Please come? It would be good to hear a good voice. Most of the people who get up are drunk, so slur their words a bit. I mean, it's all good fun, but man, I'd love to hear you belt out a tune."

"Maybe after a few drinks to loosen me up," I say, to appease him rather than because I mean it. "Need a hand getting stuff into the bar?"

"Oh man, that would be great. Thanks."

It feels like the least I can do after he drove me into town and back, even if he said he was going that way anyway.

Helping lug boxes in is thirsty work. Damien offers me a beer, and I take a cold bottle off him with pleasure. It goes down nicely as I take a large swig.

"Cheers, buddy. Much needed after all this," I say, gesturing to the boxes piled up.

"Tell me about it. I usually do it all on my own. It's hard graft getting the beer barrels into the cellar, never mind having to change a barrel or two while I'm down here."

I help him carry some mixers up to the bar and stack them where I see a couple of each already.

"You don't have to do that, man. I can do that."

"It's no bother, really. Like you say, I'd be cooped up in my room at the B&B otherwise."

"On a sunny day like today? You wanna be taking advantage of the beer garden out back."

"That would be good."

I admit, I miss the guys back home. When we're not up to the eyeballs, we like to sun ourselves in the beer garden of our local pub. It's odd being here without their company.

A text chimes, so I pull my phone out, knowing it can only be one of three people.

>Hey, man, you should know Gordon is on the warpath. Says we're going to continue the tour without you, tell people you have pneumonia or something. He's really in a spin this time. Talking about losing money and fans not turning up to see just the three of us. Reckons the record label are gonna come down on him like a ton of bricks.

Well thanks for that, Jude. You just burst my bubble.

>Sorry, man, I can't help. Been burning the candle at both ends for too long now. Need this break. Sorry if I've put you guys in an awkward position.

I wait and see three dots.

>It's all good, man. We've got your back. But you have to know that Gordon was talking of dropping you permanently if you weren't so idolised by the fans.

I try to break the tension:

>Good job I have a pretty face then, huh?

>Damn good job, bro, I'm tellin' ya now.

Would Gordon really drop me? Fuck knows what goes through that man's mind. Well, except for money and women, that is.

>Okay. Chat soon. Got to go. Lending a helping hand.

>Oh yeah? She pretty?

>It's not a woman, you perv. Met a guy who owns a pub, just giving him a hand lugging crates and shit.

>Oh, okay. Have a good one. Oh, and Brent, you do deserve a break, we all know that.

>Thanks, bro.

Sometimes I don't know how I'd get through stuff if it wasn't for Jude. He might be a joker, but he's all heart really.

I know that the other guys deserve a break just as much as I do, and I know I shouldn't have upped and left mid-tour. But I was sick of having anxiety over every little thing.

When we first started the band, it was for fun. We tried different genres of music, but we found our niche in country music. It's like we were made for it. We got some ribbing in college over it, because all our friends were into rock and stuff. But when they heard us play, they understood why it was the right fit.

"What do you say to a Johnnie Walker?" Damien asks. "It's got to be five o'clock somewhere, right?!"

"Sounds good to me."

He pours us both a glass, then takes a seat at the bar. I settle next to him.

"So, should we order a takeaway later while we binge *The Witcher*?"

"Sounds like a plan. What's good around here?"

"Well, nothing in River's Edge. Luckily for us, places in Pedmore deliver. There's a great Chinese, or if you like pizza, there's this one place that does the best stuffed crust I've ever eaten. Or there's curry. Take your pick."

"Pizza with wings and potato wedges?"

"Sounds like a plan, my man. I'll take the beers I got earlier in town back to mine."

"You didn't get a bottle of JW did you?"

"I did. I noticed you were a shorts man rather than beer last night, so I wasn't sure what you drank."

"Anything alcoholic, bro. Beer and JW is all good. Unless you have an imported bottle of Macallan anywhere?!"

"Jeez, I wish I did. Last time I had that was when I was in the States."

"Snap."

We end up talking about some of our favourite spots in the US. I accidentally mention a couple of places the band have played but managed to play it off as having seen good bands there.

"You ever been to the Grand Ole Opry?"

"Yeah, man. What a place. Saw Garth Brooks there in 2005."

"Didn't have you pegged as a country man."

"Well, not just country, but when Garth plays, you go and watch him."

"Yeah, he's pretty fucking good alright. What's your favourite song of his?"

"You're putting me in a spot here, bro. Man," I scrub a hand over my face as I think, "I guess I'd have to say it's a toss up between 'Papa Loved Mama' and 'The Thunder Rolls'. You?"

" 'Callin' Baton Rouge' or a track he did on his album *Sevens*, called 'Belleau Wood'."

"That song, man. It gives me all the feels."

"You know it?" he asks with a tone of surprise.

"Yeah, I own all his albums," I confess with a wry chuckle.

"He's one talented dude."

"That he is," I agree a little too enthusiastically. "There's this one song called 'The Dance'. It was my sister's favourite growing up."

" 'If Tomorrow Never Comes' was my grandma's favourite. Guess she's the reason I know who he is."

I feel a pang in my heart as I listen to his words. My grandma must be furious to hear I'm not on tour doing what I love. She gave me my passion for music and has always been my biggest fan.

Pushing those thoughts away, I swig my scotch and smile as Damien pours me another.

"Last one, man. Otherwise, I'll be three sheets to the wind. I haven't eaten bar a croissant I snagged from breakfast at Audrey's."

We chat a little longer, nothing more than small talk about our families and how much I miss mine when I'm away. He's the kind of guy I could find myself admitting too much to if I'm not careful. He's just so open and friendly, it makes me feel at ease.

I don't think he's the kind of person to ring the press and tell them there's a celebrity in his town—god how I hate that word *celebrity*—but it's not a risk worth taking. Especially as Gordon would descend on the town like a goddamn storm cloud, zapping me with lightning for good measure.

***

I'm three chapters into my book when my phone chimes. I almost don't bother looking, but I pick it up from the bedside table.

>Buddy, Gordon is talking about suing your ass for breach of contract.

I am sick of hearing those last three damn words.

>He's all fur coat, no knickers. He won't do shit. Not if I can butter him up.

Evan replies:

>Wouldn't you have to answer the phone to do that?

>I'll send him an email. Just need access to a computer.

>Dude, you can email him from your phone. Unless you bought a

burner or something.

>No, I just changed out the SIM. Yeah, okay, I'll write him an email in the next day or two.

>You better make it sooner than later dude. I'm covering for you as best I can. He blows hot and cold. One minute we're going on the tour as planned and pretending you're sick. Next minute he's talking about suing your ass.

>I appreciate you covering for me, Ev, I really do. But man, when I said I needed space, I meant it. I need some space to think. Just please try to tamp down the flames of his temper until I can put into words why I did what I did.

>Sure. Look, I'm not a monster. I know you need a break. I've seen touring taking its toll on you. It could have come at a better time, sure, but it is what it is, and we'll deal. Whatever Gordon says, we're in this together.

>Thanks, bro. I really mean it. You're a good friend. Too good to me sometimes. I promise I'll tell Gordon and try to smooth things out.

>'K. Just take of yourself, kid.

I roll my eyes. I'll give him kid. I'll put him on his ass.

I pull myself up off the bed, grab a towel and head into the en suite. Turning back, I grab my iPod and put it on shuffle.

"Shameless" by Garth Brooks plays first, and I find myself singing along as I get in the shower. It's the kind of song you find yourself belting out. I feel sorry for the people in the room next to mine.

Fresh from the shower, I grab some clean clothes and dress quickly. I go to pull on my cowboy boots but change my mind at the last second and pull my Vans out of my suitcase. Then I splash on some aftershave, look at myself in the mirror and try to tame my still wet hair.

I decide to stop by The Lock first for a quick drink. And maybe a little bit because I want to see the pink-haired angel I have been dreaming about.

Deb serves me a Pepsi, but there's no sign of Caleigh, so I nurse my drink in the corner for a while, deciding it would be suspicious if I just left.

After what I consider a reasonable amount of time, I down the rest of my drink and head out to Damien's. Thankfully, he gave me directions earlier. Not that I think I could get lost in a town this size.

As I'm walking in what I hope is the right direction, I see a flash of pink hair. I slow my pace when I see her with a little boy, who must be about five or six years old.

"Hi," Caleigh says as she comes to a stop in front of me. "How are you enjoying your stay?"

"Hi, Caleigh, it's good to see you. Yeah, I'm liking the place so far. Nice and quiet."

"Sorry, where are my manners? Rhett, this is Hardin. Hardin, this is Rhett."

"The man you met on the plane, Mummy?" he asks as he gives me a quizzical stare.

"Yes, baby, that's right."

"Hi, Rhett."

"Hello, Hardin, it's nice to meet you," I say as I hold out my fist for him to bump, which he does after a long second.

"Rhett's a funny name."

"Hardin, that's not nice. Remember what we say about manners?"

"They cost nothing, Mummy. Sorry, Rhett."

"Honestly, buddy, I agree with you. It's after a character in a film my mum loves."

I feel bad for not telling the truth about my name, but I told the truth about why it was chosen. Little consolation really, I know.

"My mummy loves The Rock."

"Oh, does she? Well, I'm glad my mum didn't name me that. It would be a funny name to go around with."

"It's not his real name, silly. It was his name as a wrestler. His real name is Dwayne."

"Oh, well that's a much better name."

So Caleigh goes for the ripped kind of man, does she? That rules me out. I mean, I don't have a bad physique, but nothing compared to the muscles Dwayne Johnson has. I'm sure the dude's muscles have muscles.

"Where are you off to?" Caleigh asks. She flashes me a beautiful smile and I could melt.

"Just off to binge watch a series on Netflix with Damien."

"Oh, right. Cool. What are you watching?"

"*The Witcher*. Full disclosure, I never played the game or read the books. Though I am three chapters into *The Last Wish*. I bought it when I went into Pedmore today." I don't know why I'm rambling.

"You went into One Last Chapter?"

"I did. Your uncle is a very nice man."

"How do you know we're related?" she asks as a bemused look crosses her face.

"Ted told me. Actually, he asked me to give you a message when I next saw you."

"Oh, I see. What did he say?"

"He wanted you to know that Miriam is away for another week at her mum's."

"Oh." Her faces falls slightly. "I'd hoped my great-aunt would be better by now."

"I'm sorry it's not better news. He did ask me to say hello to you, though, Hardin."

"Mummy, can we go and see if Uncle Ted has any new books for me?" Hardin asks in a pleading tone.

"Maybe next week, baby," Caleigh says, smiling down at her son. "Thank you for passing the message on, Rhett. We should let you get going to Damien's before you're late. Full disclosure, *The Witcher* is phenomenal."

"Does it live up to all the hype? I'm quite late to the party, I know."

"It depends on how you look at it. I've never played the game or read the books either. I just looked at it as a new fantasy to sink my teeth into, and I loved every second of it. It didn't hurt that Geralt was so handsome."

"Oh, so weird colour eyes and long grey hair is your thing, huh?" I ask with a wink.

Caleigh's giggle is melodic. God, could she get any more perfect?

I really need to stop thinking of her like that. It could never happen, even if she liked me that way. Long-distance relationships are tricky, then there's the fact that she doesn't know who I really am and the fact that she has a kid. I'm not bothered she has a kid, it's more that if we got attached to each other and then I had to go away all the time, it would make it that much harder.

Plus, there'd be the whole telling Hardin why I lied about who I am in the first place. It's hardly a good thing to lie to a child.

"I'd hardly say I have a type, actually. I like who I like. It's not so much what's on the outside that counts."

"So, Henry Cavill could approach you and if he was a"—I catch myself before saying *dick* in front of Hardin—"an idiot, then he wouldn't stand a chance?"

"Hmm," she ponders, rubbing a hand over her chin for effect. "If he looked like that but was as dumb as a box of frogs, or if he didn't have a sense of humour, then no he wouldn't stand a chance. A man has to be kind, intelligent, funny, loving, respectful—"

"Sounds like you're describing me there."

"Someone's full of themselves," she replies with a tinkling laugh.

Her emerald eyes sparkle with mirth and I feel drawn to her by some invisible force. I'm the moth and she's the flame. If I fly too close, I'll get burned.

"Nah, I just know I possess all of those traits."

"Hmm, I'm sure you do."

She looks me over from head to toe, her gaze scrutinising me, and I feel like I'm under a microscope.

"Well, since you didn't swipe right, you'll never know," I tease.

The blush races across her skin, making her cheeks pink. Just when I thought she couldn't get any prettier, she goes and proves me wrong.

"Mummy, what's Rhett on about?"

"Nothing, baby. It's just a joke from when we met."

"Oh. Well, I don't get the joke. Aren't jokes supposed to be funny?"

"Manners, Hardin," she chides quietly.

"Sorry, Mummy."

"We'd really better be going. You're probably already late. We'll let you get on with your evening."

"Oh, yeah, sure. I'll see you around."

"That you will. It's a small town, in case you hadn't noticed."

"Are you singing for karaoke night at The Lock?"

"Ohmygod no." She rushes her words out and blushes beet red. "I can't hold a tune."

"Ah, tone deaf. Only ever sings in the car or the shower?" I ask.

"Exactly. Will I get to hear you sing?"

"Not a chance. I can't carry a tune either."

"Doesn't mean you can't come and grab a Jameson and watch the locals as they try to belt out Whitney Houston or something."

"Are you trying to make it sound appealing? Because if you are, I'm afraid to tell you that you're doing the exact opposite."

"Okay, well, then I cordially invite you to bear witness to the Royal Philharmonic Orchestra."

"You know they play instruments and don't sing, right?"

Her cheeks pink again as she smiles at me. It's a goofy kind of smile, but beautiful all the same.

"I know that. I just couldn't think of a group of awesome singers. I was trying to make it sound more appealing to you."

"I'm afraid I'm busy that night."

"Do you even know what night it is?"

She's got me there. Damien didn't tell me when, just that they have karaoke.

"Okay, you've got me there. No, I don't know."

"It's Tuesday. And Wednesdays are 'curry and a pint for a fiver'."

"It looks like all my Tuesdays just got fully booked washing my hair. Sorry."

Caleigh pokes her tongue out at me, and Hardin just looks at us in confusion. I don't blame him; adults are confusing sometimes.

"I'll see you on Wednesday for the curry."

"Aww, don't be a spoilsport!"

"I'll see if I can pencil something in on my calendar."

I pull my phone out of my pocket and pretend to scrutinise my calendar.

"Looks like my Tuesday evening could be free. It all hinges on if there's some kind of incentive for me."

"And the incentive would be?" she quizzes.

"That's for you to decide."

"How about a Jameson, on the house?"

"Sold. I'll see you then, if I don't bump into you before. I really should go; I've just noticed the time. I told Damien I'd be there ten minutes ago and I still need to find the place."

"Carry on straight down this road, turn left and it's the third house on your right."

"Oh, awesome. Thanks. Hard to get my bearings in a new place."

"Everyone knows everyone in this town, so if you're ever lost, just ask someone to point you in the right direction."

"Thanks, Caleigh, I appreciate it."

"No worries. Have fun."

"You have a good night. Hardin." I lean down towards him. "Have a good night, little man. It was good to meet you."

He gives me another fist bump and a grin that shows he's missing a tooth. He's so cute, but then with his mother's genes, I shouldn't have expected any less.

"See you soon, Rhett," he says over his shoulder as they begin to walk away.

"See you soon, Hardin."

I wave and watch for a moment as they walk away. *Please look back,* I think to myself. And she does. She looks over her shoulder and offers me a smile before turning around and walking away. God, her ass looks so good in those jeans.

Chapter Five

Caleigh

I spent Sunday with my parents and Hardin for our usual roast dinner. Then yesterday, I busted my ass at the pub.

Tonight it's karaoke, so I'm prepared with ear plugs just in case. Not that I could bring myself to tell the regulars they can't sing, and actually some of them can. But there are others that can't hold a tune, usually because they're steaming drunk. One shot of liquid courage turns into more, and by that time they're slurring their words when they sing. All good fun, I suppose. But you wouldn't catch me dead on that stage.

"Hey, Caleigh, we got any more slimline tonic water? I can't see any on the shelf," Deb says from behind me.

Well, that's unusual; we normally have plenty.

"Let me go check out the back."

The stock room is dark, so I turn on the light and search for more slimline tonic. It's got to be in here somewhere.

"Whatcha looking for?" Damien's voice booms from over my shoulder, making me jump out of my skin.

"Jeez, boss, give a girl a heart attack why don't you?!"

"Sorry, Caleigh," he says with a smile and eyes that show contrition. "Can I help you find something?"

"Slimline tonic. We're out behind the bar."

"Shit! I forgot to get any at the wholesaler," he says as he scrubs a hand over his face in frustration.

"It's okay, boss. I'll pop to the shop and see what they have."

"Thanks, Caleigh, I'll go back to the wholesaler tomorrow. I don't know what I was thinking."

"Everybody has off days and forgets things, Damien. Don't beat yourself up about tonic water."

He hands me some money and I put it in my pocket as I make for the back room to grab my coat.

The air is cool as it hits me. Suddenly I'm grateful I remembered my coat, as I pull it tighter around me to fend off the wind.

"Hey, Caleigh," a voice says, startling me.

I turn to see it's Rhett, and I swallow my heart from where it jumped up into my throat. And here was me thinking I didn't spook easily.

"Evening, Rhett. You coming to the pub?"

"Yeah, I was headed that way now. Are you not working?"

"Yeah, I am. Damien just forgot something at the wholesalers, so I'm just walking to the shop to see if they have some. Must have used the last of it last night I guess."

"Ah, well, let me help you back with whatever it is."

He falls in line with me as I head for the shop. My heart beats a staccato rhythm because he's so close. He's so close I could touch him. But I shouldn't. I shouldn't even *want* to, but I do.

"What is it?"

"What is what?" I ask, confused.

"That he forgot. He said something on the trip back about feeling like he'd forgotten something, but he didn't know what."

"Oh, sorry. Umm, just some slimline tonic water."

"He forgot it, but he sends *you* out to fetch it? Not very gentlemanly," he says with a soft chuckle.

"That's Damien for you. Manners of a pig. But actually I offered this time."

"Still, he could have said no and come out himself."

"Too scared the cold would shrivel up his already microscopic cock and then women would have to use an extra-strength magnifying glass to find it."

Rhett bursts out laughing, and I'd be lying if I didn't say that even his laugh is perfect. Everything about him is so ... dreamy. *Shut the fuck up, Caleigh,* I think to myself.

"I won't tell him you said that."

"Trust me, I'd say it to his face."

"You're a feisty one, aren't you Caleigh?" he asks, his voice suddenly husky—or is that my imagination?

"My mum would tell you I'm too damn sassy for my own good. My dad would tell you I'm his little firecracker."

"And I'd believe every word."

We find the aisle with the tonic water and I grab as many packs as I can handle.

"Here, let me," Rhett says as he takes them from me.

"Thank you."

I pick up a few more packs, just to tide us over in case Damien forgets again. The man's brain is like a sieve sometimes.

We pay and grab the bags. Rhett carries both of them, so I carry the two packs we couldn't fit in. Walking back to the pub, I tell Rhett all about the many wonderful singers he can expect tonight and some of their song choices—the regulars like to sing the same songs most weeks. Honestly, I wish they'd change it up a bit.

Rhett helps me carry the water into the stock room, then I open the packs and grab some bottles to stock behind the bar. He kindly helps me carry a few through, so once I'm back behind the bar, I pour him a Jameson.

"It's on the house, man," Damien says from the end of the bar.

"That's not necessary," Rhett replies.

"Oh, but it is, my man. I should have gone instead of assuming Caleigh could carry it all back alone."

"Honestly, it was my pleasure, bro."

"Why don't you grab a beer and come join me?"

I hand Rhett a bottled beer and he thanks me before heading towards Damien's end of the bar. I watch as he takes a seat next to him and they start chatting.

After serving the line of customers, I ponder what brought Rhett here. It has to be one of the quietest little places in the country. Is he just after peace and quiet, or is he escaping something? From his demeanour tonight, he doesn't seem like he's troubled, but there's something about him. I can't put my finger on it, but it's like something is bothering him. I tried asking him stuff on the plane and he changed the subject swiftly, probably thinking—or hoping—I wouldn't notice.

Maybe he's just an extremely private person. I don't know. He's like a riddle I can't solve and that bugs me. It would be nice to peel back the layers of him a little bit, get to know more about him. But we only seem to make small talk.

It's that time of the evening when Tina takes to the stage and belts out Alanis Morrisette's "Ironic". I love the song, and Tina has a pretty good voice. She doesn't have to be steaming drunk to get up on that stage and give it her all either. She has confidence by the bucketload.

Next up is Joshua, who always sings "With or Without You". Another song I love. But then after him is Maddie, who always signs up to sing "Unbreak My Heart". She had her heart broken by a guy a while back, and ever since she's seemed like she's drowning in misery. She's one of the people with a voice powerful enough to hit every note, but it makes me sad to see that she's still struggling.

I know what it's like to lose a guy. I mean, okay so it's a little different because Angelo passed away, but it's really hard to come to terms with shit like that in the beginning.

It's hard to accept that they're gone. It's really hard to accept that they'll never come back to you. Loss is loss, whether it's death or just the end of a relationship. I've had both and been hurt by both. You grieve the loss of all the things you had planned together but never got to do.

I moved back to River's Edge to get away from the sympathetic looks and the many people who gave their condolences. I didn't want people's pity. I wanted to just be allowed to be me.

I lived here as a little girl, and Angelo lived here too, but we moved away to start afresh somewhere bigger when we realised that we were going to have Hardin.

Three years ago, when he passed away, I moved back here to be closer to my parents and other family members. I wanted Hardin to have family around to help him after losing his daddy. Thankfully, he was only young when it happened; he was just two years old. But that doesn't mean he wasn't affected. We both were, and we both needed our family around us.

But I digress. My point is that we all deal with loss in different ways. And Maddie sings her heart out every other week at karaoke night. She only comes every other week because her mum looks after her daughter, Janie.

My heart pangs with the memory of my own loss as she sings.

The crowd gathered applauds loudly as the song ends, and Delia gets up to sing a song by Whitney Houston. I discreetly stick in my ear plugs and serve a couple of customers. It's easy when you already know their usual and don't have to make them shout to be heard beyond the ear plugs.

I watch as Damien laughs with Rhett. And I wish I could hear that lilting laugh of his. Grabbing a bottle of Johnnie Walker, I head down to pour them both a healthy measure.

"You should get up and sing, dude," Damien says to Rhett.

"Nah, man, I can't carry a tune. Honestly, I'd make your ears bleed," Rhett replies with a laugh.

"Come on, man, just one song. I promise I'll stop nagging if you do. And, to sweeten the pot, drinks on the house for the rest of the night. Not the cheap stuff either!"

"Man, you drive a hard bargain to hear me murder a tune."

"Go on, Rhett. Just the one," I butt in.

He smiles at me, and man does my heart start racing. His pearly white grin, all Hollywood and perfect. It just does something to my insides, turning them into a pool of gelatinous goo.

"Aw, man, not you too. You know this is harassment, right?" he asks, still smiling.

"I promise we'll stop if you let me put you down for one song," Damien says.

"And I get to pick my own song?"

"Of course. I wouldn't set you up, man."

Rhett looks resigned to his fate. Poor guy.

Another couple of singers get up before it's his turn. When the melody begins to play, I just know I won't be putting my ear plugs back in. "Take It to the Limit" is a song I grew up listening to. I defy anyone to say they don't like The Eagles, whether they're country fans or not.

His voice pins me to the spot. Suddenly Rhett is all I can see and hear. He belts it out in a heavenly voice. So much for not being able to hold a tune. He even hits the higher notes perfectly. I feel weak at the knees.

When he takes his seat back at the bar, I let out a breath I didn't know I was holding.

"What the fuck, dude? Thought you said you couldn't sing," Damien says as he claps him on the shoulder.

Rhett has the grace to blush.

"That was …" I trail off, floundering for the right word. "I've always loved that song. My mum brought me up on The Eagles, amongst others. You had me believing you couldn't sing and then … then you go and bring the house down."

The raucous applause is still ringing in my ears. The crowd loved it every bit as much as I did.

"I think he should sing another for telling us a lie," Damien says to me.

"I second that."

"Oh no. No way. You promised you'd back off if I sang one song. *One*," Rhett replies, looking between us both.

"No can do, buddy. Sorry. But you tell a lie like that and you have to pay the price."

I laugh as he looks completely horrified at the thought. He knows he won't get out of it, because Damien is not the kind of guy to back down. He'll go toe to toe with him until he gets his way.

"And I say one of us gets to pick the song," I say, with a wink at Rhett.

"Damn straight," Damien agrees, slapping him on the back.

"Fuck," Rhett says as his shoulders slump.

Damien leans over the bar to conspire with me over song choice and I'm almost tempted to choose "Let It Go" from Frozen, just to be a complete bitch, but I don't. I hate that song, for a start.

"How about something like one of Panic at The Disco's songs?" I whisper.

"Nah, man, something that needs a really strong voice. I've got it, hold on."

He leans over to Rhett and asks if he's seen *The Greatest Showman*. Rhett nods and then Damien leans back over to me.

" 'From Now On'. What do you say, Caleigh?"

I nod emphatically and clap my hands in glee.

Rhett graces the stage once again without knowing the song we chose. The melody starts to play and his eyes flash with recognition.

He starts singing softly, just like Hugh Jackman would. Then it starts to get stronger and louder. His voice carries throughout the room and the crowd sit enraptured. My heart races, and I feel tears sting my eyes. I've loved this song since the moment I first heard it. It really has all the feels when you watch the film. Hardin and I might just be a little obsessed with the film and its soundtrack.

The room bursts into applause as Rhett finishes singing and I clap along with them. I clap so loud it makes my hands sting. He really is one talented guy. He obviously hides his light under a bushel. Not only can he pull off covering The Eagles—which is no mean feat—but a song from a bloody musical too. Christ alive, this man gets more and more amazing the more I see him.

Damien tells me to pour the man a drink, so I do.

***

I'm shattered. What a long night on my feet. But it was worth every ounce of pain just to hear Rhett sing. Man, he had the crowd begging for more but declined after his second song.

I collect Hardin from Mum, pack his snacks in his new school bag and make sure everything is ready for tomorrow.

"Brush your teeth for the full two minutes, mister. Don't stop until that timer goes off."

"I will, Mum," he garbles around his toothbrush.

"Good boy."

I finish packing his lunch and hear the timer go off in the bathroom. Hardin runs into the room and shows me his gleaming white teeth.

"Choose a bedtime story and I'll be up in two minutes."

"Okay, Mummy."

"And don't run up the stairs."

"I know," he says on a sigh, like I've told him a million times before. Probably because I have.

"I chose *Room on The Broom*, Mummy," he says excitedly as I sit next to him on the bed.

"Did Grandma buy you this?"

"Yeah, we got it today. She took me to see Uncle Ted. He gave me the new Snowman book too, Mummy. Wanna see?"

He clambers out of bed and rushes to his bookshelf. It's crammed with all the books Ted and my mum spoil him with.

There's nothing more wonderful than teaching him to read and sitting to read bedtime stories together. I hate it when I can't tuck him into bed at night, because I miss our bedtime stories. When we don't have anything new to read and he doesn't fancy one we've already read, we make up stories together. This kid has quite the imagination.

Climbing back on his bed, he shows me the new Snowman book and it takes me back to being a kid. I watched it every Christmas without fail. Now I watch it with my baby, just the way my mum did with me.

"We can read this another night baby. Did you thank Uncle Ted?"

"Of course I did, Mummy, I'm not silly. You always tell me to have good manners."

"Good boy. Now, lie down and let me tuck you in and we can get started on tonight's story."

He snuggles down under the covers and I tuck him in. I place a light kiss on his forehead before settling down next to him and opening the book.

As Hardin falls asleep, I lean down and kiss his soft cheek and brush a strand of hair out of his face. These are the moments I cherish most. There's nobody I could ever love more than this little bundle of joy.

I say little, but he's not so little anymore. Soon I'll blink and he'll be eighteen and moving out. I don't want to miss a single second of joy in the moments between now and then.

Padding softly downstairs, I walk into the kitchen and grab a bottle of wine from the fridge. I reach for a stemless tumbler and pour myself a small glass. It's almost too peaceful down here. It makes me miss the nights in with Angelo. I think that it's his companionship I miss as much as anything else.

I could get an early night, but it's a bit *too* early. So, instead, I pick up my Kindle and start a new book I've been dying to dive into. It's one of a series about cocky alphas, and I just love anything by the two authors.

Just as I'm getting to the good stuff, my phone rings, totally breaking the spell. The phone flashes with the face of my best friend who moved almost two hours away last summer. I answer and see her gorgeous face light up with a smile as she sees me.

Lord knows why she had to move so far away. I mean, yeah, she had a daughter and a husband, and they wanted to live somewhere bigger. Her husband, Lewis, is a hotshot solicitor and he didn't want to keep commuting to the city. I get that; Angelo and I wanted to be somewhere bigger when we had Hardin. But I miss her like crazy, and although she's a stay-at-home mum, we don't get to get together often enough. Fuck, it's good to see her face and talk about everything and nothing.

After Rhiannon fills me in on the things I've missed in her life, she quizzes me like she thinks I have something worth talking about. She asks me about my non-existent love life, and I tell her that there's simply nothing to tell. Ever the perceptive one, she doesn't miss a trick. So, I tell her about the hot guy passing through town on his way to who-knows-where.

"Nothing's going on though, Rhi. And it won't. He's not sticking around, so I'm not getting attached."

"Sure, nothing going on at all. That's why your skin is a deep shade of cerise right now."

"Rhi, I'm telling you, there's nothing going on."

"But you'd like there to be?"

"Hey, I can't help that he's hot. And to think I didn't look twice at him when I saw him on Tinder."

"Tinder?" she gasps. "Oh no, girl, please tell me you didn't meet some random weirdo off a hook-up app?"

"It's not like that," I sigh, before proceeding to tell her how we met.

When she finishes laughing her ass off at me, she hears Luna calling her. We say our goodbyes, but not before she makes me promise to—and I quote—keep her apprised of any update in the situation.

It's an empty promise, because nothing will happen, but I agree in the hopes of keeping her from hounding me about it.

***

After dropping Hardin off at his classroom, I make my way to the shop before heading home. I make my way to the till, but bump into a wall of muscle, and almost send everything in my arms flying.

"Shit, sorry. I should really look where I'm …" I trail off as I look up to see I've bumped into none other than Rhett. "Going. Sorry about that."

"No need to apologise," he says in a voice that makes my insides do somersaults. "Here, let me help." He takes a couple of things from me and carries them to the till. "You really ought to get a basket next time," he says with a wry chuckle.

"I didn't realise I'd need one. Typical of me, really. I come in for one thing and leave with about twenty."

I don't know why I'm rambling, but I can't seem to stop whenever I'm around him.

"Let me help you home with the bags."

"Oh, there's really no need."

"I'd like to though."

"Wasn't there something you came in for?"

"Oh," he says, as if he's completely forgotten his reason for being here. "Yeah, umm … let me just grab something and I'll be right back."

He walks off in the direction of the fridges at the back of the store before returning a few moments later carrying a couple of bottles of kombucha. I've never tried that stuff myself, but just the thought of a cold tea drink makes me want to puke. If you're going to drink tea, make it the hot kind with sugar and milk.

"You ought to try something before you decide you don't like it," Rhett says, causing me to frown.

Shit! I must have said that about tea out loud.

"I … umm … I didn't mean to voice that out loud."

"You didn't say anything, it was clear from the look on your face."

"But you knew I haven't even tried it."

"Lucky guess. Probably because I've seen the look on my friends' faces when I drink it. They're all about beer or whiskey, and normally so am I. But somebody told me about this stuff and, what can I say, it's good."

The cashier rings up our purchases and we bag them up before leaving the store. Rhett carries the bags, even though I told him not to fuss.

"So, what are you cooking?" he asks as we walk back to my place.

"Oh, umm, I'm making turkey nuggets with sweet potato fries. I ran out of courgette and carrots though, hence the trip to the store."

"Courgette?" he asks as he makes a funny face.

"You know, you really ought to try something before deciding you don't like it," I parrot his earlier words back to him.

"It just … I don't know; it looks revolting."

"Hardin says the same, but he eats it every time I make these nuggets. He has no choice really because I grate it and put it in with the turkey mince and grated carrot."

"Huh?"

The puzzled expression on his face makes me giggle.

"Wow, you've never made your own nuggets, have you?"

"Umm, that would be a hard no."

"You really should. They're much healthier than frozen crap. I make sure Hardin eats as little frozen food as possible."

I'm rambling and I'm probably boring the pants off him, but he listens with a smile on his face all the same.

"What's with the megawatt grin?" I ask when I can't bear it any longer.

"Nothing, it's just that you remind me of my mum. She wouldn't allow me to eat frozen food often either. She made everything from scratch almost every night when I was growing up. She'd let me have pizza or nuggets if she was really rushed off her feet, but a lot of the time she made her own pizza and froze it, so it was still the healthier option."

"Sounds like a woman after my own heart. It's this house just here," I say, pointing down the path to my front door.

"Nice place."

"Yeah, we like it. And my mum lives just a couple of doors that way," I say as I gesture to her house, "which makes it easy when she watches Hardin while I'm at work."

"Where is the little man?"

"He's at school until three-thirty. I'm a mess because it's his first week and it's weird that he's not here with me. But I want him to get a good education and make friends."

"You're a good mum."

"H-how do you figure that?" I stutter.

"Well, you want what's best for your son. You want him to get an education, to make friends and to eat healthily. I think that counts as being a good mum, don't you?"

I feel the blush colour my cheeks. "It's just the same as any mother would want."

"Not every mother, trust me. There are some women that have kids and neglect them. There are some that beat their kids, have them taken away by social services because they can't be bothered to look after them."

If he hadn't just told me about his own mother, I'd say he was talking from experience. He has this kind of weird expression on his face, like he's been hurt but is trying to hide it. Whatever it is, the deep frown mars his handsome features. But almost as soon as it appears, it vanishes again, leaving a smile in its place.

"Would you like to come in for a cup of tea? You know, the hot kind?"

Shit. I don't know why I'm inviting him in, but I can't retract my words now I've said them out loud; that would be rude.

"I don't drink tea, but if you have coffee, I'd love one."

"Sure, yeah."

I open the door and stand aside to let him in. He won't let me take the bags from him, so I show him to the kitchen where he places them on the side.

As I'm unpacking the bags and putting things away, I turn to fill the kettle and grab two mugs from the overhead cupboard. This place might not be as big as our old house, but it's home. It's big enough for Hardin and me, plus it's close to school and work, as well as my mum's place.

I watch as Rhett looks at the family photographs on the wall. He smiles as he looks at baby pictures of Hardin.

"Who's this?" he asks as he points at our family portrait.

"That's my husband, Angelo."

His face looks crestfallen, but I don't get time to wonder why.

"I didn't realise you were married."

"Oh, umm, I'm not. I'm widowed, actually."

"Shit. I'm sorry, Caleigh. I didn't know."

His shoulders slump and it looks like somebody kicked his puppy or something from the way he looks at me.

"It's okay, you weren't to know. He died a few years ago. He had cancer. We thought he had more time, but it spread faster than wildfire, and he was gone before I could process what was happening. He was always happy though, right up to the end. He was never maudlin, never got upset in front of Hardin. It was hard, because he was so little when it happened. One minute he's got a dad, the next he's gone."

I stop talking long enough to swallow back unshed tears and make those coffees. I carry them through to the living room and Rhett follows.

"He was a great dad, you know. He lived for Hardin. He was the apple of his eye. We were so lucky to have a guy like Angelo in our lives," I continue as we take a seat.

"Hardin has his eyes," he remarks quietly.

"Yeah? People say he's my double."

"In his baby photos, he looks just like his daddy."

"He was Angelo's shadow. He literally followed him everywhere, all the time. Angelo loved to read him bedtime stories, and he was especially good at making them up off the top of his head. Much better than I am, that's for sure. I try. I read to him every night. He usually picks a book or asks me to tell him stories. A lot of them include his daddy in one way or another. I'll tell him about things we did when we were young, or I'll tell him about a prince in a magical kingdom far, far away."

"Does he remember him much?"

"I'm not sure. I know he knows who he is because of the stories I tell or the pictures on the wall, but I'm not sure about real memories of his own."

I wipe a stray tear and Rhett gives me a pained look.

"I'm sorry, Caleigh. I didn't mean to pry."

"Oh, gosh, no. It's fine, honestly."

He takes my small hand in his and strokes the back of it with his thumb. That small gesture calms me. It's weird, because it should feel wrong coming from anyone other than Angelo, but it doesn't. It feels nice.

Turning to face him, I smile as he wipes away another tear from my cheek. He's tender and sweet, and it makes my heart flutter like it has wings.

Before I can fully think it through—and probably overthink it and chicken out—I lean in and ghost a kiss across his lips, waiting to see if he'll respond.

He doesn't do anything for a second, and I wonder whether I've misjudged him being attracted to me. Maybe it's all in my head.

I start to pull back but then his lips meet mine in a kiss so soft and gentle it makes my heart skip a beat. The butterflies in my stomach are going crazy as I lean into the kiss and part his lips with my tongue.

He moans quietly as he gives in to the urge to deepen the kiss. His tongue dances with mine as if we've done it a thousand times before.

His one hand comes up to the back of my head whilst the other palm cradles my cheek. My blood sings in my veins as his kiss turns from tender to passionate, consuming me the way my thoughts of him have these last few days.

Breaking the kiss, Rhett pulls back and looks at me through hooded eyes. His irises are darkened with lust and I see myself reflected back in them.

"You are so beautiful," he says in a husky voice that melts my insides.

I feel the blush creep across my cheeks.

"Even prettier when your cheeks tint to match the colour of your hair," he whispers as he ghosts a kiss over my lips.

"Hey, my cheeks don't get *that* pink," I respond defensively.

"Not quite, but they are beautiful and rosy."

He touches his forehead to mine, and it's like I can see into his soul as I get lost in his gaze.

"I've been wanting to do that ever since we met in the airport."

"You have?" I ask, surprise evident in my tone.

"I have. Ever since you swiped past my picture on Tinder."

"Ugh. Don't remind me," I sigh. "I actually can't get over doing that. My mum always told me never judge a book by its cover, but I did exactly that. Well, not *exactly*, I mean, your bio didn't give much away, and your picture was kind of dark. You're better looking in real life."

"Thank you," he says as he ghosts another kiss across my lips.

He pulls back and looks at me. He runs a hand through his long dark hair, giving him a slightly dishevelled look. I like it. I mean, I like it a *lot*.

"You are too beautiful for words to accurately describe."

Now I feel myself blushing even harder. "You say the kindest things."

"I only say them if they're true."

His tone and the look on his face are sincere. It makes my heart race as I take in what he said. Caleigh Rae Flynn: too beautiful for words to describe. Words that have never been said to me before.

Chapter Six

Brent

I don't know what made me kiss her. No, that's a lie, I *do* know. She's breathtakingly beautiful and I have wanted to know the taste of her lips since we met. I wasn't wrong, she tastes like strawberry lip gloss, but also something uniquely Caleigh. And for once it wasn't me who initiated things; it was all her. Ghosting a sweet kiss over my lips, making my cock twitch and my heartrate skyrocket.

Truth be told, after finding out she's widowed, I wouldn't have initiated the kiss. Not for any other reason than timing.

"Your coffee's gone cold," she says, jarring me out of my thoughts of where else I would like to feel her lips.

"Yours too," I reply with a chuckle.

Caleigh's quiet for a beat and it makes me wonder what she's thinking. Is she regretting the kiss? Is she wishing I'd be polite enough to get up and leave? Is that what I should do? Make an excuse and go? Or would that be rude and make her feel slighted after kissing me? Man, these thoughts are giving me a headache.

"Who are you, Rhett?"

The question shocks me. Does she know who I am? Is she expecting me to confess all?

"What do you mean?"

"Don't answer a question with a question. My grandmother always said that was rude," she replies with a smile. "All I meant was, who are you? You know, like, you aren't from around here. You're a mystery to me."

"I'm just a guy," I say with a shrug. "What do you want to know?"

"I don't know. How about how old you are?"

"I'm thirty-four. How old are you?"

"Same age. Where are you from?"

"A galaxy far, far away," I say with a wink.

"So, you're an alien? Are you just visiting our planet, or do you intend to stay?"

"It depends. I might stay, given the right incentive."

"Oh, really? And what would that be?"

"It depends on humans," I say with a grin. "I mean, are they all they're cracked up to be? Do I really want to assimilate with humanity? What can they give me in order to make me stay?"

She smiles at me and it's a goofy grin, but it's fucking adorable.

"Well, I can only tell you what this human can offer."

"Pray tell, what *would* this human offer?"

"Well, lunch would be a start," she says, surprising me.

That wasn't what I thought she'd say. I might be wrong, but it felt like her walls were coming down, but then she clammed up and slammed them back up again.

"Depends what's on the menu. Not sure I can digest human food, after all."

Caleigh smiles at me and her eyes twinkle with mirth. Maybe she's not completely erected those walls after all.

"I would love to say that I have some alien food in the cupboard for when they pop by unannounced, but I don't. I must have run out." She pokes her tongue out at me and I laugh. "How does Welsh rarebit sound?"

"Umm …"

"Don't tell me you don't know what Welsh rarebit is?"

Her puzzled expression makes me laugh even harder.

"I'll be honest. I haven't got the foggiest notion as to what that is. You could make it for me and enlighten me though. I'm always open to having my horizons broadened."

"Well, the layman might call it cheese on toast, but it's a little bit more than that."

"Mmm, cheese on toast with tomato ketchup …" I trail off as she cuts her eyes at me.

"No, no and no. It's far superior to that. Here, let me show you."

She rolls her eyes at me before getting up and walking into the kitchen. I follow hot on her heels.

I watch as she grabs a ton of ingredients and realise it must be much more than just plain old cheese on toast.

She melts butter in a pan, then adds in some flour once it's melted. As she stirs that in with one hand, she picks up a bottle of milk with the other.

"Is there anything I can do to help?" I ask, feeling like neither use nor ornament standing here.

"Sure, grab a knife from the block there and slice that tomato. We want two slices each. Make sure they're not too thick but not wafer-thin."

"Are you always so precise?"

"I can be. I'm usually very organised, but to err is human after all. We're all flawed."

"Good to know that even a woman as beautiful as you can make mistakes."

My god, why did I say that out loud? I grab a knife and she looks at me like I'm insane, before reaching over and pulling a different one out of the block.

"You can slice it better with this," she says as she hands it to me.

She completely ignores my compliment, and I'm glad she doesn't address it.

"Oh, sorry. Okay, so four slices."

I turn to her chopping board and grab the tomato, unsure that I'll even get four slices out of it. That's how bad my kitchen skills are.

I turn to look at Caleigh and see her pour milk into the pan.

"Uh-uh, back to slicing, mister. If you want to know what I'm doing, I can tell you as I do each thing."

I start to slice the tomato and she tells me as she reduces the heat and adds Worcester sauce. That makes me quirk an eyebrow at her, but she tells me to trust her, so I do. She then adds mustard, paprika, salt, pepper and finally cheese, as I finish up slicing the tomato and wash the knife.

"You keep the pan over the heat until the cheese is melted. Now, I have another pan here to fry a couple of rashers of bacon. One each, unless you'd rather more."

"I'll trust your recipe. Though I do love bacon."

Caleigh smiles at me as I come around to watch her frying the bacon whilst simultaneously watching so that the cheese doesn't burn. I take the spoon from her and begin to stir so she doesn't have to do both at once.

"Just don't let it burn."

"Yes ma'am," I say with a salute.

She grins another goofy but sexy grin at me. She really is so beautiful.

Caleigh reaches over and pops two pieces of bread in the toaster next to her. I almost want to say that it's cheese, tomato and bacon on toast, but resist the urge, knowing it would probably earn me another dirty look.

After plating the toast, she puts the bacon on top and then asks me to pass her the slices of tomato. I grab the plate I put them on and hand them to her, watching as she lays two pieces on top of the bacon.

How is it that she looks this sexy cooking me lunch? Well, more like *brunch*, as I only had a croissant at Audrey's earlier and it's a bit too early to be lunchtime.

"Now pass me the melted cheese."

I carefully hand her the pan and watch her use the spoon to help pour the cheese over the slices of toast.

"So, it's like gourmet cheese on toast then?"

"Don't let my grandmother hear you say that. She'll cut off your balls and wear them as earrings."

"Ooh, feisty. I'll have to protect my manhood around her then."

She giggles, and the sound makes my cock stir. Why? I don't know. It's just that everything about her is undeniably sexy.

"Et voilà," she says with a flourish of her hands. "You could top it with a sprig of parsley or something, but I see no point in garnish that adds no real extra taste. It's perfect as it is."

"I trust you implicitly," I reply with a wink.

Her skin colours pink as she takes the plates from the worktop.

"Knives and forks are in that drawer." She juts her hip in the general direction.

I grab cutlery and follow as she leads me back into the living room.

"We could eat in the dining room, but it doesn't make sense for just a light brunch."

"That's fine by me."

We sit and make small talk as we eat. She was right. Cheese on toast pales in comparison to the taste sensation currently exploding on my tastebuds. I'll have to remember this for when I go home. It's something I can see myself being able to make without too much hassle, although I have been known to burn cheese on toast. The boys in the band can attest to that.

"That was delicious," I say as I rest my knife and fork on my plate.

I stand and take her plate from her, take them both into the kitchen and make quick work of washing them up.

I walk back into the living room and I sit next to her. I can't help but notice as my thigh brushes hers and electricity seems to crackle in the air.

Caleigh looks at me and bursts out laughing.

"Want to let me in on the joke?"

"Sorry, you just have some ..." she makes a gesture to the side of her mouth.

I wipe at my mouth and she laughs even harder.

"I meant this side. Here, let me," she says as she reaches out a hand.

I was wiping the wrong side. I blame her for making me make a fool of myself.

"It's just a little cheese."

She pulls her hand away, but I stop her and before I can think it through fully, I suck her finger into my mouth.

Her skin colours pink but doesn't pull her hand away.

I feel my grin split my face as her eyes darken with desire as she looks at me. She casts her gaze over me, appraising me. Her eyes roam from my eyes down to my lips, then to my abs and back up to lock gazes with mine. Her emerald green eyes sparkle like the most exquisite gems. Rare and beautiful, just like the rest of her.

"There's something I've been wanting to do since you got here," she says quietly.

"Oh, and what would that be?"

"This," she whispers, barely audible, before leaning in and slanting her lips over mine.

Gone is the sweet kiss from before. This time it's fiery and passionate. Her tongue demands entry, and when I grant it, her tongue dances with mine. Her hands come to cradle my cheeks and I wrap an arm around her waist as the other hand goes to her pink tresses and cradles the back of her head.

Caleigh's hands begin to explore my abs over the top of my t-shirt. But as her kiss becomes bolder, so does her touch. It's like she's testing the waters out by dipping her toes in before she decides to go for a swim.

My cock stirs and I can't help its reaction to her very proximity.

One of her hands traces down my chest to the hem of my t-shirt. She slides her hand underneath to glide over the ridges of my torso before dipping to the waistband of my jeans. I only have a moment to question whether or not to let this happen. But that moment is gone when she expertly undoes the button and slides down the zip.

Her hand glides down beneath the denim, slipping underneath the material of my boxers. Her skin is like the softest silk as she caresses me.

I momentarily feel guilty—like, somehow, I'm taking advantage of her—but that evaporates as she kisses me more fiercely. She wants this as much as I do.

My cock hardens as her touch drives me crazy. Suddenly, she moves to straddle my lap, keeping her hand on me.

My hands are in her hair and I pull her head back to expose her throat. Pulling away from her lips, I pepper her throat with kisses, earning me a soft moan. Her whimpers turn to soft cries as I nip at her earlobe.

My hands roam from her hips up her sides to cup her breasts. Caleigh arches her back, pushing them closer to me, so I brush my thumbs over her nipples as I kiss down her neck to the hollow of her throat before following the trail down to the valley between her breasts.

Caleigh tugs at my hair until I relent and look up to meet her gaze. Desire swims in her eyes, but I don't get long to process it before her lips slam down over mine and she leads me in a sensual kiss—a kiss so hot I am susceptible to spontaneous combustion.

She moves her hand so that she's gripping the base of my now throbbing cock. I lift her from my lap and lift my hips from the couch so that I can slide my jeans and boxers further down my legs.

"Shit, wait, I don't have a condom," she says in a mildly panicked tone.

"Wallet. Back pocket."

Now she probably thinks I carry one on me in case I pull some rando in a bar, but it doesn't seem like she cares as she pulls the foil packet from my wallet and tears it open.

This isn't how I imagined sex with her might go—because let's be honest, I've dreamed of this moment and it was nothing like this. It was in a bed, for a start. But I haven't got it in me to care as she slides the condom down over me and seeks out my lips once more.

She lifts the dress she's wearing and pulls her lace panties to one side, guiding the tip of my cock through her wet folds with her left hand.

A throaty moan escapes me as I feel how wet she is, even without foreplay. It's enough to drive a man to the brink of insanity.

Her right hand still in my hair, she slides down onto me, slowly, torturously, inch by inch.

I want to take my time with her, but it's impossible. All I can see is here and now. All I know is how wet she feels and how she stretches to accommodate me, so in the heat of the moment, I reach up and tear the side of her panties.

Her shocked gasp is swallowed as I kiss her like it's the last time— and who knows, it might well be. If all I have with her is this one time, then I'm going to make the most of it.

I tear the other side and discard the material. Now I can be as close to her as I actually want to be.

My hands reach up underneath her dress and unhook her bra. The straps fall down her shoulders, so I take a moment to pull them completely free and discard her bra along with her torn panties.

I brush my thumbs across her nipples, and they pebble under my touch. She arches her back and I cup her breasts.

Her pussy feels so damn good as she moves as though she's going to let me slide all the way out of her, before slamming back down onto me, causing me to groan. She moves again and again, each time slamming her hips home, the slap of her ass against my thighs echoing.

I run my hands down her silky skin to grab her hips. Bucking to meet her thrusts, I'm rewarded with throaty moans. She lets her head fall back and I watch as her chest rises and falls with her laboured breathing.

Jesus Christ, she feels so fucking good that I can't help but wonder if this *is* a dream after all. I goddamn hope not, but if it is, I intend to stay asleep and see it through to the end.

Caleigh's moans get louder with each thrust home. Her pussy is soaking, and my cock is rock hard. I need to chase her climax before my own, but it'll be damn hard to resist the urge.

"Kiss me, Rhett," she says as her eyes meet mine.

"I want to, but there's something I want to do first."

"Oh?" she asks.

"This," I say as I stand with her wrapped around me.

Her legs grip tightly around me as I turn to face the couch. I'm not sure I can lower her without breaking contact, so I palm her ass and hold her tight to me as I lower her to lie on the couch.

Caleigh sighs as I manoeuvre myself between her legs.

"Now will you kiss me?"

I answer her with a white-hot kiss. Our mouths meeting in a frenzy, tongues duelling for dominance over the kiss.

She pushes at my chest and I have no choice but to break the soul-searing kiss. I move back and watch as she unbuttons the front of her dress. I watch her deft fingers make easy work of undoing them and then she slides the spaghetti straps off her arms.

Her hands move to the hem of my t-shirt and I lift my arms so she can pull it over my head. It is pure torture being so still when I'm inside her, but I can exert a little patience—as long as it's only a little.

When she's discarded the material on the floor, she looks up at me, her gaze intense.

Leaning down, I claim her lips in a soft, tantalising kiss. I part her lips with my tongue and explore her mouth. She has me hypnotised as she tries to gain some friction against me.

Her legs hold tightly around my waist as I begin to move slowly inside her. A groan reverberates through my chest as I feel her walls constrict around me. Goddamn, this woman is driving me crazy.

"Fuck, Rhett, I'm so close," she says as I break the kiss.

"Hold on, baby."

Baby? I've never called a woman that in my life.

I build a steady rhythm and she never falters as she bucks her hips to meet me thrust for thrust.

My eyes never leave her hooded gaze as I buck harder and faster. Her nails dig into my shoulders as she grips me. I feel the heels she's still wearing dig into my ass and my god if there isn't something to the whole pleasure-pain theory. I've never cared to test it before. Never met a woman that drives me so wild with lust.

"Rhett," she cries out.

Fuck how I wish I could hear my real name fall from her lips. But there's no time to ponder that any further as she repeatedly shouts out my assumed name.

I feel her shatter beneath me and watch as she rides out the little aftershocks. She closes her eyes and I lean down to kiss her, a chaste kiss, a promise of more to come.

Upping my pace once again, it's time to chase my own release. Caleigh is so hot and wet that it doesn't take me long before I'm crying out her name as I freefall into the abyss.

Stilling, I slide out of her to remove the condom. I tie a knot in it and leave it with her torn panties as I lie down on the couch beside her.

She moves so that I'm lying flat on my back and she's lying on top of me.

Her mouth meets mine in a soft, tender kiss. It's the polar opposite of what I've experienced with her so far. It feels more romantic instead of frenzied. Her tongue dances softly with mine as I hold her close.

"We should shower," she says, breaking the kiss.

"Together?" I ask hopefully.

She rewards me with a grin before moving to stand and hold her hand out to me.

I'm experiencing a whole lot of firsts with this woman, and I find myself actually wanting more. I usually can't wait to get away, but with Caleigh, I want to stay for as long as she'll let me.

Chapter Seven

Caleigh

I don't know what came over me with Rhett. We'd been talking about Angelo—although I didn't say much on that subject—and then I cooked us brunch. That was supposed to be all, but it turned out to be so much more.

I can't deny I've wanted him since the first time I saw him—well, saw in the flesh, not on my phone screen on a hook-up app. But what made me so brazen as to make love to him? And it was in the middle of the day, on the couch, no less.

I'm normally known for taking what I want, but not when it comes to men. I've pretty much been a nun this last three years, only without the vow of celibacy.

What makes Rhett so different? My mind is spinning with questions, but also with images of what we did and memories of how amazing it felt. It felt good to be wanted, to be touched, to feel him inside me. But now I'm not sure what happens next.

He didn't say anything about it after our shower together, and we made small talk a little longer before he left. He didn't exactly seem in a hurry to go, which surprised me. I'd thought he would get dressed and leave as soon as it was over, but he proved me wrong.

It seems he's proving me wrong in all kinds of ways. I didn't think I was ready to look at another man, let alone to have sex. I also didn't think I'd feel any sort of connection; it was just sex after all. But as he made me feel cherished, desired, really wanted, I began to feel something.

It's like I've been sleepwalking through my life and Rhett was the one to finally wake me up. Maybe that's all it was. There were no emotions behind it, there couldn't be because I barely know the man. But damn if my heart doesn't skip a beat just thinking of him.

Rhiannon would psychoanalyse me here and say something like it's all because he's the first person I've truly seen in that way since Angelo passed. She'd tell me that it was just me blowing away the cobwebs or getting back in the saddle or something. She's like that. Irritating, annoying me, because she talks sense. But I have a nagging feeling that she'd be wrong. Call it naïveté or call it intuition, but it felt like there was something connecting us, like an invisible cord tethering us together.

I should call Rhi and ask her advice, but I don't want her to pour a bucket of cold water over me. I want to revel in this feeling a little longer before coming back down to earth with a bump.

It's quiet here in the house now that Rhett's gone. I know we took a shower together, but I feel like a long soak in a hot bubble bath. So, I head upstairs to my master bathroom, where I have the most beautiful claw-footed, rolltop bath. It's deep and I can actually submerge myself as opposed to the bath that came with the house, where my knees were constantly above the water level.

As the water runs, I grab my iPod dock from my room and hit shuffle. If there's anything I love, it's to listen to music. Anywhere, anytime, I just have music in my soul. It's a part of everyday life. Or it is for me, anyway.

Turning off the taps, I sink into the water and fully submerge myself. I come back up with wet hair and wipe the water from my eyes.

You were all I ever needed, but you left me feeling broken…

The words float through my iPod dock and I can't help but sing along.

My heart exposed and open, you took my love and left me cold…

As I listen to the voice, it feels like déjà vu. If I didn't know better, I'd say the voice sounds a bit like Rhett when he was singing karaoke the other night. But I know that can't be true. After all, this is a country band I used to listen to with Angelo.

It feels like a lifetime since I've been able to listen to them without crying—and for some people, three years *is* a lifetime.

Some say it's better to have loved and lost, but they're so very wrong…

I can't say I agree with that line. It's better to have loved, to have been loved and lost it, than to have never felt love at all. If I'd never loved Angelo, my life wouldn't have been so full, so happy. His love made me feel whole.

My thoughts turn to this afternoon with Rhett. *Should I have done what I did? Was it wrong to want to feel again? Did I only do it to stop me feeling numb?* No. I did it because there's this inexplicable, yet undeniable chemistry between us. I haven't felt anything like it in a long time and I want to explore it. I don't know *how* or *when* it will end. I know he has to leave eventually, but what if he didn't have to? What if there was a reason for him to stay in my small corner of the world? Is that wishful thinking? *Maybe.*

I wash myself and my hair—again—before standing to grab the towel I laid out. I wrap myself in it and step from the tub. Pulling the plug, I let the water drain while I dry myself off and get redressed.

Sitting at my vanity, I comb through my hair and grab my hairdryer. Once I'm done, I apply a little makeup and pull my hair up in a ponytail. I find myself making a bit more effort, knowing I could bump into Rhett around any corner, thanks to living in a town this size.

Before I know it, it's time to fetch Hardin from school.

"I got all the answers correct, Mummy," he informs me as we talk about the maths questions they did at school.

"That's fantastic, baby."

"I got a star sticker from Miss Pearl. She said that I was the only one that got them all right."

"You don't get your ability at maths from me then. I was rubbish at it. I *still* am."

"What was your favourite subject at school, Mummy?"

"Oh, well, that would probably be English. I got an A star on my GCSE."

"What's a GCSE, Mummy?" he asks, looking up at me with a puzzled expression.

"It's like a big test when you leave high school, sweetie."

"And is an A star good?"

"It was the best score, yeah."

"I wonder if I'll get an A star in maths."

"Well, the way they grade the tests has probably changed a lot since then, but I bet you'll get the best score there is. But that's only if you pay attention every day. You need to keep practising to get really good at something."

"I will, Mummy. I promise."

"Good boy."

"Are you at work tonight, Mummy?"

"I am, baby. You'll be staying with Nanny and Grandad and they'll take you to school in the morning."

"Okay."

He skips along the pavement as we walk home. Staying at my mum and dad's he gets to sleep in what he calls a "big boy bed". It's a cabin bed that my mum bought him recently. He's tried nagging me into getting him one for his room at home, but I don't have the money saved at the moment. That's another reason I want to get the job I interviewed for.

Unfortunately, the waiting period is going to be about a month from the date of my interview. Niamh, the lady that interviewed me, said they'd get back to me whether I'm successful or not, so that I'm not left hanging. But she was super positive at the time.

I won't lie, I'd love to work for the company. It would be better money than just working in the pub, but it would also leave me with enough time to still put a few hours in at the pub each week without putting a strain on my time with Hardin. I don't really want to leave The Lock, because Damien and Deb have become like family to me in the time I've been there, and I'd hate to have to give it up completely.

We walk into the house and Hardin asks for a snack. I tell him that he needs to get changed out of his uniform first, so he runs upstairs to grab himself some clothes.

While he does that, I grab some bread, the Nutella spread and a banana. I think it's a weird combination and I'm not the keenest on bananas, but Hardin loves it. I pop the bread in the toaster.

I soon hear footsteps coming back downstairs. I cut the toast into triangles before spreading the Nutella and slicing the banana to go on top.

Hardin comes into the kitchen dressed in his favourite Curious George t-shirt and a pair of jeans.

"Hey, baby."

"Hi, Mummy. I'm dressed. Can I get my snack now?"

"You certainly can," I say as I place the plate in front of him at the breakfast bar.

"Yay," he says as he claps his hands together.

He climbs onto the stool and tucks into his favourite snack. The chocolate spread ends up around his mouth and his teeth are chocolatey as he smiles at me. He flashes sticky fingers at me before diving into the second piece.

"You'll need to brush your teeth before going to Nanny's."

"Why?" he asks around a mouthful.

"Don't speak with your mouth full. You'll have to brush them because they've gone all chocolatey."

He nods his head instead of answering me. Sometimes he forgets not to speak with food in his mouth. It's a good job he's only little and there's time to instil it in him.

***

It's been a week and, unable to resist temptation, I've slept with Rhett another twice. He's incredible in bed. There's just something about the chemistry between us that I've been unable to resist. It's like some gravitational pull between us.

But it's not just the mind-blowing sex. It's the conversation and everything. He's told me a bit about his family and his friends. I've told him more about Angelo, Hardin, and my other family members. It's begun to feel like the start of a *real* relationship, and I'm not going to lie, I'm scared that I'll be brought back down to earth with a bang when he inevitably leaves. I'm trying not to think about that day, but I'm a weird mix of optimist and pessimist. I'm realistic, but I try to remain hopeful. My head is definitely not in the clouds, unless it's after an afternoon in Rhett's arms, when he makes me feel like I'm on cloud nine.

I've seen him at the pub, and we've spent time together when we're not in the pub and also not in bed. We've watched films, talked, laughed. He's been back to my uncle Ted's bookstore to buy rest of the series he's reading, but he admitted he hasn't had much time to read, since he's been spending his free time with me.

Unfortunately, neither Damien nor I have been successful in getting Rhett up on the karaoke since last week, which is a shame because from what I heard, he has an amazing voice.

When I asked him why he said he couldn't hold a tune, he said he's shy about singing in public. I assured him he didn't need to be, but even then, I couldn't get him to agree to a repeat performance.

Mum has noticed a change in me since the first time I spent the afternoon with Rhett. She asked if it was a man, and I didn't want to jinx things between us by saying yes. I didn't want to look a fool if it was a one-off thing, and now I don't want to look like an idiot when he ultimately says goodbye and goes back to his *real* life.

I'm getting ready to cook lunch for him, singing along—totally off-key—to a little bit of Luke Bryan. Damn, that man has an incredible voice, and he's so handsome too.

My ideal man would be a man who can sing and play an instrument—preferably guitar, but any instrument would do really, except maybe a brass instrument, that is.

"Country Girl" plays, and I can't help but shake it like Luke asks his country girl to. I must look like a fool, but having the house to myself, I couldn't really give a damn.

A knock at the door interrupts my dancing around like a loon. As I open the door, I'm greeted by a bouquet of flowers. Rhett lowers the flowers so I can see his handsome face. I feel a smile tug at my lips.

"Hey gorgeous," he says in that husky way of his.

His voice is enough to turn my insides to liquid.

"Afternoon, handsome."

"These are for you … obviously." He hands me the bouquet and I notice an assortment of flowers. "I wasn't sure of your favourite flower, so the florist helped me choose an arrangement for you. I hope they're okay?"

"They're beautiful, Rhett, thank you so much. Come in. I'll put them in water."

I inhale the beautiful scent of the flowers as we walk into the kitchen. I place them on the breakfast bar as I find a vase and fill it with water. It's been so long since anyone bought me flowers. My mum makes a thing of getting me some from Hardin for Mother's Day, but other than that, I haven't been bought any for a long time.

The flowers themselves come as a surprise, but it isn't a surprise how sweet and thoughtful Rhett is.

"Luke Bryan, huh?" he asks with a smile.

"Yep. I do love a man who can sing, and boy, this man can really sing. Have you heard that song he covered with Jason Derulo?"

"Can't say as I have."

"Oh, it's awesome. Give me a second."

I grab my iPod and turn on the Wi-Fi so I can find the song on YouTube, considering they never actually released it together, which is a real shame. I would buy it in a heartbeat.

"Want to Want Me" plays over my iPod dock and I use the control to turn the volume up. This song wasn't meant to be played quietly.

Rhett takes my hand and pulls me to him. Sliding his hands down over my dress, he grips my hips and sways me in time to the song. He smiles at me and I swear my heart beats so fast it's like it's trying to break free. He dips me as the song ends before pulling me up and claiming my lips in a sweet, but dizzying kiss. Jeez, could this man get any more perfect?

No, Caleigh. You will not get attached. He's leaving. This relationship or whatever the hell it is comes with an expiration date. I mentally chastise myself.

"What's for lunch?" he asks as he pulls back, allowing me to finally breathe.

I don't know what it is, but every time he kisses me, it's like I forget to breathe, like he's all that matters.

"Rainbow beef salad with an Asian-inspired dressing. I hope you like steak. The recipe normally calls for it barbecued, but I don't own a barbecue and I don't really fancy going around to my parents' place to use theirs."

"Sounds lovely. Depends how you cook your steak though."

"Medium-well," we both say at the same time.

"If you have it any other way, you're a monster," I say as I poke my tongue out at him.

Seriously, though, I hadn't particularly thought about how he'd want it cooked. I had a hard enough time trying to decide what to even cook in the first place.

"And what makes it a *rainbow* salad," he asks, air-quoting the word.

"Just the pop of colour from things like the lettuce, radish, carrot, cucumber, tomato, avocado … Tomato isn't actually in the recipe I found, but I love them, so I added cherry tomatoes."

"Cherry tomatoes?"

His puzzled expression gives me a clue as to his complete lack of cooking skills. How on earth does this guy live on his own?

"Yes, they're little ones, like the size of a cherry, hence the name."

"Oh, that's better than what I envisioned when you said that. Seriously, I had some kind of hybrid of a cherry and a tomato in mind, and that sounded revolting."

"Jeez Mr. Butler. How on earth are you a bachelor?"

"Well, takeaway, good friends who have girlfriends that don't mind cooking for my sorry ass. Umm … my mum brings me by a lasagne or shepherd's pie or something once a week."

I crack up laughing as he lists all these people that do it all for him.

"You don't cook at all?"

"Well, I have been known to burn beans on toast. But I can cook scrambled eggs in the microwave."

"The microwave?" I interrupt his answer.

"Yeah. How else are you supposed to cook them?"

"Rhett Butler, I swear, I will make it my mission to convert you by teaching you how to cook them properly before you leave."

My heart squeezes like it's in a vice as I speak that last word.

"And how, pray tell, does one cook them properly."

Again, with the air-quoting of words. It's a good job he's so darn cute.

"In a saucepan, of course."

"A microwave works for me."

"Well that's because you haven't had them any other way. Boy, I can see I have a lot to teach you. They taste much better done my way."

"I won't argue with you. I'm sure you're right. But whether or not you'll convert me to cooking them your way in future is yet to be determined."

"Fine, come for breakfast in the morning and I'll give you a demonstration."

"It's a date. Now, about lunch …"

"What about it? Don't tell me you don't like avocado; that might be a deal-breaker."

"I was just wondering," he says as he comes and wraps his arms around my waist, "whether"—he peppers my neck with kisses—"you might reconsider cooking."

"Why?"

"Well, I thought that"—he kisses up the other side of my neck to my earlobe and bites—"we could have dessert first?"

"Oohhh."

I am so dumb sometimes. And I'd be lying if I said his suggestion wasn't appealing.

"So, what do you say?"

He ghosts a kiss over my lips, and I have to wrap my arms around his neck to stop him from breaking the kiss.

"I'd ask if I can think about it," I reply with a smirk.

I take his hand and lead him to the stairs. He smacks my ass with his free hand, and I'd be a goddamn liar if I said I didn't want him to do that again when I'm naked.

Chapter Eight

Brent

Every time I see Caleigh, it's harder to hear her call me by my stupid assumed name. She was screaming out my name only minutes ago, but what I wouldn't give to hear her call me by my real name, Brent Lachlan Ryder.

I feel like an utter asshole for lying to her, but I came to this town for anonymity, and it's worked well for me with everyone but her. I want her to know who I *really* am. I don't know whether she's heard of the band, but if I tell her who I am, I'm going to have to tell her why I lied. She's a really great woman, but would she understand? I'd like to hope so.

"Earth to Rhett," Caleigh says as she waves a hand in front of my face.

"Sorry, did you say something?"

"I just asked if you fancied a shower before finally eating lunch."

"It depends on whether I'm allowed to make you dirtier before you get clean."

She smiles that heart-warming smile of hers and I feel like I'm a goner. Hook, line and sinker. But I can't be. It's impossible. I didn't come here to start anything and when we did, I always knew this … relationship—is that the right word?—came with an expiration date. But my racing heart would beg to differ.

"And just how would you do that?" she asks with a raised eyebrow.

"Let me show you," I reply as I part her legs and climb in between them.

Her eyes light up as I move further south. If there's one thing we haven't done in our time together before now, it's oral.

It's not because I haven't wanted to, rather because we've both been too impatient, and she's always been so wet from just kissing or me using my fingers. I didn't know it was possible to get a woman so aroused from merely kissing until I met Caleigh, but now I'm learning anything is possible.

I slide further down the bed and pepper a trail of kisses from her naval down. Using just my thumb on her clit, I feel her legs start to quiver. It's easy to make her squirm like this after we've already had sex. That much I do know from time spent with her.

We may have only spent a couple of afternoons together so far properly—not counting the time we've spent in the pub or the times we've just talked or chilled with a film—but in that time, I've learned that after her first orgasm, she's easily aroused again.

I plan to use this to my advantage as I lick her in long, languid strokes. Her breathy moans are a turn on, and I look up to see her looking at me through a hooded gaze.

As I suck her clit, I hear her panting and it only stokes the fire burning within me. Fuck, this woman is just incredible.

Her hands come to my hair as I part her with my fingers and lick her once more. I look up to see her back arching off the bed and I watch as her pert breasts move up and down with her breathing.

"Fuck, Rhett," she whispers as I suckle her clit before licking her again.

"Yes, baby?"

"Make me come, I'm begging you."

"Begging? But I've only just begun."

"And I can barely … take it."

She has to pause when I use the opportunity to slide a finger inside her. Fuck, she's so hot and wet. I can feel my cock getting hard again. It's a good job I went and bought condoms when I was in Pedmore the other day. I couldn't buy them from the local store—I'd have the locals whispering about who I'm sleeping with—so I made sure to stock up while there wasn't anyone around to care.

"Caleigh?"

"Yeah?"

"Hold on tight, baby."

I withdraw my finger and replace it with my tongue. Her cries are enough guidance to know she's enjoying it.

Rubbing my thumb over her clit, I make her squirm in the most delightful way possible. She tugs on my hair and it spurs me on. It also gives me an idea. I take her hand from my hair and guide it down to her pussy.

"Play with your clit, baby. Let me watch as you squirm."

"Fuck!" she cries, and she slowly circles her clit while I bury my tongue inside her once more.

God if I died today, I'd go a seriously fucking happy man. But not until I've chased her orgasm, followed by another of my own.

***

When we finally got around to having lunch, it was a taste I won't soon forget, but not nearly as much as Caleigh herself is.

She had to go and get Hardin from school, and though I've already met him that once in the street, I didn't want to hang around to meet him as more than just the guy with the funny name. We're not there yet, and if I'm honest, we never could be.

I said I'll meet her later when she's working in the pub, under the guise of going in to see if Damien wants a drink, so we don't start some kind of rumour mill. Stupidly, and completely unlike me, I've already chosen what to wear so that it looks like I'm making an effort without making too much of an effort. Like I said, stupid really.

My phone chimes as I'm reading the second book in the series I started. I went back to One More Chapter and saw Ted, where he laughed and said I should have known to buy all the books at once. I'd also passed by Strings and Things again and looked longingly at the Stratocaster.

I pick up my phone in the hopes it might be Caleigh. No such luck though.

>Brent, dude, have you seen the news?

>Nah man, better uses of my time. What's up?

>They're saying you boarded a plane; someone took a picture of you in the airport. There's speculation as to where you are and, of course, that now means nobody is buying the story Gordon fed that you're ill.

Fuck. Thanks for that, Ash.

>Well I'm not sure what I can do about that now, Ash, man. Gordon will have to douse the embers of that story before it becomes flames.

>Gordon is freaking the fuck out, man. He's gone ballistic at the rest

of us, saying we must know where you are or have a way of contacting you. He's demanding answers.

>And what have you told him?

I start to get mad as I wait for a reply. Finally, it comes through.
>We covered for you, man. Even Evan, albeit begrudgingly in his case. We said you've cut us off just like you have him. Told him we've had complete radio silence. He said a man of your age cannot possibly go without a phone this long, so he reckons you bought a new one.

>Did you tell him anything, and I mean ANYthing?

>Nah man, we got you. We're your brothers, we'd never tattletale to 'Dad'. You promised us you'd email him though. You need to keep your head down though, dude. Having your face splashed everywhere won't help you keep your anonymity wherever you are.

>I know I said I'd email him, man, but I've been busy. And don't worry about me, I've dyed my hair.

>Busy chasing tail? And WTF, dyed your hair?

I chuckle at his question, but then find myself offended. Caleigh is not "tail". She's special. But Ash doesn't know that. It's not like I've told anyone, even them, about her.
>Nah, none to be found, more's the pity. And yes, dyed my hair and haven't shaved. I'm staying in a small town where, hopefully, nobody will recognise me.

>Don't try and play me, player. I know you've probably got a different girl for every night of the week. I'm not knocking you man, just making conversation.

>I seriously haven't. No word of a lie.

>Man, you're the worst liar I know, even by text.

>Shut up, Ash. You don't know what you're talking about.

>So, tell me…

For god's sake. I should know by now that Ash is the worst of us.
He's like a dog with a bone. I consider telling him another lie, but he's
just too persistent. So, I choose to tell him a version of the truth.

>There has been one woman since I've been here.

>One as in you can't get more or you don't WANT more????

I scrub my hand over my face as I swallow hard. Deciding honesty
is my best bet, I tell him the truth of it.

>I haven't wanted or needed more.

>Wow, Brent, my brother, are you losing your touch or just getting
old? ;)

>No, just…

I begin typing, then delete it and try to put my thoughts into words.

>Look, Ash, I'll level with you, okay? But please, for the love of God,
just accept it at face value and don't ask any more questions because I
don't want to argue with you

I hit send.

>Shit, you're serious about her??!! What's her name?

>I haven't known her long enough for it to be "that" kind of serious,
but I do really like her.

>You really gonna leave me hanging like that, bro?

>I said no more questions…

>Bro, all I wanted to know was her name.

>It's Caleigh…

I run my hand through my hair as I consider what I'm about to
tell him. I trust Ash though. I would trust Evan and Jude with a lot of

things, but Ash gets me on a different level, and I know he won't open his mouth to anyone about it.

>She's a single mum. She has a son who is five. His name is Hardin. But dude, you can't tell anyone, especially Gordon. I don't want him trying to use that information to find me.

I finish typing the text and hover over the send button. Taking a deep breath, I hit it before I can reconsider.

It's a long moment before he responds. I bet he's sitting with his mouth opening and closing like a goldfish. I'm never serious about a woman, like, *ever*. Much less a single mum. I don't have a bias against single mums at all, it's just that I don't do relationships, and kids add an extra level of complication that I've tried really hard to avoid because I don't want people getting hurt.

Any woman I normally sleep with knows it's a "one and done" deal, and we've normally moved onto the next stop on the tour before they can try for a repeat anyway. They may have even had kids, but I wouldn't know because I don't ask anything beyond their name and age.

>Dude! WTF? I mean, no offence, but how can you be involved with her when you're planning on leaving? Won't that affect the kid too? I mean, shit, dude!

>Look, I'm going to tell you this and then I really mean it, NO more questions.

>I'm sorry, buddy, I really don't mean it negatively. You can't help who you like, but man, kids make it hard in terms of attachment and leaving. He'll be crushed when you have to go.

>I've only met him once, in the street, and we just said hi. Caleigh and I have been secretive about meeting up and we only see each other while he's at school. He doesn't know me as someone Mummy is seeing, he just knows me as the guy with the funny name.

>Oh, I see. Well in that case, good for you. But man, if you're serious about her, it's going to make leaving that much harder.

>Trust me, bro, I know that. I haven't been here long, but already I know it's going to be hard to come home. I'm going to miss the peace and

quiet, the solitude of the place I'm staying in, cos I'm enjoying sitting in my room and reading. But most of all, I'm going to miss Caleigh, and if I stay much longer, it's going to hurt that much worse.

>I don't mean to piss on your parade bro, you know that, right? Man, I can't believe it though. Brent Lachlan Ryder can do real feelings.

>Yeah, well, just don't tell anyone, not even the guys. Please Ash, I'm not asking for much, just a little longer without having to answer a million and one question
ns.
>Asher Richards knows how to keep a secret, man.

>Dude, stop talking about yourself in the third person. It's an annoying habit. The only person capable of pulling it off is Terry Jeffords!

>Man, I haven't caught up on the latest season of Nine-Nine. Too busy busting my balls on tour. You know they asked me to step up as lead singer, right?

>No, nobody told me that. But it's a good call, dude, you've got what it takes. I could retire and it wouldn't matter. Oh, and I've not caught the latest season yet either.

>You'd retire? Man, this woman must really have you mooning like a lovesick teen if you're considering that bold a move.

>I'm not hanging up my Stetson, bro. I just need some space and time. I'll be back, I just don't know how soon.

>You've always been the one out of us that likes the limelight the least, which is funny considering you're the lead singer. Do you miss your guitar?

>Oh yeah! I saw a Fender Stratocaster in town and was practically drooling.

But I left mine behind on purpose. I'll be honest, Ash, I feel stunted or something. I can't quite put it into words properly. All I know is I haven't written anything new in months. I'm struggling to find inspiration. It's like the well has dried up or something. As for the limelight, I'm just a bit fed up with it. It was great when we were younger, but now I'm getting older, I'm less than thrilled with chicks thinking I'll screw them so they can sell their story to the paper.

>That has happened to all of us at one time or another, dude. Gordon does what he can to put out the flames in those cases. As for inspiration, yeah, I feel you. I know what it's like, you know that. Either way though, dude, I've got your back.

>Thanks, man. Look, I've got to go, but I'll be in touch. And yes, before you say it, I'll send Gordon an email, but not before I'm ready. He'll only hound me about when I'll be back and I don't have an answer, so ...

>I know, man, and we'll do what we can to keep Gordon off your case. Speak later bro.

I don't know what compelled me to tell Ash all that, considering I didn't want to spill the details to *anyone*. But I admit, it was nice to be able to tell him without the level of crap I'd anticipate from the others.

It makes me question how I truly feel though. I haven't really thought much about it until now. I mean, I'm a man, and *some* men might think that it shows weakness to open up about emotions and all that shit, but the way *I* see it, if you can admit to your feelings, if you can *show* that you actually do *feel* like any other person—then that's a goddamn strength.

Chapter Nine

Caleigh

I swear to god, every time the pub door opens, I look up in the hopes it's Rhett. He said he'd be in tonight but didn't say what time. I think Damien might have noticed my clock watching, and I know he's seen me look up at the door because he's caught my eye a couple of times. I keep trying to resist looking up, but I can't. Lord help me, I'm like a lovestruck teenager mooning over her crush. But I'm not either of those things. For one, I can't be lovestruck because I've only known the guy for five minutes. For two, I am definitely not a teenager anymore. I haven't been for a long time now.

I shouldn't even care whether he comes in tonight or not; it shouldn't matter to me one way or another. But I can't help it. There's something magnetic about Rhett. He's handsome, smart, funny. He makes my afternoons that much sweeter when he comes to visit.

I'm not reliant on someone else for my happiness, far from it. But I learned a while back that liking someone and having them in your life doesn't necessarily make you co-dependent.

There was a time when I thought that having relationships took something away from you, from your independence. I thought it meant losing part of yourself. There are these lyrics of this one song that Angelo used to love, that talk about it only being when you lose yourself in someone else that you find yourself. But I think I interpreted those lyrics differently or maybe just disagreed with the words. To me, it isn't in someone else that you find yourself. You need to stand tall, on your own two feet, to find yourself. But that doesn't necessarily mean that you lose a part of yourself if you're in a relationship. I don't know, maybe I'm not making any sense.

I don't know whether I believe in destiny or fate or whatever people call it. I think you are the master of your own destiny. You are the one behind that wheel, steering your life where it's meant to be. But I do believe that the people that you meet along the way are part of what shapes you. Whether it's something good or bad that happens to you, it has an impact on your life, though to what degree, you won't know at the time.

Maybe meeting Rhett has taught me that I can be open to finding and accepting love again. But it doesn't have to mean that if I have a relationship I have to lose my independence. I don't know whether relationships equal co-dependency, or whether it's just a matter of there being a degree of independence you give to the other person when you give them your heart. Like, you agree—in an unspoken way—that you are both dependent on each other to a degree, but you both still know how to stand on your own two feet. You don't rely on the other person for every little thing in life, every little moment of happiness, because then you really are likely to lose yourself, and if you do that and then you split up with them, how do you start to pick up the pieces?

If you're in a relationship and it ends, you need to know that you are fully capable of being independent again.

When I lost Angelo, it took a long time to accept he wouldn't be around anymore, that I would never see his face again, or hear him laugh or read Hardin a bedtime story. I had to stand up and be strong for both myself and my son. I had to do everything for Hardin that Angelo used to. But that's part of being a parent. But when it came to me, I had to learn to adapt or be engulfed by my grief. I had to learn to do a lot of things again, and that's what made me scared of relationships going forward.

However, I learned along the way that relationships with people might help define you, be it a relationship with a man, a friend or a family member. But helping to put you on the right path, to help define you as a person, to learn things from those relationships, that isn't a bad thing. You're still you, you're just forging a path to becoming the best version of yourself that you can be. So no, in my opinion, you don't lose yourself, your sense of identity, by being in a relationship.

The door opening pulls me out of my thoughts as my eyes snap up to meet that cerulean blue gaze I've come to love staring into. They say eyes are windows to the soul, and if that's true, then what I see is a pure and beautiful soul, untainted by the world around it. I'm sure he's been hurt, but if he has, he hasn't let it colour who he is as a person. He hasn't let the world leave its cruelty imprinted on his soul.

"Hey Caleigh," he says with a wave as he approaches the bar, "is that boss of yours in tonight?"

"Hey, Rhett. Yeah, he's through the back sorting out a supplier issue. They didn't bring us enough barrels. I'm sure he'll be out once he's done on the phone."

"I'll take a bottle of beer while I wait then, please."

He sits at the bar and I turn to grab him a bottle from the fridge. Budweiser seems to be a favourite of his, so I take off the cap and hand it to him.

"Thanks. How are you?"

"Good, thanks. You?"

"Yeah not too bad. Got my head stuck in a book, otherwise I might have been here earlier."

"Must have been a damn good book."

"It's the second book of the series that the Netflix show *The Witcher* is based on."

"Ooh does it have pictures? I do like Geralt."

"No, but there is a series of graphic novels. But you do know the drawings won't be of that Cavill? It was written by a Polish author, Andrzej Sapkowski. It was originally a series of novels and short stories and then a video game, if I'm right. I don't know whether the game preceded the graphic novels or the other way around though."

"Damien says you guys binged the whole series in one night," I say with a smile, already knowing everything he's telling me, but unable to give the game away at work.

"We did. It was a long night. I only planned to stay for a couple of episodes, but it was so good that I didn't want to be left hanging for the next one. Damien told me as much before I started watching, but I have to be honest, I'm not one for hype over things, be that books or TV shows."

"Oh? And why's that? Surely hype is good and lets you know something is worthy of reading or watching."

"Nah, not me. I might be in the minority here, but if there's that much hype about something, I give it a wide berth in case it falls short of my expectations. I know everyone can't like the same things, otherwise it would be pretty boring if we did, but I've been burned several times with the whole 'oh my god, this show is amazing,' only to watch it and wonder to myself whether or not I'd watched the same thing. When the buzz dies down, I will decide whether I want to watch or read something on my own."

"I guess that's a good way of being, actually. I never thought of it like that, I suppose."

He chuckles, and the butterflies in my stomach begin to take flight.

"Like I say, we aren't all wired the same. Are you the kind of person who reads reviews before buying a book?"

"Umm ... I mean, sometimes, yeah. Though not always. Depends what it is, I suppose. If it's by a favourite author, I just one-click on Amazon without reading the blurb, never mind reviews. But if I've never read anything by the author, then yes, I'll read a mix of one and five-star reviews."

"And why do you do that? Read a mixture, I mean."

"Well because I'm wary of books that have nothing but five-star reviews. Although there aren't many I've read that are like that, if I'm honest. I read the lower rated reviews because we don't all read the same book and have the same feelings about it afterwards."

"Exactly. We don't all love or loathe something. You may like something, but I may not, and vice versa. So, when literally everyone is raving about something, I just don't trust that hype. There *have* to be people that didn't like it, so I wait a while and see if they come out of the woodwork before making up my mind. Ultimately, whether I enjoy something or not is not dictated by either good or bad reviews. I like to give something a go and decide for myself. But it can take a while before I take the leap. Does that make sense?"

"Totally. I'm the same about it being ultimately my decision whether I read a book that other people have hated. I'll read it because it appeals to me. And whether I enjoy it or not is not based on other people's viewpoints. So, yeah, I get it."

I'll be honest, I enjoy finding things out about him, even the little things.

"Working hard, I see," Damien says, making me jump.

"That would be my fault, sorry, buddy," Rhett answers before I can speak.

"And why's that?" he asks as he grabs himself a beer from the fridge and walks around the bar to sit on his favourite end stool.

"I was waffling on about reading the *Witcher* books."

"Oh, buddy, I feel you. I love the books. And that's coming from a man who rarely finds the time to read. I devoured those books one a night until I was done. I have the graphic novels too. I probably still have the game somewhere too, although I don't get as much time for games as I used to."

"Did the supplier agree to rectify the mistake?" I ask, interrupting their bonding time.

"No. They agreed to deliver extra tomorrow, but at an extra cost. So, we'll have to make do with what we have until then, which shouldn't be hard. They basically said that it was signed for by Deb, so she should have been more aware of how many barrels were on the order. It's my own fault though, but I didn't realise that until *after* I'd had a go at the guy on the phone."

It's unlike Damien to make a mistake. He's the most organised person I know, but I guess we're all flawed and prone to the odd mistake.

"Oh?"

"Yeah, I, umm … well, I ordered the wrong number of barrels. I missed off a number on the order. Stupid rookie mistake really. I should know better. But I've been getting headaches for a while now and looking at a screen just doesn't help."

"Headaches, boss? Are you okay? Should you be going to the doctors?"

"More like the opticians, I think. I should stop being vain and realise that if I need glasses, I need glasses. I just don't want to admit to getting old, I guess."

"Dude, I need reading glasses too," Rhett says. "I have done since I was twenty-one. I was the same at first, embarrassed by the need to wear them. I was young and dumb. Vain, like you say. But if you're getting headaches from being on the computer and stuff, you should get yourself an eye test."

"I will, man, just been so busy lately. And yeah, vanity doesn't help. I guess I have to face facts and just get it done."

Honestly, vain men refusing an eye test. How typical.

***

As I finish my shift, I send Rhett a text before I can reconsider.

>Fancy coming to mine? We could have a nightcap, maybe …

I wait as three dots appear on the screen.
>I'd love to. Are you sure? Don't you have Hardin?

>No, Mum is taking him to school in the morning. Any time I finish as late as this, she takes him for me so that he can go to bed at the proper time and I don't have to wake him to bring him home.

>In that case, shall I meet you there?

>There's a spare key to the back door inside a fake rock right next to it. Let yourself in. I'll give it another ten minutes before I leave. Just make sure you aren't seen, please, for me? You know people in small towns know everything about everyone.

>Sure. I'm just leaving now. Damien is talking my ear off though.

>He's a good guy. Harmless unless you get on the wrong side of him.

>Yeah, well, I'm just going to tell him the text was important, and I need to make a call. That way I can get going. Give me two minutes.

I feel myself grinning from ear to ear. Sure, I want to keep things between us hush-hush for now, but he's the kind of guy that I could see a future with if he wasn't leaving town. If he was staying and things got serious between us, then I could see my parents being happy for us. He's the kind of guy a woman could take home to meet the parents and they'd get on like a house on fire.

My heart pangs in my chest as I think of his departure. I don't know how imminent it is and I don't want to burst our little bubble just yet.

Why does it hurt so much to think about what happens when he's gone? Why did he have to come into town and catch my eye? Other guys have come and gone since Angelo, and I haven't so much as batted an eyelid. I've been asked out and turned them down. I've been asked for my phone number and never given it to anyone. Why is Rhett Butler different? I've given him my number, I've cooked him lunch, I've slept with him; he's the first man I've been to bed with since Angelo. If he wasn't just passing through town, I could see us going on real dates. I could see a future. More than that, I find myself *wanting* to see a future in which we're together. How the hell do I make sense of these feelings?

>I'm waiting at yours. Haven't turned any lights on in case anyone sees.

I smile as I read his latest text. I can just see him sitting in the dark, waiting for me.

>Give me five minutes to say goodnight to Damien and walk home.

>See you then xx

My heart takes flight as I see those little kisses. Sure, it might seem insignificant to some, but it's the first time he's put kisses on a text, and it makes me happy. I guess little things really do make a difference.

Grabbing my coat and bag, I walk back into the bar and spot Damien sipping his whiskey, still sitting on his favourite stool. He's nothing if not predictable.

There was a time, a while ago, when I thought he might see me as more than a friend. I guess it was my mind playing tricks on me though, because he's never made a move on me. He's just always been a friend, and now my boss.

"Night, boss. See you tomorrow afternoon."

"Night, Caleigh. Have a good one."

"You too, boss."

"Those barrels should come around three-thirty. Please do me a favour and tell Deb I'm sorry I thought it was her mistake in signing for the delivery. I'd tell her myself, but I'm off to see a band play over in Pedmore. I'll talk to her when I'm back at work the following morning, but I don't want her thinking I'm mad at her or anything."

"Will do, Damien. If I were you, I'd book that eye test soon. Don't worry about Deb, it'll be water off a duck's back. Anyway, a nice long soak to soothe my aching bones is on the cards, so I'll be off."

"Night, Caleigh."

I make the short walk home and let myself in quietly. I don't know why I'm tiptoeing around when it's my house, but I find myself doing it anyway.

"Hey," Rhett says as I turn the light on in the living room, making me jump out of my skin.

I knew he was here, but he still scared the shit out of me.

"Hey."

"I don't think I was seen. I think we'd have the police here with their blues and twos if the neighbours thought there was an intruder."

"Can I get you a drink?" I ask as I toe my shoes off and feel instant relief.

"Sure."

"Alcoholic or coffee?"

"You did offer me a nightcap," he says as he stalks closer to me.

"I have beer in the fridge, but I also have a bottle of whiskey in the cupboard."

"I'll take a whiskey," he replies as he wraps his arms around me.

I place my arms around his neck and tug gently on his long hair. I say long, it's shoulder length. I'm almost jealous because it's so thick and gorgeous. I'm thankful he doesn't wear it in a scruffy topknot. I know it suits some people, but I don't think I'd like the look on him.

Ghosting a kiss over my lips, he tastes like whiskey. I inhale deeply and smell something sort of woodsy. I love that he smells so masculine and sexy. Is it weird that I like it that much? Maybe, but I don't care.

He gently coaxes me into a deeper kiss, and I submit, parting my lips and allowing his tongue to dance softly with mine. It's soft and tender, yet there's a hint of desperation. Like he's seeking solace in my kiss.

"I thought you wanted a nightcap?" I ask as I break the kiss.

"I want something else more," he replies huskily.

Even the timbre of his voice has my insides liquifying.

"And what would that be?" I play dumb.

"Well, I could tell you, or I could *show* you. You choose."

"How about you tell me, *then* you show me?"

"Well now, I think I could do that," he says with a wry chuckle.

He tugs my hair and tilts my head back before leaning in and stealing another soul-searing kiss that has my toes curling into the carpet.

"I think first of all," he says as he peppers kisses down my neck, "I would peel you out of these clothes. Then, I would lie you down and use my fingers and tongue to draw out your first orgasm. I'd watch you squirm as I suckle your clit, whilst my free hand would roam up to your breasts and play with your nipples ..." He trails off to kiss up to my ear.

My body already feels like somebody lit the match and is just waiting for me to combust, and he hasn't even done the things he's talking about.

"I'm imagining you're already hot and wet, so I'd slide two fingers inside you and fuck you with them until you can't stand the overwhelming sensation anymore. Then,"—he ghosts another kiss over my lips before pulling back and looking into my eyes. He holds my gaze as he continues—"after you've come for me, I'd strip naked and watch my hard cock as it sinks inside you. I would trap your hands above your head with one hand, while I take my time, build a steady rhythm. My free hand would grip your hip as you buck to meet me thrust for thrust."

"Fuck, Rhett."

"I'd seek to build a punishing pace, fucking you good and hard until you're screaming out my name like a goddamn curse and a prayer."

I squeeze my legs together, but it doesn't abate the feeling at all. Warmth pools in my abdomen, and pretty soon, I'm sure it will consume me whole.

"Does that sound like something you'd want?"

"Yes," I say on a sigh.

I can't fathom another thought except him fucking me so hard I'm seeing stars. I want to seek oblivion with him.

Suddenly, he sweeps me off my feet with his hand beneath my legs. Cradling me to his chest, he walks to the bottom of the stairs before pausing.

"I forgot condoms."

"There are some in my drawer. I might have gone into Pedmore and stocked up," I say as I feel a blush creep across my cheeks.

"We had the same idea then, because I did that too."

His face morphs into a sexy grin before he leans in for a chaste kiss. He carries me upstairs and pushes my bedroom door open with his foot.

Lying me down reverently on the bed, he peels my skirt off, followed by my red lacy panties. I blush again as I realise that I wore a matching lacy bra in the hopes that he'd be peeling me out of my underwear tonight. I couldn't know for sure, but I know I *hoped* it would happen.

I sit up so I can take my top off, but he shakes his head at me, and I drop my hands.

Rhett moves up the bed and sits next to me, pulling me close for a kiss before his hands grip the hem of my top and pull it up over my head.

His eyes dart to the red lacy bra and I swear his eyes bug out of his head as he looks at my cleavage. Bringing his hands up, he cups my breasts and brushes his thumbs over my nipples, making them pebble instantly.

Leaning to one side, he kisses down my neck to the hollow of my throat. He trails kisses down to the swell of my breasts and then in a line down the valley between them. At the same time, I feel him unhook the clasp of my bra and the straps fall down my arms.

He sits back up, pulls the straps from my arms and discards it to one side. He looks at me, his gaze intense. An emotion I don't have time to decipher flits through his gaze before he pushes me back to lie on the bed.

I lie still, my naked flesh breaking out in goosebumps as he trails a hand over my body. He starts at my collarbone and then makes his way down to the apex of my thighs. It makes me shudder and gasp as he moves deft fingers over my skin. I can't seem to stop watching him, my eyes are glued to his every move.

"You are so beautiful, Caleigh."

I want to speak, but it's like I don't remember how to form words. My brain is just a fog of lust.

"I want to make love to you, not just fuck like rabbits. I don't want sex for the sake of sex. I want more."

My heart races as he confesses his desire.

"Rhett, I …" I trail off as he dips a finger between my legs and toys with my clit.

I can't form a coherent thought, never mind words, when his touch threatens to consume me.

***

The kitchen smells like fresh coffee while I walk around in just a t-shirt and a pair of panties. I gather ingredients for the perfect fluffy scrambled eggs and some bread to toast.

Rhett sits at the breakfast bar drinking his coffee, but I feel his eyes burning a hole in the back of my head.

"Are you going to come and learn how to make the best eggs, or are you going to keep staring at my ass?"

"That's a tough choice," he says with a laugh.

I turn to face him, spatula in hand. "Get your ass over here and watch the master at work, so that you can learn to cook for yourself."

"Yes, ma'am," he says with a salute.

I don't know what made me let him stay the night. I don't even think it was a conscious thought, it just felt natural. Plus, I ended up waking this morning with him spooning me, which felt pretty goddamn amazing.

We ended up collapsing, exhausted and satiated in one another's arms after he made love to me just like he promised. But then I awoke at three o'clock this morning because he was trailing a hand over my body and I felt his fingers dip between my legs. I pretended to be asleep as he slid one finger inside me, but I couldn't help as I began panting when he rubbed his thumb over my clit and worked me into a frenzy.

That ended up in rough, fiery, passionate sex. The kind of sex that makes your whole body come alive and start to burn from the inside out.

"So, first of all, you can crack the eggs into the bowl in case you end up getting any shell in there," I say as I hand him the eggs and an empty bowl.

While he cracks the eggs, I let my mind wander back to the events of last night.

I can't remember a time when I'd ever been so wanton. I mean, sex with Angelo had always been amazing, but he'd never held his hand around my throat in the middle of the night whilst he fucked me so hard that I began to see stars and thought I might pass out.

It had been my idea for Rhett to do that. It wasn't so much a suggestion, it wasn't discussed, I just took his hand and put it to my throat. He didn't hurt me, but holy shit, he'd made me come so hard.

I've read books and seen things played out on TV, but never thought I'd experience them first-hand. Never thought I'd *want* to. But Rhett brings out something in my I didn't know existed. There was something raw, primal even, about the way we acted. It was pure ecstasy, powerful and addictive.

"What next?" he asks, breaking my train of thought.

We cook the perfect eggs, light and fluffy, just like they should be. We pile them on top of the buttery toast and eat at the breakfast bar.

After a second cup of coffee, I stand and wash the dishes. Rhett stands beside me with a tea towel and dries them ready to be put away. Such a routine, mundane thing to be doing, but as I watch him in my peripheral vision, I feel this happiness fill me.

If life is short, and moments are but fleeting, then I want to capture each moment and squeeze as much joy from it as possible. I'm beginning to think that life is about creating passionate, happy moments, and I shouldn't let anyone stand in my way of enjoying every last one of them. I've stood in my own way until now, and I'm making a conscious decision not to do that anymore.

"Hey, whatcha thinking?" Rhett asks as he nudges my hip with his.

I realise I've been holding onto the plate for too long whilst being stuck in my own head.

"Just daydreaming, I guess."

"About how I'm going to take you back to bed and we're going to stay there until you need to shower before work?"

"Oh, are you now?"

"Yes."

His answer is firm, accepting no argument from me. Not that I'd *want* to argue with spending the day in bed with this handsome, amazing man.

"Then let's go."

I place the plate I'm holding on the draining board and take Rhett's hand in mine.

Once we're in my room, I strip myself of what little I was wearing, before turning to strip Rhett out of the t-shirt and boxer shorts he's wearing. When we're both naked, we stand facing each other. We're not touching, but I can feel his gaze sweep over me from head to toe as though he's tracing the lines with his fingers. It's tangible, and the air feels electrically charged as he moves to stand toe to toe with me.

Reaching out my hand, I cup his cheek. He rubs his scratchy short facial hair over my palm, and it tickles. I run my other hand over his taut muscles. His body is built like some kind of Greek god. I could stand and marvel at it all day, but I'd rather enjoy the way it feels when his body is on top of mine. Or underneath me. I don't care which, as long as I get to feel all of him.

I sit down on the bed and pat the space next to me. Rhett sits but doesn't do anything. It's like he's waiting for me to take charge. So I do.

As I straddle his lap, I push him back so that he's lying down on the mattress. Leaning down, I kiss him. Our tongues dance together in a slow, sensual tango. My breasts push up against his chest and I feel my nipples pebble.

Sitting up, I grind myself against him, earning me a throaty moan that I feel reverberate through his chest where my palms are placed.

"Caleigh ..." he whispers.

I grind myself over his erection and feel that warmth bloom in my abdomen.

"God, Caleigh ... I-I need you s-so bad."

Reaching down a hand, I take hold of his thick cock and rub it over my clit, moaning as it stimulates me.

Rhett reaches for my bedside table where there's a packet of condoms, but I put my hand on his arm, stopping him. I want to feel him, all of him.

"I have a contraceptive coil fitted," I inform him when his puzzled gaze sweeps over mine.

"But they're not one hundred per cent effective, let me just—"

"I'm clean, if you're worried. I haven't been with anyone since … Angelo." I whisper my late husband's name.

"Are you sure you want to?" he asks.

I don't answer, I just slide down onto the tip of his cock, moaning as I slide down and he fills me torturously slowly.

Rhett moans loudly as he feels me stretch to accommodate him. It feels so fucking good to feel him inside me without a thin sheen of rubber between us. Some people say they don't feel too different, but honestly, this feels so much better than the previous times we've been together.

I want him to feel my walls clench around his bare cock as I ride him. Our cries mingle as he bucks his hips to match my every movement.

"Fuck, Caleigh, you feel like heaven."

I increase my pace, making us both pant for breath. I watch as his chest rises and falls beneath my hands.

This connection I feel between us is as electrically charged as a bolt of lightning.

"Caleigh, I-I c-can't hold out much l-longer …"

My head falls back as his fingers dig into my hips. I buck against him and he thrusts inside me harder than I've ever felt in my life.

A guttural growl comes from Rhett as he bucks up to meet my hips.

"Caleigh."

"Rhett."

I snap my eyes to his and it's like he's trying to convey something without actually saying it. In a flash, he manoeuvres so that I'm beneath him. He positions himself between my legs and pushes them back towards my chest before lifting my calves so that they're over his shoulders.

When he finally moves—after what feels like an eternity but is really only a few seconds—he feels deeper inside me somehow.

He leans down to kiss me and it's a hot, messy, brutal kiss. It steals all the oxygen from the room, and I feel a fire raging inside me as he leans in to lick and suck my nipple before biting down. It stings, but my word, it is pleasurable, not painful.

"Rhett, I-I'm going to—"

I don't get to finish my sentence as my orgasm tears through me. It feels like a tidal wave and I'm riding the crest of it.

He doesn't give me time to recover as he ups his pace, in search of his own climax. When it takes hold of him, he cries out my name and stills his movements.

I feel it as he comes inside me and I can't help the grin that slowly spreads across my face. *That* was what we were missing. Or at least I know *I* was. This whole time, that was the thing I wanted to feel most.

Chapter Ten

Brent

I can't believe we just did that. Part of me—a big part—hadn't wanted that to happen unless she knew the *real* me. But when Caleigh said she wanted that, I couldn't hold back any longer.

I'm not stupid. I'm clean. I've been for checks since the last woman I slept with on tour. Plus, I've only ever not used a condom a couple of times when I've been really drunk or too horny to give a damn.

But I didn't want to do that with Caleigh still calling me fucking Rhett. That godforsaken stupid name that I gave myself to protect my anonymity here. I wanted her to cry out my *real* name as I came inside her. I've dreamed about it. I've touched myself in the shower to visions of her doing that. Ultimately, I was too weak-willed to stop it though. I wanted her more this time than any of the times we've been together before.

This woman will be the death of me, of that I'm certain. Absolutely fucking positive.

Caleigh curls up into my chest as I lie on my back, exhausted.

"Caleigh?" I ask quietly.

"Yeah?"

"You're the most perfect woman on the face of this planet. I hope you know that."

"You're too sweet. I'm not perfect, nobody is. We all have flaws, some more than others, some bigger than others."

"Then you are imperfectly perfect. Don't argue."

"Oh, Rhett," she sighs.

My heart feels like it's trapped in a steel vice with a thousand white-hot needles piercing it. I need to tell her my real name. I don't know if she'll understand, but I have to have hope.

"Caleigh, I have something to tell you."

I get no response, so I look down at her and see her eyes closed, her face relaxed in sleep.

"My name is not Rhett," I whisper. "It's Brent."

***

I walk around town aimlessly. Caleigh had to go to work and I didn't want to prop up the bar all day just to see her. I have a feeling that even if other people didn't notice, Damien would cotton on to what's going on between us.

I'm not stupid. I've seen the way he looks at her when he thinks nobody's watching. I've looked at her the same way, so it's impossible that I'm mistaken.

My feet come to a stop and I look up to see the beautiful black Fender Stratocaster in the window of Strings and Things.

Before I can stop myself, I push the shop door open and a little bell alerts the shopkeeper to my presence.

"Hello, sir, is there something I can help you with?" he asks.

"I-I don't know. I was l-looking at the beauty in the window." I almost trip over my own words. I feel like an idiot.

He walks to the window display and removes the Fender. He cradles it gently, like any man with a love of guitars would.

"Do you play?" I ask.

"Oh, I used to. Not so much with the arthritis taking hold of my hands."

"I bet you miss it. I can't even imagine not playing. I started learning—I say *learning*, but maybe it was more like messing around— when I was about nine. My parents got me a tutor after they saw me playing on a friend's guitar one day."

"I've seen many a child that age start to play. I, myself, was a little older than that, but I started in high school. I think I was maybe twelve. Did you want to handle this beauty and see how she plays?"

I shouldn't. I promised myself this time here without a guitar. But …

Before I realise what I'm doing, I say yes and take it from him. I sit on the stool he points to and strum a couple of chords. My fingers move like muscle memory. They fly over the strings like they have a million times before and I start to play a melody I'm all too familiar with.

" 'Hotel California', what a song," the guy says as I continue to play. "Haven't played that myself in years."

"It has some of the best guitar riffs in music today," I respond without missing a beat. I lose myself to the music, tuning out to the world around me.

"You have an amazing voice, son," he says as I finish playing.

I hadn't even realised I was singing along.

"Thanks."

"Where are my manners? My name is Tom," he says with a toothy grin.

"Hi Tom, I'm … Rhett."

"Rhett? Unusual name. Haven't met anyone with that name before."

"Yeah, my mum named me after a guy she liked."

"The only Rhett I've ever heard of is the one from *Gone with The Wind*."

"That's the one. She had a crush on him. It's her favourite film of all time."

"My wife loves that film too."

I feel like I got punched in the gut. I haven't gone this long without speaking to mum in my life. Even when I'm on tour, we speak to each other every day. What must she be thinking? And with the news apparently reporting that I got on a plane … She must be going mental. Shit!

I check my watch so as not to seem too rude.

"Ah, man, I didn't realise it was that time already. Sorry, Tom, I'm running late to meet my girl. I'll be back soon though."

"Don't keep the girl waiting. Go on, skedaddle. I'll still be here whenever you want to come back."

"Thanks," I say as I shake his outstretched hand.

I hand him back the guitar and make like I've got a rocket up my ass.

I walk back through town and sit on a bench by the clock in the centre of all the surrounding shops. Pulling my phone from my pocket, I scroll through my contacts and hit Call before I can chicken out. I know she's going to flip her shit, but I deserve it.

She answers on the fourth ring.

"Hello?"

"Hi, Mum, it's Brent."

"Brent? Whose number is this? Where the hell are you? What's going on? Why did you ditch the tour? Why aren't you returning Gordon's calls or texts? He's rung me, you know, asking if I know where you are. I told him I didn't because that's the truth, but he didn't believe me at first. It was only when he could tell how upset I was that we hadn't spoken that he backed off. And that's another thing, young man, why aren't you returning *my* calls? Me, of all people. I'm your mother, for Christ's sake!"

"Woah, slow down, Mum. One thing at a time. Look, I'm really sorry that I haven't called you. I'm an asshole, there's no denying it—"

"Language, Brent." She butts in to chastise me for what she calls my "potty mouth".

"Sorry, Mum, my bad. Look, I'll fill you in, but long story short, I'm in a small town where nobody knows me. I had to leave the tour, I just had to get away. It wasn't any one thing; it was a culmination of things. I haven't been feeling right about music for a while. I've lost my passion somewhere along the line. Anyway, I've not answered Gordon for two reasons. One is that I don't want to answer his barrage of questions because I don't know the answers myself. The second reason is because I've bought a temporary SIM card for my phone. I haven't given him the number."

"And that's the number you're calling off?"

"Yes, keep this number to contact me until I return home, okay? I'm really sorry I haven't called, Mum, I truly am. I haven't got any excuses, because that's all they'd be—excuses. The truth is, I want to stay here for a while, and I want to do so anonymously. I'm liking being somewhere that nobody knows my real name."

"I'm just glad that you're okay, son. A million scenarios ran through my head. I would have contacted the boys, but Gordon says they don't have a way to reach you either."

"Yeah, that's a lie. They have this number now. *Please*, before you shout at me for giving it to them and not you, listen. I was worried you'd be disappointed in me for ditching the band and running away like a coward. You always taught me to confront my problems head-on, and I haven't. Instead I've run in the opposite direction."

"Son, I'm not disappointed, I'm worried. I've been worried that something happened to you, until I saw the news with pictures of you in an airport."

"I don't even know how they knew it was me. I've dyed my hair and haven't shaved."

"Baby, you are recognisable. But it wasn't just that, it was someone working at the airport that knew you'd bought a ticket—that's what you get for using your card instead of paying cash."

"Someone at the airport needs sacking," I say with a laugh.

"Sorry, son, no grounds to sack them on. They told a friend who told a friend. You know how gossip trees work. They were only doing it because they were excited to see a celebrity."

I bristle at her use of my least favourite word.

"I know, Mum. I just wish I could get some goddamn peace and quiet."

"I get it, son. You have always been the one out of the four of you that liked the limelight the least."

"Funny, you're the second person to say that to me lately."

"Well, it's true, son. Goodness knows why you agreed to be the lead singer. But what's done is done, right? So, anyway, tell me how you've been."

I tell my mum about the quiet little town, and although I think twice about it, I tell her about Caleigh too. She grills me for more information, as mums always do. I allow her to ask what she wants but limit my answers. I want to keep Caleigh to myself for as long as possible.

When we hang up, I promise I'll call her in a couple of days. I feel like a complete douchebag for worrying her, but she forgave me for it.

Feeling better after talking to the one person that really gets me, I walk to the taxi rank and get a taxi back to River's Edge.

We pull up outside Audrey's and I pay the fare. I want to go and see Caleigh, but I won't … yet. I'll grab something to eat first and then I'll decide what to do about going to The Lock.

This afternoon, I was left wondering whether she'd heard me when I told her my real name, but I fell asleep next to her, and when we woke up, she made love to me and cried out "Rhett", so I don't think she could have heard me—unless she's damn good at pretending. After all, she didn't look like she was faking falling asleep in my arms.

If she'd heard me, surely she would have questioned me instead of making love to me. And she certainly wouldn't have cried out my fucked up assumed name.

That leaves me with a question on my mind about whether to tell her or not. Well, no, that's not quite right, I *will* tell her, but it's a question of *when*.

***

It's been a couple of days since I saw Caleigh. I was going to go to the pub the other night, but I felt too weird—okay, more like cowardly—to face her after the whole saying my name out loud, even though I'm not convinced she heard me.

I've finished books two and three in the series I've been reading. I haven't dared leave my room at Audrey's except to eat.

Damien texted me about going to see some live band over in Pedmore, but I wasn't feeling it after the talk with my mum. We spoke again this morning, and I even talked to Dad for a bit too. That might not mean much to some, but my dad and I don't have the closest relationship. I think it's because he never wanted me to actually tour with the band. He wanted me to get—and I quote—a real job.

My dad, Don, he owns this big corporation, and as his male heir, I was meant to "take over the empire someday". But that was never going to happen.

He thought music was a hobby and I should start working for his company, learn the ropes and allow him to retire. He didn't like it when I told him it was literally the most boring job I could think of and I would rather shoot myself in the head than take over from him.

Maybe I shouldn't have said it like that, but I was young, and music was what I was passionate about. I wanted it to be more than my hobby, I wanted to be a famous singer and guitarist. But now that I am … I don't know. I mean, I love my job. I love the fans. The fact that we've sold multi-platinum records. The record label loves us. Gordon took a chance on us and helped us become one of—if not *the*—most famous country bands the UK has seen. That's all amazing and everything, but I do sometimes wonder what would have happened if I'd chosen Dad's path instead.

I would be stuck in an office with a view of the London skyline. I would be wearing suits, making decisions about the future of the company. I'd have a secretary to bark orders at, like my dad. Would that be a comfortable life? I mean, he makes good money, but it isn't about the money. The boys and I aren't exactly poor. I didn't choose this path because I wanted to be rich. I'd still want to be part of the band if we weren't as successful as we are. Music is in my veins. Okay, the writing has been all dried up recently, for me anyway. But that's why I'm here in River's Edge. I'm just a little burned out, but I'll get back to what I love the most … in time.

I check the time and decide to get a taxi into Pedmore. I need to do something to stave off cabin fever, which has set in over the last couple of days of being stuck in my room.

As I open the door, Tom greets me with a warm smile.

"Hey, Rhett, good to see you again."

"Hey, Tom."

"Back to play me another song?"

"Actually, I'm back to buy the Fender."

"Oh, that's great news, son."

He grabs Bess from the window—I know, it's weird to name a guitar, but I've done it anyway—and brings her to the counter.

"I'll be sorry to see it go. It's been here for a little while now."

"She's going to a loving home, Tom, don't you worry."

Tom rings up my purchase and places Bess into a black case. He looks a little forlorn as he hands her to me, but he smiles as I reverently take her from him.

"Thank you, Tom. And seriously, don't worry. I'll treat her with the love and respect she deserves."

"I know you will, son. I know."

"Take care, Tom. Who knows, maybe I'll see you again soon."

"And you, Rhett. Have a good day."

He smiles and waves as I turn to look at him as I exit the shop.

It wasn't a conscious thought to come back and purchase Bess, more like an instinctual thing when I got to town. I strap the case to my back and pull my phone out to text my mum. We spoke yesterday, but I'm used to speaking to her every day, so I send her a text to let her know I'm thinking of her.

My phone chimes and I smile, expecting it to be mum, but it isn't.

>Hey stranger. How are you? Haven't seen you around for a couple of days now.

My smile spreads as a warmth. Runs through me. Shit, how I've missed that sweet girl.

>Hey Caleigh. I'm good. Just needed a couple of days to chill out, you know?!

>Are you busy today?

>Not really, I'm just over in Pedmore. Was about to get a taxi back.

>How about I come fetch you and we go somewhere for lunch?

The warmth I felt blooms.
>That would be great. Where shall I meet you?

>There's a diner called American Honey. They do great pancake stacks. I know I'm normally about healthy eating, but I could just eat some pancakes with bacon, eggs and maple syrup.

>Bacon and eggs with pancakes sounds a little too weird, but adding syrup? You're a monster, Caleigh Flynn ;)

>Don't knock it until you try it. I'll make a monster out of you yet.

>Where am I headed to find this diner?

She gives me directions and I walk around town, looking for the shops she tells me about, to make sure I'm headed in the right direction. A light bulb goes off in my head as I realise that I can use Google Maps. I'm such an idiot.

"Howdy stranger," she says, startling the ever-loving shit out of me.

I turn around and see long legs that seem to go on for miles. My cock twitches a little as the thought of those legs wrapped around me plagues my mind. Looking her over, I see her tiny denim shorts and a tight purple tank top. Damn, she looks too good to be true.

"My eyes are up here, perv," she says in a teasing tone.

Looking up, I see her gorgeous green eyes glistening with mirth.

"Can't a man appreciate a fine-looking woman?"

"That depends if she can eye-fuck him right back."

"Oh, I'd say that was allowed. In fact, scratch that, she'd be actively encouraged to eye-fuck the shit outta him."

"What's that?" she asks, gesturing to the case I'd forgotten I had on my back.

"Oh, that? It's this thing made of wood and some strings."

Caleigh raises an eyebrow at me and puts her hand on her hip.

"Don't sass me, boy."

I poke my tongue out, earning me a light chuckle in response.

"It's not an *it*. Her name is Bess."

"You're cheating on me with someone called Bess?"

"I happen to believe there's room in my life for two ladies, or more accurately, three."

"I don't believe in polygamy. Are you seriously trying to tell me you're polyamorous?"

"There's plenty of me to go around," I reply with a wink.

She cocks her hip to one side and just stands there, looking at me. "I'm afraid I'm a selfish bitch. I like it when my man is *my* man."

Her man? Really? Is that what I am?

"Well, I'm sorry, but any woman who loves me has to love Bess and Jeri-Lynn too."

Loves me? What the fuck am I even saying? It's like my brain isn't sending the correct signals to my mouth like I have no filter. What the hell?!

"Who the hell is Jeri-Lynn? Isn't that a woman from *Star Trek?*"

"Damn straight it is."

"You're telling me you're dating an actress?"

"No, silly, I just named my beauty after her."

"I'm starving, let's go eat while we debate your polyamory."

I hold out a hand, and Caleigh takes it. Her small, soft hand fits snugly into mine like it was made purposefully for me.

Walking into the diner, we spot a free booth and take a seat. Caleigh snuggles up close and ghosts a kiss over my lips. My cock stirs, so I try to discreetly rearrange myself under the table.

"Hey," she says as she sits back and grabs a menu. She hands it to me and tells me to decide what to order, because she already knows what she wants.

I take a moment to look over the menu but decide to be brave, and when the waitress comes over, I order the same as Caleigh—a short stack of pancakes, crispy bacon, eggs and maple syrup. It makes Caleigh chuckle as I ask for the syrup on the side so I can taste test before pouring it over.

"So, are you going to introduce me to Bess?"

I open the case and Caleigh looks over my "other woman" as if appraising her to deem her worthy of my affection.

"She's a beauty alright. But I must ask, why the name?"

"We had a dog named Bess when I was little. She was black and tan, just like this Bess."

"Aww, you're sentimental. How sweet."

I lean in and brush a strand of hair out of her face before cupping her cheek in my palm. Looking into her eyes, I feel hypnotised. I ghost a kiss over her lips then go to pull away, but she draws me in for a deeper kiss. I gladly submit to her strawberry-lip-gloss-tasting kiss. Inhaling deeply, I smell her strawberry shampoo and the floral undertones of her perfume. She really is hypnotic.

It's only when the waitress coughs that we pull apart. Caleigh blushes as she realises we were being watched. She smiles up at the waitress as she hands us our food, then she thanks her. My manners escape me as I am too enthralled with watching Caleigh.

"Thank you," I call belatedly to her retreating back.

"This all smells great, but I'm still not sure I can get my head around the sweet and savoury combination."

"Just eat, will you?"

I do as she commands and actually—although I'm loathe to admit it—the combination of sweet and savoury isn't as bad as I thought it would be. I was a bit of a fussy eater as a child. I said I didn't like things when I hadn't even tried them. My mum would pander to me, but my dad told me I could eat what I was given or go to bed starving. But as he can't send me to my room as a man in my thirties, I've become a bit fussy again.

"So?" she asks as she finishes her food.

"Hmm," I pretend to ponder, scrubbing a hand over my chin for good measure.

"Just answer me, you jerk," she says as she nudges me in the ribs.

I pretend to be winded and Caleigh gives me a hard stare.

"I liked it, okay?"

"Only like, not love?"

"Love is pushing it."

"Oh please, it's the best thing invented since carbs themselves."

"I submit, okay? It was delicious."

"Well, you seemed to enjoy the syrup. You might as well have licked the plate clean."

I pick up my plate and Caleigh reaches out to stop me, but she's too little too late as I stick out my tongue and lick the plate a little.

"Eww, Rhett, stop it."

She bats her hand at me, and I can't help but laugh. She's got her nose all scrunched up and her mouth in a grimace. She's so damn cute.

"Okay, okay, you win." I put the plate back down and reach for my milkshake. Slurping it through the straw makes Caleigh cover her ears, so I do it again, only harder.

"You're such a jerk, Rhett Butler. Do you know that?"

I'd be insulted if I thought for one moment that she meant it.

"A cute jerk, though, right?"

"I don't know about that."

"Well, at least Bess and Jeri-Lynn won't have to fight you for my affection."

"You never told me you played. Are there really no ends to your talents?"

The change in topic throws me off for a second.

"I've played since I was a kid. But I don't know about my talents. I mean, you make it sound like there's a long list of them."

"Oh, there are. Trust me."

"Name one."

"You've got the voice of an angel."

"I don't know about that. Name another."

"You play guitar."

"Ah, but you didn't know that. So, name another."

"Y-you …" she begins as she squirms under my gaze. "Y-you …"

"Haven't got all day, Miss Flynn. Spit it out."

"Well, you're extremely good with … you know …"

"Nope, got no clue what you mean."

"*Fuck.* Are you really going to make me say it? *Jerk!* You're really good with your … tongue," she finally whispers the last word.

"Name another."

Her cheeks become the darkest shade of pink and I can feel my cock beginning to stir as I look at her. She's so goddamn beautiful.

"You … you make me laugh."

"Uh-uh, not a talent. Try again."

She squirms in her seat and I find myself happy with how uncomfortable she is.

"You're incredible in bed," she whispers.

"Why thank you," I reply as I lean in to kiss her neck. I tuck a stray strand of hair behind her ear before kissing my way up to her ear and biting gently.

"What do you say I get you home and treat you to a repeat performance?" I whisper in her ear.

"I'd say let's pay the bill and get the hell out of here."

"I was hoping you'd say that." I stand and pull out my wallet.

We walk to the counter and pay the bill before walking hand in hand to her car.

"Drop me at Audrey's and I'll sneak down the path by the river."

"Don't keep me waiting," she almost begs.

"I promise."

I push Caleigh up against her car, and before she can protest, I slam my mouth down over hers and demand entry with my tongue. She submits all too willingly, and fuck if it doesn't make my cock harder just knowing that she's so ready and willing to comply.

Tracing a hand over her hip, I left the hem of her top and run my fingers along the waistband of her tiny shorts. Caleigh sucks in a sharp breath as I dip my finger between the material and her silky skin.

"Rhett, we could be seen," she says, breaking the kiss.

"I don't care," I reply before slamming my lips back over hers in a brutal, punishing kiss. We haven't been public about us, and God knows we could be seen by anyone from River's Edge if they were here shopping, but I can't find it in me to care. I'm hers and she's mine.

I slide my finger underneath her panties and her breathing is ragged. She wants to resist, but she's not going to. She's too far gone to care.

She's wet as I slide a finger through her folds. God how I want to strip her and fuck her over the bonnet of her car. My cock hardens just thinking about it and I grind myself against her.

"Shit, Caleigh, get us back to town. Now!"

Chapter Eleven

Caleigh

It feels like a lifetime before Rhett finally slips in through the back door. I'm in the kitchen, waiting for him, wearing nothing but a silk kimono. His eyes bug out as they land on me.

"Fucking hell, Caleigh, are you trying to give me a heart attack?"

"No, baby. I'm giving you this," I say as I drop the material to the floor and stand before him completely naked.

It takes him all but a nanosecond before his mouth crashes into mine. His arms come around my waist and he slaps my ass hard enough to leave a handprint. I'd be lying if I said that wasn't hot as hell.

"God, you're so beautiful," he says as he comes up for air.

"Strip."

That's all I say, just one word. More of a command really. And yet, he's eager to comply. He stands back and starts to peel off his shirt. Good god, I could stare at him all day. He's too perfect. I know I told him before that nobody is perfect, but he is—and if he's not, he's as close as anyone will ever get.

"My eyes are up here," he parrots my words from earlier.

I don't bother making eye contact, though. I just watch as he kicks off his jeans and stands before me in all his naked glory.

His hands are on me and all I can think is that I can't wait to get up to my room. I want to taste him. Now. But he doesn't give me chance when he lifts me effortlessly and sets me on the breakfast bar.

"You're mine, Caleigh Rae Flynn," he says, before kissing me until my toes curl and my blood sings in my veins.

I wrap my legs around his waist and my arms around his neck, drawing him closer to me. I don't know how we've gone from not labelling whatever this is between us to me being *his*, but I can't find it in me to care as he aligns himself with me and grips my ass. As he sinks into me, a moan escapes me. It's pure bliss. It's like we were just made to fit.

Rhett fists my hair in his hand and tugs my head back to expose my neck. He kisses me, his lips as delicate as a butterfly's wings as they trail down between my breasts and then across to suck my nipple into his mouth.

It's like an out of body experience as he thrusts into me and bites me at the same time. I can't describe how it feels, because there aren't enough words in the English language.

"Shit, Caleigh," he whispers, kiss breath fanning out over my skin, leaving a trail of goosebumps in its wake.

"R-Rhett, I'm so c-close, baby."

His grunts punctuate each thrust of his hips. He fills me in the most delicious of ways. My head falls back as he grips both of my hips in his hands and thrusts faster. My breathing becomes more and more ragged as he pushes me closer to the brink. It's not the brink of an abyss, because an abyss is nothing. This—this is *something*. The way he makes me feel is beyond compare.

I dig my heels into his ass and buck my hips to meet each thrust. He's pushing me higher and higher towards my climax and I know I can't hold on much longer. I've held it back as long as I possibly can to stop this from ending too soon.

"Shit, Caleigh, I can't hold back much longer."

I look up and see his hooded gaze watching my breasts bounce, but he must notice me staring because he looks up at me with a gaze so intense it could very well burn me alive.

Leaning all my weight on one arm, I reach down with my other hand to play with myself. Rhett's eyes follow my hand and he watches me as I touch myself. He leans down over me to bite my nipple again, and it's like a detonator switch as I feel my orgasm roll through me like thunder.

Rhett reaches around me and palms my ass before pulling me close to him. I wrap my arms around his neck, and he lifts me effortlessly. I don't know what he's doing until my back comes into contact with the cold wall.

I keep my legs around his waist as he begins to thrust inside me once more. He ups the pace, but it isn't long until his movements begin to falter. He slows his pace down, but each thrust is harder than the one before it.

I clench my walls around him, really feeling him as deep as he can go. He leans in and claims my lips in a white-hot kiss before pulling back. His hips slam into me and my cries can probably be heard from a hundred miles away, but I don't give a damn. He said I was his and he was mine—well, he's right.

"Fuck me, Rhett, fuck me. Do you hear? Are you scared I'll break?"

"Hell, Caleigh," he rasps out before doing exactly what I told him.

He fucks me so hard it's now me who's scared I'll break. But I don't care if I do, because Rhett will put me back together again piece by piece like he did the shards of my heart.

When I fell, I couldn't tell you. I can only say that I fell hard. As hard as humanly possible.

The moment Rhett comes inside me, all I can see is his face. All I can feel is his hard body pressed up against mine as he comes to a complete still. All I can hear is our ragged breathing. If I could freeze one moment in time, it would be this one. The one where I finally admit to myself that it truly is possible to love again.

I never thought there would be another man who could make me feel like I was the centre of the universe. But I was wrong.

The only question is, does he feel the same?

***

After showering together, Rhett and I collapse into bed and wrap ourselves around each other. I could lie here forever, just a tangle of limbs. I know that isn't possible, but the mere fact that I am already in love with him means that I can never lose him. If I did, then the heart he pieced back together would be broken irreparably.

I survived losing my first love. Could I survive losing my second? My last?

I doze off into a peaceful sleep as Rhett lies stroking my hair. The little gestures really do mean the world.

Chapter Twelve

Brent

Caleigh and I have spent another amazing week together, and although I haven't said it out loud, I know the truth of how I feel inside.

We were made for each other, her and me. I may not be her first love, but I want to be her last. I want her to fall in love with me the way I have fallen for her. Hard.

My phone disturbs my peace, so I reach over, fumbling around on the bedside table without looking.

>Dude, Gordon knows where you are. I don't fucking know how. It wasn't one of us though, I swear. You didn't even tell us where you were, remember? So, if I was you, I would say goodbye to that girl of yours and get your ass on a plane before he comes to you.

Shit. Fuck. Bollocks. It can't be true.

>How could he do that, Jude? My own mother doesn't know where I am and nor do any of you. The only people that knew were … fuck … the airport staff. He must have paid them off.

Holy crap. What the hell am I meant to do? I launch myself out of bed and grab my clothes, dressing in a hurry.

>I'm coming home. Tell him I'll be there. Do not let him come here, Jude. I mean it.

>You know I can't stop him when he sets his mind to something, Brent. None of us can.

>So, what does he intend to do? Drag me home by my ear? I'm not

a goddamn child that he can order around.

>He can when he's your goddamn manager. Hell hath no fury like a manager scorned.

>I thought that was a woman? I type out, trying to lighten the mood.

I scrub a hand over my face before hastily packing my case. *Shit!* What am I going to do about getting home? I guess I could always use my credit card to buy a plane ticket now that my cover is about to be blown to smithereens anyway.

How the hell am I supposed to say goodbye to Caleigh? I don't have the words. I never got to tell her who I was, and now I have to explain the fact that I'm leaving without being able to tell her why.

How on earth did I let myself get caught up with a woman? It should never have happened. I was never meant to stay. But someone saw fit to put Caleigh in my path and I fell head over heels, lost myself in time and space, only finding myself when I was with her. My true self, that is. Whoever I was before was gone, and I discovered the real me in the arms of Caleigh Rae Flynn, the only woman who has ever held my heart.

They say it's better to have loved and lost, and who knows, maybe they're right, because I wouldn't swap the time I've shared with Caleigh for anything in the world. But to lose her? It's going to mean complete and utter devastation. It will literally annihilate my heart to tell her goodbye.

The thought flits through my mind that maybe I should just go without saying goodbye. But I know I could never do that, not to her and not to myself. I want to steal one last kiss from her before leaving. A kiss that will have to sustain me a lifetime without her.

I leave my case at the door to my room. If I take it with me to see Caleigh, she might see it and bolt, not giving me a chance to explain.

Grabbing my phone, I pull up flights. Nothing? How can there be nothing? I check other sites, in search of anything, even economy class would do. I don't care as long as it's a seat on a plane. But I can't find anything. What the hell? Is this like the busiest day of the year to travel or something?

I look up flights for tomorrow. There are only a few available, so I grab the first one I can. What harm can one more day do?

Deciding to go and see Caleigh anyway, I close the door behind me and head downstairs.

"Good morning, Rhett. I trust you slept well?" Audrey asks in her ever-chipper tone.

"I did, thank you. I wanted to let you know that I'll be leaving tomorrow morning."

"So soon? I do hope you'll come back again sometime."

"Yeah, something came up at home, but I'll be back, I'm certain of it."

I've never been as uncertain of anything, but I can't tell her that.

"See you later, Audrey. Have a good day."

"You too, Rhett. If it's your last one, I hope you're making it count."

"Oh, Audrey, out of curiosity, is there a reason you can think of why there wouldn't be any flights today?"

"It'll be because of the air show, dear. They close down our airport to any inbound or outbound flights. It's an annual thing."

Well, that would do it.

"Thanks, Audrey. See you later."

As I walk out into the morning sun, I close my eyes and inhale deeply. What can I do with Caleigh to make our last day count? If the air show is a big draw for people in town, then maybe I can get her all to myself.

>Morning gorgeous. Fancy doing something today?

I see three dots on the screen, and it brings a smile to my face. At least she's still talking to me until tonight.

>I'm doing the stocktake, remember? But I'm free as a bird afterwards.

>Is Damien in the pub?

>Yeah, why?

>Because I can pretend that I'm coming to see him.

>Now?

>Yes ma'am. I'm already on my way.

I smile to myself as I pocket my phone and decide to take the river path. I know it takes longer to get to The Lock, but it gives me a chance to take in the sights of this place one last time.

Taking my phone out, I snap a few pictures. A pink-haired goddess looks at me from the wallpaper on my phone and I can't contain my grin. My heart races like it's about to burst out of my chest. I take advantage of feeling it while I can, because twenty-four hours from now, it will never beat again.

As I walk down the road to The Lock, I see a rental car parked outside. At least that means I'm not too early for the pub to even be open. I hadn't thought about that when I said I'd drop by.

"No, he's not been here and trust me, it's a small town, so I'd know it if he was," Damien says to someone as I walk through the door.

I open the inner double door and come face to face with my worst nightmare. I spin around on my heel but it's too late.

"There he is." Gordon's voice pulls me down to earth with a bang.

Fuck fuckity fuck fuck!! *FUCK!!*

Turning back around, I look between Damien and Gordon.

Damien's mouth is hanging open and I swear, in any other circumstances, it would be funny.

"Brent, good to see you," my manager says with a shit-eating grin. "What's up, son? Cat got your tongue?"

"You've got the wrong guy, surely? This is Rhett. Rhett Butler," Damien flounders.

"Hello, Gordon," I finally respond. My feet feel glued to the floor. Or maybe it's the cement blocks I have in my shoes.

"So glad I found you, Brent. You've been gone for so long."

"What do you want me to say, Gordon?"

"Nothing, son. Don't say a thing. Just come and get in the car and we'll be on our way. Where's all your stuff? We'll grab it on the way to the airport."

"How did you even get here? The airport is closed for the annual air show."

"Who says I flew commercial? I used the private jet, touched down in a place called Brookhaven a couple of hours ago."

Damien silently watches the exchange, his eyes flitting between the two of us.

"How did you know where to find me?"

"Oh, you can thank the girl at the airport back home for that. My guess is that you thought you could fly under the radar once you got here, but you shouldn't have paid with your card for your ticket. That was your second mistake—the first being you leaving in the first place."

"Why come all this way, Gordon? What did you think was going to happen? That I'd just up and leave with you like a good little boy?"

"Son, you left us in the lurch. You left the guys without a lead singer until Asher stepped into the breach. Did you really think that I'd allow you to ditch us for some peace and quiet in Nowheresville? Just how long did you think I'd let that go on for, son?"

"Did you ever think that maybe I *needed* this peace and quiet?"

"Son, all the boys need a break, but you don't see them fucking leaving mid-goddamn-tour, do you?"

"Fuck off, Gordon. I don't have to answer to you," I seethe.

"Oh yes you do, son. You all answer to me."

"Stop. Calling. Me. Fucking. *Son.*" I enunciate each word clearly.

"What the hell is going on up here?"

My head whips around hard enough to give me whiplash at the sound of her voice.

"Seems your boyfriend isn't who he claimed to be," Damien finally speaks.

"First of all, how the hell do you know about us? And second of all, what on earth are you wittering on about?"

"Oh, I've seen you two skulking around together. Was quite the little show at American Honey, though. Some seriously heavy-petting, and in broad daylight in a public space too. And what I mean, *darlin'*, is that your little boyfriend *Rhett* here," he says, air-quoting my name for good measure, "is really *Brent* fucking *Ryder*. The one and only lead singer of Whiskey Lullaby, you know, the band Angelo used to like."

Caleigh flushes at his knowledge of us, then confusion flits through her gaze, before finally settling on hurt when he mentions Angelo's name in the same breath, as if to hurt her. I don't know whether he truly meant to be spiteful, but I want to punch the son of a bitch for hurting her.

"Don't be stupid. Don't you think I'd know if Rhett was actually Brent?" she asks finally.

"Cut his hair a little, give him a shave and dye his hair dirty blond and he's Brent Ryder alright. But if you don't believe me, ask Gordon here. He is the band's manager, after all."

Her eyes dart from Damien, to me, to Gordon.

The shit-eating grin he's been wearing while hearing this little exchange doesn't falter as he turns to her.

"Hi, darlin'. You'd do well to listen to your friend here. This guy right here," he says, pointing at me, "he really is Brent Lachlan Ryder, my front man. Guitarist and lead vocals."

"Rhett …" She trails off, the pain evident in her voice. "P-please t-tell me he's w-wrong." Her eyes are full of unshed tears.

I've never hated myself more than I do right now. I did this to her.

"Caleigh, I can explain." I start towards her, but she takes a step backwards. "Caleigh, please."

"Y-you c-can't be him. This is all a joke, r-right? A wind-up. I-It h-has to be."

"Sweetheart, please." I close the gap between us in large strides.

She backs up until her back is against the wall. She's like a spooked horse, ready to bolt.

"D-don't. Don't sweetheart me. You're a liar. A crook. A phoney."

"Baby, I'm still me. I swear. Everything you know about me is true."

I brace my arms on the wall on either side of her head, caging her between them so she can't bolt before I explain.

"*Liar*," she spits. "And to think I was going to ask if you wanted to meet Hardin properly, to introduce you to him as my boyfriend."

Her anger is palpable as it rolls off her in waves.

"Baby—"

"Don't you fucking *baby* me. Go fuck yourself, Rhett. Brent. Whoever the fuck you are."

"I'm still me, Caleigh. The only lie I told you was my name. I swear to god, I have not told you another lie, ever."

"Oh, and I'm supposed to just believe you, *forgive* you, just like that, huh?"

"You'll have to figure this out some other time, darlin', because Brent is due on a plane home with me," Gordon says from somewhere behind me.

"Go fuck yourself, Gordon," I spit at him over my shoulder before looking back to the woman I love. "Caleigh, please, just hear me out."

"No can do, sunshine, we'll miss our flight."

"I said *fuck off*, Gordon. It's a private jet; you can leave whenever the fuck you please. In fact, why don't you just do that. Go get on your fucking plane and get the hell out of here."

"Unless you want me to sue your ass for every penny you have, son, then you'll be leaving here with me."

"I'd rather be penniless than be without"—my eyes bore into Caleigh's as I choose my next words carefully—"the woman I love."

"*Love?*" she asks, her voice at least two octaves higher than normal.

"Yes, Caleigh, *love*. I love you. I should have told you sooner. I should have said it every minute, of every hour, of every day since we got on that plane."

"You lied to me from the moment we met. How is *that* love?"

"Oh, sweetheart, the boy here doesn't *love* you. He's just trying to sweet talk you. He says it to every piece of skirt he's ever fucked. And let me tell you, the amount of—"

"Gordon." I cut him off. "Don't listen to that son of a bitch, Caleigh. I'm begging you to hear me out about *why* I lied. I had to. *Had* to. I didn't know you then. I didn't want anyone finding out where I was. I knew this fucker would come after me if I told a soul."

"Okay, so say I buy that. Why *keep* lying to me, Brent?"

Her anger rises and I watch her chest as she takes ragged breaths. I deserve it. I deserve her anger for lying for this long. For not telling her who I was after the first time we slept together. I promised myself I would tell her, and I lied. I even lied to myself. How fucked up am I?

"I tried and failed so many times, Caleigh. Please, please believe me. I know I should have told you so much sooner. All I can say is that I'm sorry."

"When did you think you should tell me, Brent? After we first slept together? After a day, a week? After the first time I let you make love to me … *without a condom*." She whispers those last three words.

Her words are like red hot daggers being thrust into my heart.

Laughter shakes me out of my pain for a moment.

"What the *fuck* are you laughing at?" I seethe at my asshole of a manager.

"The fact that you fucked her without protection, son. Have I taught you nothing? No glove, no love, else you catch some nasty disease and give it to the next woman in the next town, and the next and the next, until it's just one giant cesspool of sexually transmitted disease. If you're going to fuck a whore, don't do it bareback, you fucking rookie."

"What the *fuck* did you just say?"

I spin away from Caleigh and stalk around to the other side of the bar. I've heard enough out of that nasty mouth. It's time someone taught the asshole a lesson.

"I said, you fuck a whore—"

The resounding crack that his jaw makes soothes me like a balm I didn't know I needed. Jesus, if only I'd hit the dickhead sooner.

"Don't you *dare* call Caleigh a whore. You *ever* do that again and you'll need somebody to pull me the fuck off you before I beat your corpse back down to hell."

Fucking Gordon Boothe. Who the hell does he think he is, walking in here and calling Caleigh that? He's always been a good man, or so I thought. But when I take some time out for the sake of my peace of mind, he turns up and shows his true colours.

I turn back to Caleigh, but she's nowhere to be seen. I run around the other side of the bar and see the back door slamming shut behind her.

"Don't do it, man. Be smart. She doesn't fucking want you, and she never will."

"The fuck do you know, Damien? You're only jealous because I've been seeing her."

I turn around and he looks right at me.

"You be careful what you say, dude. I've got a lot of respect for Caleigh."

"Yeah, so much respect you just drop her late husband's name into conversation like it won't upset her."

"She'll get over that. And I'll be here to pick up the pieces after you fly back to where you belong."

"You think she'd touch you? Please, don't make me laugh."

"You never know, dude. She's hurting, and I could be the one to help ease her pain. I swear, when I feel that tight little pussy for the first time … oh will it be like manna from heaven. It'll taste all the sweeter knowing *you* will know I'm doing it and you'll be hurting so bad—"

"I swear to god, asshole, if you lay one finger on her—"

"Oh yeah, what you gonna do about it?"

"Watch your mouth or you'll end up with a dose of what I just treated Gordon to."

"Get your sorry ass in the rental car outside and leave town, dude. Just get the hell out of dodge, because Caleigh doesn't need you, your money or your baggage."

"Fuck you, Damien," I reply as I rush off out of the front door.

It takes longer to get to Caleigh's house from the back door, so I have time to catch her … I hope.

I whisper a prayer to whoever's listening as I break into a run. Please, let her hear me out. I know I don't deserve it, but I need her to hear me. To listen, *really* listen, and hear the truth in my words.

Chapter Thirteen

Caleigh

The loud knock scares the hell out of me, making me jump as I sit with my back to the front door. I'm not in the mood to see anyone, so I sit quietly in the hopes they'll just go away.

"Caleigh, please. Please let me explain," Rhett—or is it Brent—calls.

I remain quiet and shrink myself into a ball so he can't see my shadow through the door.

"Caleigh, I know you're in there."

My chest is still heaving from my sobs. I can't bring myself to face him. Not like this. He needs to see me without tears rolling down my face. I need to show him I'm strong and his betrayal doesn't matter. But then again, I'd rather not see him at all.

"Caleigh, baby, please," he begs.

I feel myself bristle as he has the audacity to call me baby. He's a fool if he thinks he can sweet talk his way out of this.

"I know you're in there, Caleigh."

God, this guy, he doesn't give up, does he? Can he not just take the hint?

There's silence for a few moments, so I'm hoping he's just left.

"Caleigh, please," he shouts as I hear him banging on the back door.

The sound of the key in the lock makes me jump. As if he'd use my spare key. I can't believe the audacity of the man letting himself into my house after I've told him to get lost.

"Caleigh," he calls as he walks through the kitchen to the hallway and spots me sitting on the floor.

"Please, just hear me out," he says quietly, holding his hands up in a placating gesture.

"And why the hell should I do that?" I ask, in as strong a tone as I can muster. I stand with my back to the door, take a deep breath and blink back unshed tears. "Why should I listen to you when all you do is *lie?*"

"Caleigh, I swear to you, the only lie I told you was my name. You know the real me. The way I acted, the things I told you, that was all the real me. I had to lie about my name, I *had* to."

"Oh, you *had* to, did you? And why would that be?"

"To protect myself. I needed to take time away from the band, but I couldn't go anywhere where people would know me. I dyed my hair. I got on a plane to the smallest, quietest town I could find. What I didn't foresee was meeting you. You changed everything."

I suppose I understand his wanting anonymity, but what I can't get past is the lying to me after we started seeing each other.

"You lied to me, Brent. That's what I don't get. Okay, you wanted to protect yourself, but didn't you think you could trust me to keep a secret?"

"Please, Caleigh, would you just sit and talk to me over a cup of coffee?"

His eyes plead with me, and although I might come to regret it, I find myself giving in. Brent follows me into the kitchen and sits at the breakfast counter as I make some coffee. I add a nip of whiskey to mine and offer him some, but he declines.

As I pull out a stool on the opposite side to him, I look at the breakfast bar—a place where not so long ago, he gave me a part of himself as he made love to me. At least that's what I thought at the time. Sighing, I cradle my coffee cup between my hands and sit silently, waiting for him to explain.

"It's not that I didn't trust you, Caleigh. It's because I'd already lied for so long and I was scared of the fallout. I knew that something like this would come of it and I didn't want that to happen."

"So, what were you planning then? I mean, did you think we were going to live happily ever after? Were you going to legally change your name to Rhett Butler? Where did that name come from in the first place, anyway? I mean, were you telling me the truth about anything at all? How did you think this would go, Brent? The longer this went on, the harder it would have gotten to tell me the truth."

"First of all, the name came from my mum's love of the actor. I never lied about that."

"Wait, it was your name on Tinder, so that means you planned to lie all along."

"Yes, my profile was under Rhett. But that was because *before* I met you. I used the app to hook-up. I'm not proud of it, and I'm *not* defending that stupid decision. I'm an asshole who lied about his name. But I swear, when we met in that airport, I-I haven't used the app since."

"You wanted anonymity from fans, I get that. I really do. But I'm not some groupie that would have hung you out to dry. I wanted you, Brent, the real you. And I thought I had the real you. But you lied to my face over and over."

"I know. Trust me, Caleigh, nobody hates me more than I do for that. You were right. The longer it went on, the harder it got to turn to you and say 'Oh, by the way, I'm not who you think I am. I'm actually Brent Ryder'. I tried. I really did. I even told you one day, but you'd fallen asleep in my arms."

"Oh, so because you told me when I was *asleep*, that makes it okay?" I seethe.

He flinches at the sharpness in my tone.

"I'm not saying that's okay, Caleigh. I was just meaning that I did try to tell you. I didn't wait until you were asleep. I lay there with you in my arms and I told you. It was only afterwards that I realised you were asleep."

"So, if you'd plucked up the courage to tell me then, why did you chicken out when I woke up?"

"Because I looked at you and saw a woman I was falling in love with."

"That makes it *worse*, Brent. You knowingly lied to a woman you profess to *love*."

"I wish like hell I could turn back time and start over again, Caleigh, I truly do. But I can't. All I can do is tell you how sorry I am. I want to make things right with you, but I don't know how."

"I don't think you can," I say, my voice barely above a whisper. My heart feels like it's broken into a million fragments. It's like he took a sledgehammer to it.

"Caleigh, please. Please let me try. I don't know how to fix it, but I want so badly to try."

"You're *leaving*, Brent. *This* isn't your home. You already have somewhere far from here. Even if I could forgive you—which I'm not saying I can—then we couldn't make things work. You're a famous singer, part of an extremely famous band—a *huge* part of that band— and you can't juggle that with a long-distance relationship. It's just not possible."

"I would find a way to *make* it work, Caleigh. I would do anything to show you how much you mean to me. I really mean it when I say I *love* you. You're everything to me, and I want to prove that to you somehow."

I scrub a hand over my face as a sigh escapes me. I want him so much that it physically hurts. But if there's one thing I can't stand, it's people that lie.

"You can't, Brent. Look, it pains me to say this, it really does, but I can't be in love with someone I don't trust. Without trust, there's nothing."

A stray tear rolls down my cheek and I wipe it away with my sleeve. I take a large gulp of my now lukewarm coffee and am grateful for the whiskey to help steady my nerves.

"I will earn back your trust, Caleigh. I will do anything it takes. *Anything.*"

"I'm sorry, Brent, but no. It will never work. Whatever we had—it's over. We have to accept that and go our separate ways. You've hurt me, irreparably."

"Caleigh, I … I'm sorry. Truly sorry. I don't know what to do here. I'll get on my knees and beg if that's what it takes. I'm not beyond swallowing my pride here."

"Brent, please."

I sigh and stand up. Putting my cup in the sink, I take a moment to gather myself. Then I take a deep breath and turn to face the man I've loved and lost. My heart is broken, and I don't have anything left to give him. Trust is the most important part of any relationship, and I can't trust a man who didn't put any trust in me. If he'd told me from the start, or even if he'd just confessed before this shitstorm, I probably could have forgiven him.

It's not the fact that he lied to protect his true identity. I could possibly have gotten over that, but now we'll never know. It's more the fact that after we started seeing each other, I trusted him to never hurt me. I fell for him and I fell *hard*. But he didn't trust me with his secret, like I was some groupie that he hooked up with in the past. A woman to use and discard.

"Caleigh," he says as he stands and walks towards me.

I put my hands out to stop him coming any closer. He sinks to his knees and looks up at me, his eyes full of sorrow, his handsome face crestfallen.

My heart feels like it's trapped in a vice with a million hot needles sticking out of it. I want so much to forgive him—I could forgive the lies because I know he had to protect himself. But there's no trust. He broke that bond and it's beyond repair. I thought we had a future. I was going to introduce him to Hardin properly, as someone I was dating. Now I'm truly glad I didn't because whilst *I* might be able to understand his reasons, I couldn't forgive him for hurting my child.

I'm not about to allow my son to get hurt. I'm his mum, and I would protect him with my life. It hurts to know that we could have been happy, the three of us. And it hurts to know I'll never have that. Maybe never again with *anyone* else because I don't know where to begin piecing my heart back together now.

"Caleigh, please. I love you so much it physically pains me to know that I've hurt you. I want to put that right. I can't make it go away, but I can spend the rest of my life making it up to you. Just give me one chance, please? I swear on my life I will *never* let you get hurt again, by *anyone*."

My heart stutters in my chest, and I swear to god it's stopped beating.

"I can't, Brent. Please, please just leave. Go back to your life and forget I exist. I forgive you, okay. I forgive the fact you lied. I just can't forgive how long you let it go on for, how close you let us get without allowing me to know the real you. You should have trusted me with your secret. I would never have said a word to anyone. But you treated me like I was some … some groupie that you'd use until you left town."

I watch as the first tear falls down his cheek, and my heart breaks a little bit more. I don't want to lose him. But I guess you can't lose what you never really had.

Slowly he stands, and he wipes his tears away. I want so much just to hug him. To hold him and tell him everything will be alright. But I won't placate him with lies.

"For what it's worth, Caleigh, you were always more to me than that. I'm truly sorry that I made you feel like less."

My arms ache to hold him, but I stand firm, resolute that this is for the best. I only offer him a small nod.

"I love you, Caleigh Rae Flynn. I always will. You are the first woman I have ever fallen in love with, and you will be the last. I know it's all of my own making, but my heart is broken beyond repair and I will never be able to give it to anyone else. No matter how far in the future, you will always be the keeper of my now broken heart."

With those parting words, he turns and walks away. I can't move. I can't speak. I can't tell him not to go. All I can do is watch his retreating form.

As the front door closes behind him, I slide to the kitchen floor and sob like I've never sobbed before.

Chapter Fourteen

Brent

Six weeks later

"I am sick of looking at your fucking moping face. Would you just cheer the hell up, you miserable shit?" Ash says as he throws his towel at me.

I watch him walk around naked, not giving a fuck who has to look at his junk.

"I'm entitled to feel however the fuck I please. Now would you please put some goddamn clothes on? Have you no shame?"

"Nah, man, I don't care if you have to see my naked ass. I know it's not like you wanna fuck me, is it?!"

"I wouldn't touch you with someone else's cock mate, never mind my own."

"Aw you know you love me really," he says with a grin that's pure cheese.

"Like a hole in the head."

"You need one of them. Stop your goddamn moping over Caleigh."

"Don't," I warn.

"I'm just saying, man." He holds his hands up, giving me a view of him full frontal. Just what I always wanted. Jesus, why does this jerk think he can walk around naked in my house?

"Yeah? Well, don't *just say* shit. You hear me? You don't get to mention her name."

"Lighten up, bro. It's been six agonising weeks of this bullshit."

"Just because you wouldn't know love if it bit you on the ass, that doesn't mean that I don't know how it feels."

"You just need to get laid. Best way to get over one woman is to get *under* another."

He finally wanders off to get some clothes. I hope. Leaving me to ponder his words. Maybe he's right. Maybe I need to get laid. What can it hurt at this point? It's not like Caleigh will take me back anyway.

I've tried to text, but I always chicken out at the last second. I've tried to call, but I can never seem to press the button. I got her voicemail six million times in a row during the first week, so I should get the message. But while my head knows that, my heart *doesn't* agree. My cold, dead heart, the heart I annihilated by lying. It's amazing it can feel anything right now, but it does.

"Maybe now we're coming to the end of the tour, you can find some pussy worth sticking around for," Ash says as he walks back in, thankfully fully covered.

"Uh-huh," I grunt, noncommittally.

"Seriously dude, I am telling you—"

"Yeah, I heard you the first time. Get laid."

"No woman is going to want you with that sour face though, so, would you put a smile on it? I mean, it wouldn't kill you. If you have to, just fake it. They do say 'fake it 'til you make it'."

I can't stand his crap any longer, so I fake a huge smile before hitting the shower.

***

"I still can't believe you hit Gordon," Jude says as we set up.

"Dude, that was weeks ago," Ash chimes in as he sets up his amp.

I know that people normally have other people who set their stuff up, but the four of us have always done it together. It's just something we do, because nobody knows our instruments like we do.

"Gordon still hasn't let it go though, has he?" Evan asks of no one in particular, "He's like a dog with a bone, but he has a right to be when someone fractures his jaw."

"Seriously, man, can you just leave it? Gordon agreed to drop it because I came back for the end of the tour."

It wasn't easy, but I'd got Gordon to admit that he'd acted poorly towards Caleigh, calling her things he shouldn't have. We talked on the flight home and he'd apologised when I spilled my guts and told him I really loved her. I'd apologised for hitting him and got him some ice to ease the swelling. Then we'd settled our differences like men, drinking whiskey and talking about the end of the tour and how we had to "go out with a bang".

Gordon admitted he was never really going to sue me, that he'd only said it to try and get me back on tour. He also said if someone had spoken about a woman that he loved in the way he spoke about Caleigh, he would have sucker-punched them. He admitted he deserved what he got. What he didn't know until later was that his jaw was actually fractured.

No wonder my hand stung like hell afterwards. I hadn't even noticed the swelling of my knuckles until he pointed it out and had me ice them. Maybe he did that because he cared, maybe it was because I wouldn't play the guitar well with a swollen hand. Either way, I wrapped my hand in a bandage to hold the ice in place while we sat and drank a couple of whiskeys—the good stuff, of course.

"Tonight has to blow the roof off boys. It's the last night, and we still have a lot of making up to do with the fans. Well, I say *we*, but I really mean *you*," Jude says, pointing a finger at me.

After a soundcheck, we head off to grab a bite to eat. We end up at an American diner, where I order a short stack complete with crispy bacon, scrambled eggs and maple syrup. Every bite reminds me of Caleigh. I sigh in frustration, which earns me jeers from the boys before I suck it up and finish my pancakes in silence.

"You ever gonna get over this shit?" Evan asks quietly as we exit the diner.

"Don't think I can, bro. I fucked up. I hurt her, and that hurts me. It kills me to know I am the one that pieced her back together and then tore her apart again—her words, not mine."

The only time I managed to pluck up the courage to text Caleigh was when Gordon and I were in the rental car on the way to the airport in Pedmore. I didn't think I'd get an answer, but I did, and she'd answered me saying exactly that.

"Think you can win her back?"

"Not in this lifetime," I answer with a shrug.

"Then I guess you gotta move on, my friend."

"I know, but it's hard man. I've never been in love before."

"Then woo her back with a grand gesture like they do in those cheesy Hallmark films. Watch a few romcoms for inspiration or something. Dudes always fuck up, but they always win the girl back. Every. Single. Time."

"Ev, that's just make believe. Nobody would pay to watch a film without a happy ending. But in real life, there isn't always a happily ever after. Sometimes, you fuck up the most perfect thing in your life and there's no going back."

"For what it's worth, man, I'm really sorry."

He claps me on the shoulder, and I give him a wry smile.

"It's my own fault, bro. I fucked up."

"Happens to the best of us."

"You married the love of your life. You've got it made with Julia."

"Believe it or not, there was a while there where I thought we wouldn't make it."

"Really? You two always seem so puke-inducingly loved-up."

"We hit a rough patch when we were trying for a baby. Julia got frustrated that we couldn't get pregnant. We paid to go private for tests and everything, and they all came back fine. So the doctors told us to try a little longer before thinking about more drastic measures like IVF."

"And did you?"

I can't believe I didn't know this about one of my best friends.

"We did. We tried and tried, but I have to admit, I was sick of it. I was ready to throw the towel in. She was always stressing over when she was ovulating, and I felt like sex had become a chore rather than something we enjoyed."

"But you have Jessa now."

"Yeah, because we stopped trying so hard. I'd had enough and I quit playing the game the way we had been. I refused to sleep with her, believe it or not," he adds with a chuckle. "One night, we both got angry, drank a little, screamed and shouted a little, then made up with freaking hot, angry sex. That's the night Jessa was conceived. I told her that if I'd known that's all it would take, I'd have got drunk and had dirty, angry sex with her a lot sooner."

I can't help but laugh, and Ev lets out a hearty chuckle.

"And you're thinking of trying again once we get home from this tour, right?"

"Well, if I can trust you to keep a secret," he says in a hushed tone, "we're actually expecting again. She'll be due in five months."

"What?" I ask a little too loudly, making the other boys look around at us, their heads comically on a swivel.

"Keep it down, man. We were going to tell you all tomorrow once this tour is over. That's why Julia has invited you all over for a barbecue. Don't worry, Gordon won't be attending. Apparently, he's needed elsewhere, so it will just be us boys, Julia and Jessa."

"Congratulations, Papa," I whisper, managing not to draw the attention of the others this time.

***

"Hey Jessa," I coo at the gorgeous little girl in Julia's arms.

Her long blonde hair is just like her mum's, but her eyes are all her dad's. She really is the most beautiful little angel.

"Brent," she says, struggling against Julia's hold, her arms outstretched to me.

I take her and Julia smiles. I've never thought about whether I want kids of my own, but being Jessa's godfather is one of the best things about my life. She's so cute and sweet and loving.

Her daddy dotes on her and hates it when we have to go on tour and have to leave the girls behind. Jessa's so young that she and Julia can come with us, and when they do, the three of them stay in a hotel rather than cramped up with us on the tour bus.

Evan knows that when she's old enough to start school that they'll have to stay home more, and he'll miss them when we're gone.

We're meant to have a big tour of the US coming up; it's still in the planning stages. But now Julia's pregnant again, I'm not so sure Evan will want to go. The baby will still only be young, and like with Jessa, he won't leave before he's at least experienced all the new baby's firsts: teeth, words, crawling, walking, all that jazz.

"Higher," Jessa says with a toothy grin.

I twirl her around in the air, making her squeal.

"Higher."

I hold her higher as I spin.

I'm not crazy. I spin slowly so as not to cause myself to get dizzy and drop her. She's far too precious, and Evan would kick my ass. I don't want to have to think about whether or not I could take him in a fight. But I'd probably let him beat seven bells out of me because if I'd hurt his daughter, I'd deserve it.

"Jessa, baby, time to come and eat," Julia calls.

"But, Mummy," she whines as I come to a stop.

"No, little lady, you will come and eat. Then you can play with Uncle Brent later."

"Okaaay." She draws the word out and pouts.

I hold her hand as we walk over to the table and Julia takes her and places her on the booster seat Evan set up.

Sitting at the table, I watch as Evan and Julia interact, feeling a pang of jealousy hit me in the chest as they look at each other with such love evident on their faces.

Honestly, I never thought any of us would settle down. But Evan had been in love with Julia since forever. They didn't get together until about ten years ago, but when they finally did, it was the kind of love that films and books are written about.

They say you go through a honeymoon phase, but I guess their phase is longer than others. From what I've seen, they are sickeningly in love. But from what Evan said when we left the diner, it got rough a few years ago when they started trying to get pregnant. However, they don't look any different to me now than they did all those years ago.

Seeing how much they love each other and everything they've battled through, only to come out the other side stronger for it, makes me think about Caleigh.

I've been trying not to, but I can't help it. I fell in love with her before I knew what was happening. I didn't mean to, but it wasn't as though what we had was planned. I didn't go looking for anything, not even a girl to hook up with for a while. But then I met a pink-haired goddess who changed my mind, changed my heart, and left an imprint on my soul. Why the hell did I have to fuck it up?

***

It's been a week since the barbecue at Evan's and we're gathered in the studio to record more songs for the album. I've been tinkering with a song of my own, but it isn't perfect. Far from it.

Loving you made me a better man,
Why did I ruin what we had?
You were my everything,
A reason for my heart to beat,
But now I'm broken,
I had to admit defeat.

It's hard to concentrate as I begin to play the opening chords of a song Evan wrote. All I can think of is the words tumbling around inside my own head, the myriad of emotions swirling inside me.

I did it all for love,
Something I knew nothing of,
Until the day I met you,
And you showed me the way.
But now I'm here without you,
Lost in a sea of despair.

I feel a twinge of sadness as Evan begins to sing words of the love he feels for Julia and how she is his world. He writes like no other man I've ever met. His ability to pour heart and soul into his lyrics makes me strive to write better.

Of course, we've all written our own fair share of songs over the years for the albums we've recorded, but we all know we pale in comparison to Evan. He has the mastery, the technique, the words, but more than that, he's the one of us that *truly* knows what it is to *love* another person more than anything else. Asher and Jude are eternal bachelors, and they like it that way, *want* it that way. But me? I've not been able to write a song in so long, which is why I needed a break, and now that I have lyrics rattling around my head, they're all about Caleigh Rae Flynn, the one that got away.

We wrap up two tracks at the studio before calling it quits for the day. We had to re-record due to me not knowing I was crying until it was too late. Evan's words spoke directly to my heart and drew on every emotion I have raging inside me like a tsunami rushing to shore.

Gordon was pleased with the new tracks in the end, so it was all good. Now we're one step closer to releasing the new album. But we're also a step closer to the biggest decision of my life.

Chapter Fifteen

Caleigh

Rhiannon convinced me to bring Hardin out to Brookhaven and stay with her, her husband Lewis and their beautiful little girl, my goddaughter, Luna.

It's been so nice getting away from work, and Hardin's school is on another break, so it was perfect timing.

Before I left home, Deb told me that she'd overheard a conversation that wasn't meant for her ears, something that made me want to scream and scratch out Damien's eyeballs. Pathetic scumbag made crude remarks about me, and to think I'd considered him a friend as well as being my boss.

Deb had come in early that fateful day, only to overhear raised voices between Damien, "Rhett" and someone she couldn't identify—Gordon.

Damien had made a comment about my "sweet little pussy" and how he'd piece me back together after Brent left. Why the hell he'd think that, I don't know. He's been my boss and my friend, but I've never looked at him in *that* way. I thought he'd never looked at me in that way either, until Deb told me everything she heard.

I'd been working alongside him for weeks without knowing what went down after I left. I didn't want to know. All I needed to know was that Brent was gone.

Deb apologised for not telling me sooner, but she knew I was in pain over Brent leaving and taking my heart with him. She only decided to tell me because she's watched as Damien has been overly nice to me.

I thought it was because he was being a friend, but it's obvious that he had an ulterior motive. Deb didn't want him taking advantage of me, but it's not like he's made a move on me in the last six weeks. He's been acting normally, except for being overly friendly and helpful, which now I come to think about it is probably because he's been waiting for the dust to settle before doing anything. Who knows, maybe he'll try something when I get back from Brookhaven next week. If he does, I'll quit my job and take him to a tribunal for sexual harassment. Okay, maybe I won't, because I'm not one to make waves, but I'll damn well quit if he doesn't apologise for the comments he made. Part of me believes he only said those things to get under Brent's skin, to hurt him for hurting me. But Deb said he sounded sincere—or as sincere as you can when talking about someone's "sweet little pussy".

God, just the thought of him saying that makes me feel sick. And goddamn angry.

Luna comes running up to me, squealing as Hardin chases her around the garden.

God, Rhiannon's house is so beautiful, and the garden is so big. I could easily see myself and Hardin living somewhere like this one day.

I heard back about the job interview yesterday and they want me to start as soon as possible. It'll mean more money and a better chance at getting a mortgage on a decent sized place for Hardin to grow. Our house is okay for now, but a little on the snug side as Hardin gets older.

Rhiannon has been trying to convince me to move here to Brookhaven. She said that the schools are excellent, that Hardin would be happy here. It would be a wrench to leave his friends, but she said that it's something to think about while he's so young, because he could make friends easily here.

Thankfully, the job allows me to set up wherever I want, so it's definitely something to consider.

"Hey, Mummy, which way did Luna go?" Hardin asks breathlessly.

"I can't tell you that. That's cheating."

"But Mummy," he whines.

"You're playing hide and seek. I can't tell you where she is, because then you wouldn't be finding her yourself, and that's not fair, is it baby?"

I ruffle his hair and he frowns at me, his brows furrowed, marring his handsome features.

"Okay, Mummy, I'll play fair."

"Good boy. Now go on, go find Luna before she gets fed up of waiting."

He runs off in the wrong direction and I can't help but chuckle.

"Sounds good on you, you know?" Rhiannon says as she sits beside me on the patio swing.

"What does?" I ask, confused.

"Laughter. Haven't heard it much since you got here."

"Oh," I respond with a sigh. "I guess I haven't had much to laugh about."

Rhi knows what happened back home and she's *somewhat* sympathetic, but she also says that I should have held onto Brent because a love like that doesn't come around often. She's right; it doesn't. I was lucky to have had it with Angelo, but even luckier to have found it when I least expected it. But even if I forgave his lies—which in my heart, I already have—it's the broken trust that hurts the most. That's before you even get to the rest: the fame, the distance, the women on the road—do I believe that one? I believe he was probably a bit of a playboy, yeah. But do I think he slept with them without protection like Gordon insinuated? I don't think so, because when we first met, he insisted on condoms, stocked up on them in fact. It was me that told him to stop using them because I was clean and because I trusted him—was that trust misplaced?

"What's got your face all screwed up?" Rhi asks as she sips her wine.

"Nothing. Just thinking, I guess. Maybe a bit of wishful thinking."

"Wishful thinking? About Brent, you mean?"

"Yeah."

"Honey, he loves you. I know I can only go off what you told me, but it honestly sounds like he loves you. He lied, yeah, but that was to protect his identity."

"Do we really have to go over this again?"

"Sweetie, I know I've said all this before, but I'll risk sounding like a broken record until it sinks in and you do something about it."

I sigh and take a large gulp of my wine.

"Rhi, he hurt me. He *really* hurt me. Plus, he's gone now. I have no way of contacting him even if I wanted to."

"You don't think he's kept the same number in hopes of you calling?"

Sighing again, this time deeper, I look my best friend in the eye.

"I've wanted to try and call him, but I've chickened out so many times. I was the one who told him to leave. I know he had no choice anyway because of his manager, but I told him not to contact me again. He's probably deleted my number by now. I'm probably nothing but a memory."

"Pfft! Please don't try and tell me that you believe that nonsense you're spouting?"

"Nonsense?"

"I'm probably nothing but a memory," she says, mimicking me. "Please, like you think that's true. You don't turn love off like a tap, Caleigh. It takes time and effort to put something like that to the back of your mind so much that it becomes a distant memory."

"Well, he's had six weeks. And you know what they say about how long it takes to get over a relationship—it takes the same length of time to get over it as the length of time you were together. Well, if that's the case, he's long over me by now. We only had a couple of weeks together, so…" I trail off with a shrug.

"Please, girl," she says with a laugh. "You don't really believe that bullshit, do you? It takes however long it takes, but it isn't judged on how long you were together. More like on how much you meant to that person. And if you really meant that much to him, he'll barely be able to keep his shit together right now. Just like you."

"Oh, thanks," I say in mock offence as I nudge her elbow, causing her to spill a little wine.

"Hey, careful. I like my wine in my glass or in my mouth, not wasted on the floor."

"Oh, I'm so sorry."

"Less of the sarcasm, young lady."

"Why? It's the language I'm most fluent in."

"Yeah, if you don't count your other language: bullshit."

We both crack up laughing, and I have to admit, it feels good to really laugh about something, even if it is only something little.

"Mummy, I fell over and hurt my knee," Hardin says as he limps over to me.

"Oh, baby, come here. Let Mama take a look."

He climbs up onto my lap and I look at his grazed knee.

"I'll go and get the first aid kit," Rhi says before disappearing inside.

"How did you do this, baby?"

"We were on the tyre swing and Luna pushed it hard, then I fell off."

"Aw, baby, come here."

I wrap my arms around him, and he does the same, squeezing me tightly.

"She didn't mean to push so hard, Mummy."

"I'm sure she didn't, baby."

Luna comes running over with Hardin's glasses in her hand.

"Here, Hardin. I found these on the floor," she says as she hands them to him.

"Thanks, Luna."

"I'm sorry I pushed you too hard."

"It's okay. Auntie Rhi went to get the first aid kit."

"Yeah, we'll put a plaster on that, and you'll be fine,' Rhi says as she comes back out onto the patio.

She opens the first aid kit and goes about cleaning Hardin's knee and patching him up.

***

It's been a nice day, except for Hardin getting hurt. But he wasn't bothered by it after Rhiannon patched him up. He went back to playing with Luna, and then they ate their tea and played inside for a while before having a bath and going to bed.

They were both so dirty from playing outside that I'm almost certain it was more mud than water in the bath after they'd finished.

"So, have you thought any more about calling a certain someone?" Rhiannon asks as we relax in the living room.

"Don't even go there, Rhi."

"I'm sorry for loving my best friend and wanting her to be happy," she says with a huff.

"Leave the poor woman be, Rhi, baby," Lewis chimes in.

He's not one for talking about feelings and shit, so when it comes to me pouring my heart out, he normally leaves us to it. But he knows Rhiannon has been getting on my back since I got here.

"I'll leave her alone when she does the right thing and follows her heart instead of her head."

"You do know that the heart doesn't think, right?" I ask. "It's completely illogical to think that one can follow their heart instead of their head, when it's their head that does all the thinking."

"You have to be so bloody stubborn and obtuse, don't you, woman?" Rhiannon crosses her arms and pouts at me like a child.

"I'm merely pointing out a fact."

"Well if you want to put it like that, then, I will get off your back when you wrap your *mind* around the facts."

"And what facts would those be, Rhi?"

"That you love him, and he loves you. That you should pick up the damn phone instead of being a coward, thinking he's forgotten you. One of you has to reach out to the other, and if it's not him for some reason, then you need to do it. Everyone deserves a second chance. Don't you owe it to yourself to find out if he's hurting too? To find out if you can put it behind you and move forward, *together?*"

"If I owe anyone anything, it's his manager. I owe him a slap in the face for calling me a whore."

"Oh, go ahead, ignore the question if you like. But you know I'm right. I know he lied to you, Caleigh, and I know he hurt you. He's flawed, but that's because he's human. You've seen the real him, and no, I don't mean as a liar. I mean as someone who is imperfect. Which, after all, is the one trait every human being has in common. We are all flawed in some way, honey. I am, Lewis is, *you* are."

Is she right? He's not perfect, but then nobody is. He's imperfect, like anyone else on the planet.

"I-I don't know, Rhi. I have Hardin to think of too. I have to protect him."

"Honey, what do you have to protect him from? It's not like Hardin knows any of this. He's blissfully oblivious. What you really mean is that you are worried about protecting your heart. Angelo was your first real love and he left you—*not* by choice, I know—and now Brent is the first person you've allowed yourself to feel something for since all that. That means that it hurts that much more, because you actually felt ... *feel* something for the man."

I wish this woman would shut up. I wish she'd stop making sense. I want to wallow in self-pity. Aren't I allowed to do that?

"Without trust, there is no love, Rhi."

I take a large gulp of my wine and blink back unshed tears. All this talk of Brent just makes me miss him so much more.

"But honey, trust is *earned*, not given. You could allow him the chance to earn your trust again. I'm not saying you should marry the guy. Not yet, anyway. I'm just saying that you could give him a second chance, and if he blows it, then he doesn't deserve you. But if you ask me, although he's not perfect, he *is* perfect for *you.*"

"So, he's perfectly imperfect? Is that what you're trying to say?"

"You could put it like that."

I don't know what more I can say. I feel drained. I came here because

I didn't want to talk about Brent—well, that's what I convinced myself of at first. But I guess I really did need somebody else's opinion. An outsider looking in, someone who would be objective, someone who cares about me and wants what's best for me.

"You know, I think I'm going to call it a night."

"Honey, I didn't mean to upset you," Rhi says as she places a hand on my arm.

"I know you didn't, sweetie. I just need to be alone with my thoughts. I think I need to sleep on it and look at it with fresh eyes another day. But while I'm staying here, I'd appreciate not talking about it again. Not right now, anyway."

"Okay honey, if that's what you want, then that's what you'll get."

"Thank you, Rhi. I really mean it. Thank you for giving me something to think about. I think you're right about some of it, but other stuff, I need to think longer about. I really appreciate my best friend having my back."

"That's what I'm here for, my lovely. I'm your best friend, a friend who will never pull her punches and always give it to you straight."

"And that's why I love you so much."

I lean down and kiss her on the cheek before saying goodnight and leaving her and Lewis to the rest of their evening.

As I enter the guest room, I grab a towel and my pyjamas before heading for a shower. I wish I could have a long hot soak in my bath at home; it's where I ponder things when I'm upset. But a shower will have to do for now.

***

After a week with my best friend, it's time to go home. I'm longing for my own bed, but I'll really miss Rhiannon. It was so nice when we lived closer together. That's another reason to think of moving out to be closer to her.

Two hours driving has me itching with cabin fever. I need to get out and stretch my legs. As I pull up outside the house, I look at Hardin in the rear-view mirror, only to see he's fallen asleep. He's not one for naptime anymore, but he does tend to conk out on long trips. To be honest, I would too, given the chance.

"Come on, baby, we're home," I say as I undo his seatbelt.

He stirs and looks at me through his sleepy gaze.

"Nanny and Grandad should be here in a bit to take you to theirs while Mummy works tonight."

"Do you have to, Mummy?" he whines.

"I do. But the good thing is, Mummy got a new job, so I won't have to work as many hours in the pub and I'll get more time to spend with you."

"YAY!" he shouts, nearly perforating my eardrum.

Truth be told, I'll still do a few hours each week in The Lock—if Damien and I don't fall out—because I like the social element of it. But now with my work hours being more flexible, I'll be able to be home with Hardin more. It's what I've been needing ever since I went back to work after he was born. But with little to no experience, nobody was willing to take a chance on me. So, I got the experience and now I'm qualified and that makes things so much easier all around.

After a quick snack—his favourite, Nutella and banana on toast, of course—we pack a bag for him to stay with my mum and dad.

They don't know anything about Brent or what happened. They don't even know I was seeing anyone—unless Damien has opened his mouth while I've been away. I don't want to tell them now, because I don't want to hear the questions and the advice they'd impart. I need to reconcile how I feel by myself. I know that Rhiannon loves me and gave me some advice, but I really don't need more people piling on their opinions. I need some time alone to make a decision.

If there's anything to tell them later on, then I will. But for right now I'm going to go to work and try to get on with a semblance of my normal routine.

"Hey, stranger," Damien says as I walk in.

"Hey. We, umm …" I stop and clear my throat. "We need to talk. Can we use the back office?"

"Sure. What's up?" he asks as he walks with me around the bar and down the little corridor to the little office.

"Well, there's something we need to clear up," I reply as I close the door behind me.

"Go on." He settles into the chair behind his desk and steeples his hands on the cherry wood top.

"Well, I heard something, and I wanted to find out from the horse's mouth if it was true." My throat goes dry, so I try to swallow.

"What's that then, Caleigh?"

"Is it true that you made some rather crude comments about me when I left the day that Brent's manager turned up?"

"What?" He sounds exasperated. "What am I meant to have said?"

The look that crosses his face is hard to read. I sit down in the chair opposite him and lean forward. I don't want this to be overheard.

"It seems you said something about my—and I quote—sweet little pussy, amongst other things."

Damien's face falls and I know it's true. Not that I didn't believe Deb, after all she has no reason to lie. But to see the truth on his face hurts.

"It was said in the heat of the moment, Caleigh. I'm so sorry."

"Don't you think you should have told me at some point in the last, what, seven weeks?"

"I didn't see any reason to bring it up. You were already so hurt, and I didn't want to make it worse."

"Don't give me all that. You didn't want to admit that you fucked up and said some vile things. You weren't protecting me; you were protecting your goddamn self."

"Maybe in part it was self-preservation too, but you have to believe me, Caleigh. I didn't mean the things I said. Like I say, it was in the heat of the moment. It was meant to hurt that fucker, not you."

He holds his hands up in a placating manner.

"Do you like me in *that* way, Damien? Be honest, don't BS me."

"No, I swear."

"Don't soft-soap me. I've seen the way you look at me when you think nobody's watching."

"Okay, look." He sighs as he adjusts himself to sit back in his chair. "I *did* have a thing for you. But I started seeing someone a few weeks back. It's all been hush-hush, because you know what small town gossip is like."

"That's all well and good, and I'm happy for you. But that's not what I asked. Let me make this a bit clearer. When you argued with Brent, when you said what you did, did you feel something for me at that time?"

"Yes," he says with a long sigh. "When you came back to live here and started working for me, I liked you then. I didn't act on it because I knew you were devastated by the loss of Angelo. Truth be told, I was jealous when I saw you with Brent. That time I saw you outside American Honey—"

"I think the less said about that, the better," I butt in as I feel myself flush at the memory of Brent being so brazen as to touch me in the diner car park.

"Sorry, I wasn't going to … look, umm … what I mean is that when I saw the way you two looked at each other, the love evident in your eyes … I was jealous that you'd never looked at me that way. I always secretly hoped that I would be the man you looked at with an adoring gaze. I hoped to be the one by your side as you fell in love again. But I could always see that was never going to happen, because you never saw me that way."

He pauses and pulls a bottle of whiskey out of his bottom drawer. Pouring a small amount into two glasses, he hands me one before he continues.

"I know now that what I thought I felt about you was infatuation. And I know that, at least in part, because when I started seeing Ellie, all the feelings that I had bubbling up inside me were stronger than what I felt for you."

"Ellie?" I ask in shock. "Wow. I didn't see that coming. I thought she hated you."

"Hate's a strong word. She admits to pretending to dislike me for a while, but more to keep me at arm's length than anything. Look, Caleigh, I'm truly disgusted at myself for the crude way in which I said things about you to Brent. But I wanted to hurt him because he hurt you. I don't like to see my friends getting hurt, and I just wanted to hit him where it hurt."

"I get that. I'm grateful for you sticking up for me. But I really wish you hadn't said the things you said."

"I truly wish I hadn't too. I should have just sucker-punched the asshole instead."

"I'm glad you didn't do that, Damien."

"You are?" he asks, his face registering shock. "Why would you be glad about that? For him, or because he could have got me arrested?"

"A bit of both," I reply as I sip the last of my whiskey. "Now if you don't mind, I'd like to put this behind us and get to work."

"I'd like nothing more."

I get up and place my glass on the desk before grabbing my apron and getting behind the bar.

Ellie is sitting by Damien's usual stool. Funny, I didn't see her when I came in. Deb smiles at me from her place at the end of the bar.

"Did you …" She trails off in a whisper as she comes over to me.

"Yeah, we talked. It's sorted."

"Okay, tell me later when, you know, Ellie can't hear."

"Yeah, he just told me about that. I thought she hated him."

"Me too. They make a cute couple though, I have to admit."

"How long have you known?"

"Only a few days. I was waiting until you got back to say anything. How have you been?"

"Good, thanks. It was nice to spend time with my bestie and my goddaughter. Lewis was mostly at work."

"Glad to hear it. How's Hardin?"

"He's good. He went to my mum's after a quick snack."

"Don't tell me. Nutella and banana on toast?" she says with a giggle.

"Yeah, as per. He got Luna eating it this week too. Needless to say, Rhi was unimpressed."

"I can imagine. At least it's not something weirder than that. Like, say, cheese on toast with apple slices."

"Oh my god," I laugh, bringing my hand to my mouth. "I can't believe you remember that. That was so long ago."

"Ah, but luckily for me, I have the memory of an elephant," she says with a wink.

"At least I have better eating habits now."

"Thank the Lord for small mercies," she quips and pokes her tongue out at me.

"Bitch."

I whip her ass with a bar towel before turning and serving a customer. Josh has a smile on his face, so he probably heard the tail end of the conversation.

Chapter Sixteen

Brent

I've finally finished working on the song. The title pretty much wrote itself: "The One That Got Away". It was the most obvious part of the song really.

I can't stand this pain another day,
Without the one that got away.
She held my heart within her hands,
If only I was a better man.
She doesn't deserve the lies I told,
But will she still love me when we're grey and old?
I wonder, does she think of me at all?
I miss her love; I miss it all.

I haven't played it for anyone, not on purpose anyway. Ash walked in the other day and heard the tail end of it. He told me it belongs on the album, but it's something private, something I'm not sure I can share with the world at large.

We've pretty much wrapped the album anyway, but Ash tells me we have time to record it, even if it's a bonus song only available on iTunes or something.

Yesterday, I finally plucked up the courage to look at houses for sale. I've found one in a small town a couple of hours away from River's Edge.

It's far enough away that Caleigh need never know where I am—depending on if I can actually pluck up the courage needed to contact her—yet close enough to torment myself everyday over what I lost—if I can't bring myself to pick up the phone and call her. Or rather what I destroyed. Maybe eviscerated is a better word.

I've got a viewing set up for the day after we finish in the studio. I'm getting straight onto the plane; my bag is already packed. I'll stay in a B&B and meet the estate agent the next morning. This time I'm not making the mistake of flying commercial. I've asked the boys if they mind me taking the private jet. We all part own it, but I wouldn't just take off without warning, not this time.

They don't know where I'm going, just that I'll be back without hesitation this time. How long for, I haven't made them aware. I'm still working up the nerve to tell them what I've decided to do. Lord knows how they'll react.

I don't want them to hate me, but I have to do this. I have to do it for me. Nobody else, just me. I guess I've known in my heart for a while, but it took some time for my head and my heart to be in agreement.

Today has been one of quiet contemplation. I've made some mistakes recently and I want to rectify them. I don't know quite how, but I want to at the very least try. I think. God, I don't really know. Do I ring her? Do I let her get on with her life? Is she better off in my arms or better off without me? I know what I want, but what I want in all this is not what's important—it's all about Caleigh. Will she even answer the phone? If she doesn't, do I just turn up unannounced?

I'm plagued with questions that I can't find the answers to, no matter how hard I wrack my brain.

"Yo, bro, you home?" Jude calls as he shuts my front door.

"In the kitchen."

I turn and put the coffee on. If he's here disturbing my one day of relative peace, it can't be without caffeine.

"Sorry to interrupt your solitude, man," he says as he walks in.

Him standing in my space makes the kitchen feel like it was made for a dwarf. The guy's muscles have muscles, although he's not quite as built as Dwayne Johnson. Even thinking that makes my heart feel twisted up in knots. I can just remember Hardin telling me that Caleigh loved The Rock.

"You look like someone kicked your puppy, what's up, man?"

"Nothing, bud, I'm fine. What brings you here?" I ask, eager to divert the conversation away from me.

"Just wanted to swing by for a chat."

"About?"

"You."

Great! So much for diverting his attention.

"And what in particular would you like to discuss?"

"The one that got away…" He trails off as he looks at me.

I feel small under his scrutiny. It's disconcerting.

"I don't want to talk about her, bro."

I can't even bring myself to say her name, it hurts that much. Turning back to the worktop, I pour us both a coffee.

"I don't mean Caleigh, I mean the song."

"What?" I ask, so shocked I almost spill the coffee I'm about to hand him, "How do you know…? Ash."

Damnit, he's a good friend, but I could swing for him if he was here.

"Yeah, Ash. Dude, he's only looking out for you," he rushes out as he registers the dark look that crosses my face.

I would probably piss my pants if he gave me the look that I hope I'm pulling off, but he just laughs.

"He just wants me to hear you play it. Will you do that for me?"

"I can't man, I just … I'm sorry but I can't."

"Don't make me beg. A man my size begging would look fucking ridiculous."

"Too damn right you would. But I still can't, Jude. It hurts too goddamn much."

"Okay, let's try this another way. Will you let me look at it?"

"I don't have it written down."

"What?" Now it's his turn to look shocked.

I always write my songs down, but this one hurt too much to put pen to paper.

"It's all in my head, man. I couldn't write it down. It felt like I was slicing open a vein and bleeding out."

"I'm sorry, Brent. I truly am. I'll admit, I've never been in love. Maybe that's weird for a dude my age, but I guess being away from home a lot means I've never formed attachments, never even wanted to. But even though I lack in experience, I still know it must really be breaking your heart to be away from Caleigh. I know you fell in love with her and I know you fucked up, but you could still win her back, man."

"I don't think I can," I reply softly, my tone full of melancholy, and probably a touch of feeling sorry for myself.

"You never know, bro. I know Ash said something about a big, romantic, Hallmark-style grand gesture. Maybe your song is it."

I sip my coffee as I wonder for a moment if he's right.

"It's going to take more than that, Jude. I broke her heart. I let her fall in love with me when I was lying about who I am all along. I lost her trust."

"Okay, dude, two things. Number one." He counts on his fingers. "You didn't *let* her fall in love with you, like you couldn't have stopped her if you'd tried. And number two, the thing about trust is it is meant to be earned, not just given. Oh, and number three, sorry, you have the rest of your lives to make it up to her. *Show* her, don't tell her. *Prove* you love her. It's more than just words. For example, if somehow someone took your words away, what would you *do*, how would you show her how you feel?"

"That's deep for you, dude," I respond, reverting to my fallback of joking to deflect.

"Yeah, I might look as deep as a puddle, but that's what you get for judging a book by its cover. Now answer the fucking question. What would you do?"

"I don't know, man. Like, I honestly do *not* know. I've been trying to think of something, and yet I've had weeks for inspiration to hit and it hasn't."

"Are you sitting back waiting for it to come to you? That's where you're going wrong. You have to go out there in search of answers. Stop sitting at home and moping around. Go out there and win the love of the woman you want to spend your life with."

"Jeez, when you got here, I was hoping for some other topic of conversation. I didn't expect to be made to feel like a stupid fucktard."

"That wasn't my intention, bro. Now look, I have to ask one last time." He pauses to drink the last of his coffee. Maybe he thinks he doesn't have to finish the sentence. "Would you please play the song, just for me, just this once?"

I don't answer. I turn back and pour myself another coffee.

As I turn around, I see him pocket his phone. My own phone chimes, so I pull it out of my back pocket.

>Dude, just play him the goddamn song. It's so beautiful. Don't make me beg. A.

As if I thought I could count on my other best friend to do anything other than be a traitor.

>Go fuck yourself sideways with a cactus, you traitorous douchebag.

>Harsh!

>I could have said a lot worse, trust me.

I pocket my phone and look up to see a smile on Jude's face. He thinks he's won the battle. And sadly, I admit defeat.

We walk into the living room, and I pull Bess from her case. Of course, I wrote it on the guitar I bought while I was away. It reminds me of Caleigh. It's bittersweet really.

Jude takes a seat on the couch, and boy does his size dwarf it. It looks like it was made for a bloody Polly Pocket, not a three-seater for grown-ass adults.

"Don't leave me hanging, bro. I ain't got all day."

"Patience," I warn as I run a hand over Bess.

***

Jude left not long after hearing the song, leaving me to cry in peace and quiet. I waited until I heard the door close behind him before allowing the first tear to fall, and they didn't stop until I got in the shower and washed them down the drain.

Sadly, it wasn't long before they started up again, so I poured myself a whiskey to drown my sorrows.

Three glasses of whiskey later and I've managed to take the edge off my pain. Not made it go away, just stopped it from being so razor-sharp. Maybe I should spend my days trying to find peace and solitude at the bottom of the bottle, but that would be a mistake. I need a clear mind to try and find the answers I seek. Trouble is, I don't even know where to begin.

>Open the door, bro. This food's getting cold.

I see the text and am confused. What the hell is Evan talking about?

I walk to the front door and unlock it. I'd made a point to lock it after Jude left, so that I wasn't interrupted again.

"What the hell man? Since when do you lock your door when you're home?"

"Since my friends started barging in unannounced and unwanted."

"Careful, or I'll take this back," he warns as he waves a bag in front of me.

The aromas from that bag make my stomach rumble. Funnily, I

hadn't even noticed I was hungry.

"Come in, then, before it gets cold," I reply as I move aside to let him in.

"Quite the greeting, man. Nice to see you too."

"Sorry. I'm just feeling sorry for myself, and I was enjoying the company of my bottle of whiskey."

"Don't be selfish, then. I'll plate up; you pour."

I grab him a tumbler from the cupboard as he walks around, grabbing everything he needs to dish up whatever he's brought with him.

"How are Julia and Jessa?"

"Good, yeah. They're with Jules's mum, so it was either an evening in front of the telly or force my company down your throat."

"Good job I like you then, hey?"

"I didn't know what you'd want, so I got a few things. You can have a bit of whatever takes your fancy," he replies as he puts containers on the breakfast bar.

"Ooh, is that crispy duck?"

I point to a foil container and Evan nods.

"What else are you hiding?"

"Chop suey, egg fried rice, and chicken and mushroom soup, because I know it's your favourite—besides the duck, that is."

"I didn't even think I was hungry, but man this just smells like heaven."

"Like you're headed there when life's done with you." His face morphs into his classic cheesy grin.

"Yeah, fucker, because you'd know. One day, when I'm ruler of hell, I'll make you, Ash and Jude my little bitches."

"The pay would have to be good."

Goofing around with one of my three best friends feels so good. I don't know how much longer I'll be doing it, so I'll take what I can get, when I can get it.

***

Thankfully, there was no mention of Caleigh or the song while Evan was here. I'm just assuming he knows about the song because the other two have big mouths—especially Jude. We enjoyed Chinese takeaway and a couple of whiskeys, leaving me feeling slightly buzzed.

As I shower, I can't help but think of Caleigh, though. I'm reminded of the showers we took together, pretty much every time I shower. Even when buzzed, apparently.

I let my head fall back against the cool tiles and close my eyes. A vision of pink hair falling over her full breasts plays behind my eyelids.

Ghosting my hand down over my abs, I imagine that it's Caleigh's hand touching me. Her soft silky skin roaming over the ridges of my body, down until she reaches the defined V shape she enjoyed touching so much. Slowly her palm cups my cock and strokes me up and down. Fuck! I'm hard, and there's nothing I can do except bring myself to climax to the visions of Caleigh's lithe body.

I get into bed, satisfied that I no longer have a hard-on and a serious case of blue balls, but saddened that I opened my eyes and Caleigh dissipated into thin air.

The ghost of her will no doubt haunt my dreams, just like she has done every other night since I left her.

Chapter Seventeen

Caleigh

I've finally decided to bite the bullet and look for a house closer to Rhiannon. I know it means giving up my job at The Lock and changing Hardin's school. It also means I won't have my mum and dad on my doorstep anymore, and that makes me sad. But the fact is, I've done a lot of soul searching and decided that I need to make a fresh start.

A new job, a new place to live, a new attitude. It's what I need. It'll be good for me and for Hardin.

It will be a wrench to leave my parents behind again, but as they're both retired, they can come and visit any time they like.

Honestly, the decision was prompted by Rhiannon, but it's not her making me do anything I don't want to do. I always said I would rather not live in River's Edge. Angelo and I had wanted somewhere bigger for the three of us and I only moved back because we lost him. Now it's just time for me to move on with my life. Everything has to move forward. You need to keep swimming, like a shark, because if you stay still … well, in the case of a shark, it would die, but in my case, it would mean that I'm merely existing instead of living. I need to live. So I need to do it for me, for Hardin, and in memory of Angelo, who would want me to give Hardin the best life possible.

I'm not saying we couldn't rub along just fine in River's Edge, but that's all we'd be doing, rubbing along instead of really going out there and grabbing life by the proverbial balls.

I've always known that life is a series of fleeting moments that you grab and squeeze as much joy out of them as possible. Some moments are longer than others, some are happier than others. But whatever you do, you make the most of them, because you never know when the time will come that you have no more tomorrows.

As I pull up outside the house, Hardin looks up at it, his eyes as wide as saucers. It really is beautiful. It's a house of character, not a new build with no love or care shown to it. I don't know if it's "the one", but I know it has potential.

Instead of renting a space in the town hall in Pedmore for my yoga classes, I can actually find a premises of my own. It's not like I'd drum up much business back home either. It would make far more business sense to move somewhere like here and find a location for my classes.

"Mummy, if we live here, then will we still see Nanny and Pop-pop?" Hardin asks in a small voice.

I know it's going to be hard for him seeing them less, but I'm certain we'll be happy when we settle down somewhere. We'll find a way to make it all work. We have to.

"Of course we will, baby. They'll come and visit, and we can visit them in the holidays."

"But I won't see my friends from school anymore," he adds, sadly.

His words tug at my heart strings.

"I know, baby, but you'll make lots of new friends at a new school."

"How do you know they'll even like me?"

"Oh, baby, of course they will. What's not to like? You're an amazing kid. You're clever, funny, and anyone would be lucky to have you as a friend."

"Okay."

His sadness really sucker punches me, but I take a deep breath and tell myself I'm doing the right thing.

"Come on, baby, let's go check out the house," I say as I see the estate agent standing at the front door of the house.

We climb out of the car and Hardin holds my hand tightly as we walk up the path.

"Good afternoon, Miss Flynn. I'm Jane. It's a pleasure to meet you."

I shake her outstretched hand and offer her a smile. "Hello, Jane. It's good to finally put a face to the voice on the other end of the phone."

"And who is this handsome little boy?"

I introduce her to Hardin, and he thanks her as she hands him a lollipop.

"I knew you were coming, so I came prepared," Jane says as Hardin unwraps it.

"Thank you."

"You're welcome, Hardin. Are you excited to see the house?"

"Umm … a little bit."

"I'm sure you'll be happy with what could be your bedroom."

Jane leads us into the house where we start the tour. It really is beautiful. It's spacious, there's lots of natural light, and the bedrooms are great sizes. Everything about it is what I'd want from a place to call home. The kitchen is phenomenal, a mix of old and new.

We walk into the back garden, and Hardin's eyes light up when I tell him there's plenty of room for him to play football.

"This place is amazing," I say as Jane leads us back to the living room.

"It sure is, and the previous owners made some really great upgrades that make it that much more desirable."

"How soon would you need an answer?"

"Well, I do have another showing in"—she looks at her watch—"five minutes. I've had quite some interest in this place because of the size and the price. It's very desirable."

"Could I take some time to think it over?"

"If I were you, I'd make an offer as soon as possible."

"Okay. I have to weigh up the price, considering I'm also looking to rent premises for my yoga classes."

"Just call me as soon as you can. I know this place would be perfect for the two of you."

"It really would," I agree as we walk to the front door. "I'll be in touch shortly. I'm just on my way to see the rental space."

"I look forward to speaking to you soon, then."

We shake hands, and I open the front door before taking Hardin's hand in mine and bidding Jane goodbye.

Walking down the path, I look around the front garden. It's well tended, and although there's a decent amount of space, it doesn't look like the upkeep would be too hard.

I really want to snap her hand off and take it right away, but I can't because I have an appointment to view the space for my classes. I have to weigh up the pros and cons, but as she has another viewing, I guess I'd better do it fast.

"Oh, I'm so sorry," I say as I bump into a hard wall of muscle.

"It's my fault, I wasn't looking where I was…"

His voice trails off, and I have to blink back unshed tears. What the hell is he even doing here? Is he Jane's next client? He wants the same house as me?

"Caleigh," he says softly, as if he might spook me somehow.

"Brent."

I don't have the words to say anything more to him. I nod curtly and move to walk past him, but he blocks my way.

"Please don't go," he pleads.

"I-I h-have to."

Great, so now I'm stuttering. What the hell has happened to my strength? My knees feel as weak as my voice.

"Hi Hardin," he says, causing me to move a hand to protect my son.

I know Brent isn't a threat, I just can't help but want to shield Hardin so that he doesn't feel the pain I feel.

"Hi, Rhett," Hardin replies, his voice a lot perkier than mine.

"Actually, baby, this man's name is Brent. He was *pretending* his name was Rhett."

Hardin looks up at Brent with a puzzled expression.

"Why would he do that, Mummy?" he asks, not taking his eyes from Brent.

"I was hiding in town and didn't want anyone to find me," Brent answers.

"Like hide and seek?"

"A little bit. I had to be *really* good at hiding," Brent replies in a hushed tone.

"Say goodbye, Hardin. It's time to go now."

"Bye, Brent."

"Bye, Hardin. It was nice seeing you again," he says as we go to walk past him.

A hand on my elbow halts my movements. I forgot how electric his touch felt. My traitorous heart beats faster, harder because of his proximity. The smell of his aftershave permeates my senses and I feel all the hairs on my arm stand on end.

"Hardin, baby, would you go wait in the car for Mama? There's a good boy," I say as I press the button to unlock the doors for him.

"Okay, Mummy."

He skips down the path and opens the car door. Once he's sitting on his booster seat, he waves out of the window.

"Caleigh, please—"

"Please what, Brent? Please fall at your feet like the groupies? Please forgive you for shattering my heart into a million tiny fragments? Please what?"

I take a deep breath and try to calm my racing pulse. It isn't working, even though I try over and over.

"I know it isn't worth much to you right now, but you look good. I'm shocked but pleased to see you."

"I wish I could say the same."

I choke back a sob as I hear Jane call Brent's name. He replies that he'll be right with her before looking back to me.

"I'm so sorry, Caleigh. Sorrier than you'll ever know. I will never have the words to tell you how badly I feel for what I did."

"Then don't bother trying."

My curt response is strangled by the lump in my throat that threatens to consume me.

"Caleigh, I know I don't deserve your forgiveness, I'm not asking that of you. I just ... well, I don't know, it's just so great to see you. You ... you look amazing."

"Thanks."

Why am I even entertaining this conversation? It's not like we have much to say to each other now. We're nothing but a memory. Something that was amazing, but something that will never be. We were a love that failed. Destined to crash and burn due to the course he set us on.

I watch as his eyes burn a trail over my body, and I can't help the butterflies that start to swirl inside me as his hooded gaze meets mine.

"I know I broke your heart," he says. "I know it because the moment it broke, I felt like I was being stabbed with a red hot knife. I also know I can't expect you to forgive me, let alone still love me. The pain of that alone is enough to bring me to my knees. To know I'll never feel your love again. Never feel your arms as you hold me, never feel your body pressed to mine ..."

I feel the tears fall, but I can't move to wipe them away. I'm frozen in place.

"Brent, please," I whisper.

I feel like I'm struggling to breathe, like he's stolen all the oxygen in my lungs with his words.

I have to admit, I still struggle with the same thoughts. Thoughts of never kissing him, never making love to him, never being able to lie next to him in bed and just watch him as he sleeps. It keeps me up at night sometimes, wishing upon the brightest star that I could go back in time and keep us wrapped up in our little bubble.

My brain doesn't register what's happening until it's too late. Nothing makes sense as his body presses up against mine, his arms wrapped around me. It's like it's all happening in slow motion, but warp speed at the same time. That just doesn't make one iota of sense, but it's the truth.

I can't move away from him. My traitorous body is paralysed, as are my senses.

Suddenly his lips slant over mine, ghosting a kiss over them so softly. Pulling back, he looks into my eyes. They must convey my confusion, but also the love I still feel for him, because he leans in to claim my lips once more.

It's not a sweet kiss, it's white-hot and sensual. It sears right across my soul and I relish in it as it burns deep. His tongue duels with mine, dominating the kiss, stealing all my resolve as I relax in his hold and kiss him like it's the first time all over again.

My arms wrap around him of their accord; it's like my brain is ignoring the warning signs. I play with the hair at the nape of his neck and feel my nipples pebble as he bites my bottom lip, sucking it into his mouth.

"Caleigh," he says breathlessly, as he breaks the kiss.

I look into his eyes and it's like a journey I don't have a map for.

"I love you so much."

His words shake me from my stupor. What the hell was I thinking? I not only allowed him to kiss me, I actively encouraged it. *Fuck!*

"I have to go," I say, my voice at least an octave or two higher than normal.

"Please don't," he sighs as he slips his hand into mine.

Tears fall unbidden down my face and I almost let them devour me, but at the last moment, I come to my senses.

"No, Brent. We can't do this."

I want him to hold me, to tell me it'll be alright. Internally, I'm struggling with myself. My head says no; my heart begs me to say yes.

Extricating myself from his grip, I turn and walk away. I hang my head, my heartbreak weighing heavily on me like an anvil crushing me slowly. In his eyes, I saw the missing pieces of me. It might sound crazy, but it was like for that tiny moment, I felt complete. In that brief space in time, it all wasn't true. Then reality crashed in and I was hit with a tsunami of emotions, each one wringing me out, gutting me and bringing me to my knees.

Frightened of what I might see, but what I might miss if I don't look, I turn as I get to the car. He's watching me, sorrow etched into his face like it's taken up permanent residence. Lifting a hand, he offers me a small wave and I close my eyes.

I don't want to leave. I want to run back up the path and tell him we can get past anything. To tell him that, together, we can overcome any obstacle life throws our way, dodge each curveball. But the sad reality is that we can't. There's too much in our way. Mostly me trying to prevent my heart from being eviscerated again.

I climb into the car and turn on the ignition. The car rumbles to life and I look at the dashboard. I'm running a few minutes later than I'd hoped to my next appointment. Looking in the rear-view mirror as I pull away, I see Brent standing there, unmoving. He becomes smaller and smaller until I blink, and he's gone.

All of a sudden, my fragile heart begins to beat hard against my ribcage. It begs me to turn the car around. But I can't do that. I won't do that. What's done is done and can't be undone. The past is exactly where it belongs. And Brent is in my past, not my present or my future, much to the chagrin of my traitorous heart.

Since when did I listen to Rhiannon about my heart feeling something? It defies logic, but the facts remain the same. My heart still beats for Brent Ryder, even though he'll never know it.

Chapter Eighteen

Brent

Touching my fingers to my lips, I still can't believe that it happened. It's like a very lucid dream. Did I really kiss her? What was I thinking? I wasn't thinking, is the answer. I was feeling. The strong, gravitational pull that drew me to Caleigh came back with a vengeance and it was like my body overrode the signals from my brain that were warning me against it. It was a bad idea. It would only make me miss her all the more when she inevitably left me standing all alone … and she did.

I stood and watched her drive away, unable to tear my eyes away even for a second. It gutted me all over again as she disappeared from my life for the second time. But she kissed me back. Why did she kiss me back?

Her body had moulded to mine, her tongue duelled with mine in a frenzied, white-hot kiss that I'll never forget until my dying day. My body had reacted to her closeness, my arousal prominent and pressed against her. I'm sure if I'd been able to, I would have felt her pussy dripping wet, needy, wanting me as much as I wanted her.

It was hard to go and view the house with Jane. She didn't question me about Caleigh, but I asked her how much interest there had been in the house and she'd said it was one of the most desirable houses on the market in Brookhaven.

What the hell Caleigh was doing viewing a house there, I really don't know. Is she planning to leave River's Edge? It's none of my business anymore, but I still need to know.

As soon as Jane finished giving me the tour, I offered over market value for the house. It was a dick move, I know, but I didn't want Caleigh to buy it.

I'm not a *complete* asshole, I bought the house because I fell in love with it the instant I saw it. But I can't lie, Caleigh wanting it was a reason to offer over list price. Why? That's simple. I don't want her to live anywhere that isn't with me. I can't imagine her anywhere else except by my side for the rest of my life. I might *have* to accept that, but my head and heart aren't in agreement on that. I still have visions of winning her back.

Buying a house that she was interested in wasn't part of the plan, but it buys me some time to try and win her back. If she isn't already looking at other properties, that is.

I'm lying on the bed in the B&B when my phone rings. Looking at the caller ID, I see Evan's name and swipe to answer.

"What's up, Ev?"

"Well, you disappeared. For the second time, I might add. Where in god's name are you?"

He sounds irritated and disappointed.

"I had something to do, Ev. I'll be back late tomorrow."

"So, you aren't even going to tell anyone where you are?" he asks as he sighs in frustration.

I scrub a hand over my face and sigh. I haven't plucked up the courage to tell the boys. I wanted to do what needed to be done first. I had to find a house or else I wasn't going to tell them anything just yet. Now that I've found somewhere, I know it's time. But not until I sign on the dotted line tomorrow and fly back home.

"I'm sorry, Ev, I really am. But listen, I'm not completely off the grid. You can call or text and I promise to answer. But I can't tell you anything until tomorrow. If you looked hard enough, I'm sure you probably could find me. But please don't try. I need the night, Ev. Please?"

"Okay."

"Thank you," I say as I breathe a sigh of relief.

"You owe me an explanation no later than tomorrow, Brent."

"I know, and I promise I'll give you one."

"Until tomorrow then."

"Yeah. Bye, Ev."

I hang up and see the pink-haired beauty that still graces my screen. I can't bring myself to change the wallpaper on my phone. I can't delete any of the photos we took together. It's too painful.

Pulling up a new text thread, I do something I hadn't anticipated.

>I know I have no right to ask, but I can't help myself. Are you staying in town or going back home?

I put my phone down and grab a towel. Turning the water on, I wait until it's nice and hot before stepping into the small en suite shower.

My thoughts turn to Caleigh. I close my eyes and see her naked, bent over and bracing herself against the tiles. Her hair is wet and clings to her shoulders. I grab a fistful of her luscious pink locks and inhale deeply, storing the scent of strawberries in my memories for later. A loud squeal erupts from her as I spank her wet ass. Her giggles are like music to my ears and I wrap an arm around her as I align myself with her. I sink into her and she calls out my name, my *real* name.

And that alone is enough to break the fantasy. She never did that in real life.

I dry myself off, pull on my shorts to sleep in and pick up my phone.

>Go the fuck away, you piece of shit. You bought that fucking house to spite me. You're a prick, Brent. A goddamn douchebag.

>Caleigh, I can explain. It wasn't out of spite at all. Please just tell me if you're in town tonight.

>So what if I am?

>I need to see you. Please, Caleigh, I'll come and fetch you or meet you somewhere. I just need five minutes.

>Will you explain why you bought my fucking house?

She's obviously angry because she doesn't really swear unless she's mad.

>I'll do anything you want if you agree to meet.

>Shit. I don't know why I'm saying this but … where are you? I'll come to you. I don't want you here where Hardin can see. It was hard enough explaining to him why you kissed me.

>I'm at the B&B on Whitmore Crescent. You know it?

>See you in fifteen minutes.

Fuck. She's really coming. Or is she leading me on? No, she wouldn't do that, she's not the type. I don't really know why I asked her to come. It was as surprising to me as the fact that she actually said yes.

I watch the clock as the minutes tick by. Fifteen long minutes later, my phone chimes.

>Room number?

>Six.

A minute later, there's a knock at the door. Opening it, I see a vision better than my memory could conjure up.

Caleigh is dressed in a V cut vest and painted on jeans. Looking down to her feet, I see her black Louboutins. I'd know them anywhere, considering they've left marks on my ass when she's had her legs wrapped tightly around me.

"My eyes are up here, douchebag."

My gaze snaps up to meet hers, and there's a fire in her eyes. She's blazing mad, and I don't blame her. But, for a brief moment, I remember what Evan said about angry make-up sex, and it's all I can do not to grab her and throw her on the bed. Instead, I stand to one side and allow her into the room. She huffs as she passes me and throws her bag on the end of the bed.

"So, would you mind telling me why I'm here? Why you bought my house? Why you kissed me like you were giving me part of your soul?"

"I don't know why you're here, only you can answer why you came when I asked. As for why I bought the house, it was because I've been interested in that place for a while and Jane told me how desirable it was. I made an offer and the owner accepted. The kiss … well, honestly, I couldn't help it. It was something I had to do."

"I don't know why I came. Don't know why I even answered your text, if I'm being honest."

"Do you want to leave?"

She's silent for a few moments before letting out a breath and whispering "No".

"Can I get you a drink? I can only offer tea, coffee or a bottle of water."

"I'll take a coffee. One sugar, please."

She perches on the side of the bed and offers me the slightest smile as I walk around the bed to the kettle. I'm not much of a fan of instant coffee, but the fresh brewed stuff is hard to come by in a B&B. I sit in the chair next to the bed as I hand her a mug.

"What are we doing, Brent?"

"Well, we're sitting in a room in a B&B, drinking coffee and talking," I reply, trying to break the tension surrounding us.

She offers me a small smile before taking a sip from her steaming mug.

"You know that wasn't what I meant."

"Honestly, Caleigh," I begin as I scratch my head, "I really don't know. I didn't think I stood a snowball in hell's chance of you agreeing to meet."

"It came as a surprise to me that I agreed."

"Where's Hardin?"

"He's with Rhiannon. We're staying tonight rather than make the two-hour drive back home."

"Are you honestly hoping to move here?"

I know I'm making small talk instead of saying what's really on my mind, but I can't help it.

"Yeah. I'm looking to put down roots somewhere bigger, where I stand a chance of attracting more clients."

"Clients?"

"Yeah. When we met, I was coming back from a job interview, I told you that."

"Uh-huh, I remember."

"Well, it paid off. I got the job. And that means moving to Pedmore or Brookhaven, because I wouldn't get many clients in River's Edge. I was going to use the town hall in Pedmore, but decided I'd like to look for places to rent."

"What's the job?"

"Yoga instructor. I qualified a little while before we met. It took a while to actually qualify, but I persevered. It's something I enjoy and practice at home daily—or most days, if I can't manage every single day—and something that I can fit around Hardin's school hours and holidays."

"Wow. I'm really happy for you."

"Thanks. I work for a company, but it's like being self-employed. You set your own hours; they help pay towards the rent on a premises where you'd set up the business. It's a bit like working for a taxi company. You work for the actual main company, but you rent out a room or something, like how you might rent a taxi for use. Sorry, I'm rambling."

"No, no, you're not. I like hearing about your big plans."

I also like the ease with which she's talking to me. I expected her to be more guarded.

"I know it's a big change, but I always knew I couldn't stay in River's Edge forever. I couldn't work at The Lock for the rest of my life. I've always felt like I was made for something bigger."

"I'm so happy for you, Caleigh. Grabbing life by the balls and doing something you really want to do, something that will make you happy. That's the best thing you could do."

Something crosses her gaze, but I don't have time to figure out what it is.

"So, what about you? Why did you buy a house in Brookhaven? Don't you already have somewhere back home, wherever *home* is?"

I take a deep breath. I hadn't planned to tell her this. But then I hadn't planned on seeing her at the house, hadn't expected her to come to see me, so I scrub a hand over my chin and open my mouth, afraid of what's about to come out of it.

"I'm quitting."

"Quitting what? I need more than that to go on."

"Whiskey Lullaby. The boys don't even know it yet, but I'm quitting. I just don't love what I do anymore. I thought my stay in River's Edge would give me the answers I needed. Thought I'd get over my writer's block. Hoped I'd reconsider my hatred of being in the limelight. None of that happened. Well, I managed to finish the tour and I wrote one more song. But going back to the tour and recording the album afterwards, that confirmed my worst fears; I don't want to do it anymore. Don't get me wrong." I pause to take a deep breath and finish my now cold coffee. "I've loved my time in the band. I've loved travelling. I've loved the fan base we cultivated. But, whether it's because I'm getting older or what, I don't know, I just know that my heart isn't in it now."

"I can't believe it. I thought you were going back to the groupies and whatever else it entails."

"Honestly, so did I. Not the groupies, that hasn't been doing it for me for a long time. Then I visited a quiet little town where I met a pink-haired siren who stole my heart."

Her gasp is audible, and her skin turns a deep shade of pink.

"I fell in love for the first time in my life, and it made me re-evaluate everything I thought I ever wanted. To be honest, I was never really comfortable with the limelight, but I tolerated it for my love of music. However, my time away from the band only confirmed that I am more comfortable with anonymity."

"That's why you dyed your hair and stayed away from big towns where you'd be more likely to be noticed. You wanted a taste of being anonymous."

"Exactly." God, it feels so good to get everything off my chest. It's like a weight has been lifted.

"You were the driving force, Caleigh. Your loving me for the man I am, not the fame or fortune, that's what made me really make the changes I've needed to for a long time. After making up my mind to make the move across the country and start my life afresh, I felt so much happier. I won't lie, I wondered whether I'd ever see you again. But I didn't expect to bump into you—especially quite so *literally*—today. Seeing you made my heart start beating again."

I look up to meet her gaze. I see her eyes swimming with unshed tears.

"I don't know whether I could ever make you fall in love with me again. I'm not even asking you to try; I know I don't have that right. But you being here now,"—I pause as I reach out to take her hand, tracing small circles with my thumb—"it makes my heart thunder in my chest. While I was back home, it's like it forgot how to beat. I needed to see you again to be reminded."

"Brent," she whispers.

"Caleigh, you asked why I kissed you. Well, I didn't exactly tell the whole truth before. I needed to be reminded of the way you used to kiss my lips. To remember how you held me in your arms, how you felt pressed up against me. I needed one last reminder of the love that we once shared."

I stand and close the short distance between us. Crouching so that I'm eye level with her, I bring her hand up between us and place gentle kisses on it.

"I want to kiss you, but this time, I'm not going to take what I want without your permission."

Caleigh nods furiously and that's all I need before my lips are on hers once more. I push her back on the bed and brace myself over her as she licks at the seam of my lips, and as I open to her, she bites on my bottom lip just like I did to her earlier.

She moans quietly as I taste her, my tongue dancing with hers the way it has so many times before. My hand trails up from her thigh to the hem over her vest. Her sharp breathy moan as I touch her bare skin is like kindling to a flame.

Suddenly our hands are everywhere, and I realise—quite belatedly—that I'm only wearing my shorts from earlier. Her soft hands roam the bare expanse of my skin, and my breathing becomes laboured as one hand makes its way to the waistband of my shorts.

I need one last reminder of how it feels to make love to her. I need to remind her how much she felt when we were together. How she fell in love with me. The *real* me, even if not by name.

"Oh god, Caleigh," I moan as she pushes my shorts down over my hips, freeing my erection.

She looks down, and when she looks up at me through hooded eyes, her grin is nothing short of salacious.

I want her so much it physically hurts. I'm trying to show some restraint, to draw this out so that it isn't over before I can process what's happening. I want to remember every second, every feeling, every touch, every emotion she draws out of me.

"You feel so good," I whisper as I reach to pull her vest off over her head.

My eyes fall to the red lacy bra she's wearing. I've peeled it off her before. Boy does it make her cleavage look enticing. But then, she could be wearing a damn bin bag and she'd still look amazing.

Her pink hair falls over her shoulders and I reach to brush it back, wanting an unobstructed view of her lithe body.

"I want you so damn much, Brent."

God, my heart wants to soar as I hear my real name fall from her lips. I've waited so damn long to hear it, and now my heart wants to burst from my chest.

I undo the jeans that act like a second skin on her, and she lifts her ass from the bed so that I can wiggle them down over her hips. Pulling them down to her feet, I remove her heels before discarding the jeans and placing the heels back on her feet.

I look up at her; she's wearing the red lacy thong that matches the bra. She looks fucking incredible.

Kneeling at her feet, I nudge her legs further apart before trailing kisses up each thigh in turn. Caleigh whimpers as I kiss her navel and run a finger along the waist of her thing.

As I look up, I see her watching me. Her breasts move up and down with each ragged breath, and I swear I have never seen anything more beautiful in my life. She's perfect. The creamy expanse of her skin, the emerald green gaze that swims with emotion, her luscious pink tresses, the swell of her breasts—I could die a happy man just to have known her for this short time.

Her tattoos each tell a story, and she wears them well. They add to the mystique of her. I find myself wanting to hear the stories behind each and every one. And, who knows, maybe if she comes back to me after tonight, I'll get to find out.

I tug her thong down her legs, off one foot and then she kicks it off the other.

Before I can help myself, I reach out to toy with her clit. I watch as her body writhes on the bed. I love the way it's *my* touch that does that to her.

"Brent, I can't wait," she calls out as I slide a finger inside her.

Truth is, I can't wait either. But I need to exercise a little patience. Good things come to those who wait. Or so I'm told.

Caleigh's his buck as she rides my fingers. Her walls clench around them, and god does she feel good. No, strike that, she feels *exquisite*.

"H-harder Brent," she pants.

I am only too happy to oblige, so I up my pace and hook my fingers to hit the spot over and over until I feel her legs quivering. I know she's so close.

Her hands fist the sheet as I look up. God, she takes my breath away. And this is where she belongs—with me.

"B-Brent ... I-I ..."

At the last second, I withdraw my fingers and she cries out in frustration before I replace them with my tongue.

So much for the angry sex I thought I was about to get, but hell, I'll take it however I can get it when it comes to Caleigh.

Her hands come up to fist my hair as I use my thumb to tease her clit. It acts like a detonator as she comes long and hard, crying out my name at the top of her lungs.

My god, could she get any more perfect? Could my heart be any fuller right now? I really don't think so. I stand up and look down at her. She's so beautiful it steals all the oxygen out of the room. She's flushed pink, and her lithe body turns me on now more than ever. My cock is rock hard, and I have to fist it a couple of times to try and get some relief.

"Come here," she whispers, looking up at me through her long eyelashes.

Without hesitation, I move to the bed. Bracing myself over her, I lean down to kiss her. She moans as my tongue dances sensually with hers.

I don't waste a moment as I align myself with her. I break the kiss so that I can look deeply into her eyes. Watching her eyes light up as I sink slowly inside her is something I could get used to. There's a deep sense of satisfaction as I stretch her to accommodate me and sink fully inside.

I still for a moment, giving her the chance to change her mind. I get my answer when I feel the heels of her shoes digging into my ass. Her arms wrap around my neck and she tugs at my hair as I begin to move inside her.

I feel her fingernails drag down my back, no doubt leaving marks, but I don't care. She can mark me as hers, because that's exactly what I am.

Upping my pace, I feel Caleigh meeting my hips thrust for thrust. She feels so damn perfect and I want so much to come deep inside her, but I have to hold back somehow.

I stop suddenly, making Caleigh cry out in frustration.

Leaning in, I kiss her so deeply it's enough to make her toes curl, then I pull her legs up onto my shoulders. I feel deeper inside her from this angle, and I'd be lying if I said the feelings swirling inside me don't make me want to cry—happy tears, not ones of sadness.

I've missed this, missed us. I've needed this since that fateful day when Gordon helped speed up the process of blowing us apart. Not that I can blame anyone but myself for the fallout. He just made it happen quicker. But now here we are. What comes next is anyone's guess. That being said, all I can find it in me to care about right now is the here and now. The woman lying underneath me.

I feel that familiar tingle, telling me how close I am. But I must chase her release first.

"H-harder, Brent ... p-please."

Withdrawing almost all the way, I thrust back inside her, making her cry out my name.

"A-again," she pants.

I do the same thing another couple of times before stopping and leaning down to bite her nipple. Her back arches off the bed and she moans in ecstasy. Moving inside her again, I build a punishing rhythm, pushing us both closer and closer to our limits. Beyond them, even.

With a final thrust, we both cry out as we reach our climax. Never has anything felt so right. This woman will be the death of me, pure and simple. But I wouldn't have it any other way.

Lying curled up together under the blanket, we stay silent except for our ragged breathing.

"Caleigh," I say softly. "I love you so much. I don't want to be without you."

"Brent, I … th-this … this was a mistake." Her voice breaks as she utters those last four words. Four words that are like daggers to my heart.

"Wait, Caleigh, what?" I cry as she jumps up from the bed and begins to dress.

"This was a mistake. It can't—*won't* happen again. I'm sorry."

"B-but you wanted this as much as me. Didn't you?"

"I did. But that doesn't stop it from being a mistake."

"Y-you regret it?"

I look at her as she pulls her clothes on in a hurry. Her face is sad and my heart splinters. Why is she doing this?

"I … no, I don't regret it. Sex with you is … well, it's beyond amazing. But it can't happen again."

"Caleigh, I—"

"Don't." She cuts me off with a hard stare that penetrates my soul.

"Tell me you don't love me, and I'll let you go without a fight."

"I-I c-can't say that, Brent. You k-know I can't."

"Then don't go. Stay with me and we'll figure it out together."

"I have to go. Rhi is looking after Hardin. I need to get back to them. I'm sorry."

She pulls her shoes on and walks to the door. Turning to look back at me, she opens her mouth but quickly closes it again.

"Please," I beg.

"I'm sorry."

And with that, she leaves my room without looking back, taking my heart with her.

I lie back on the bed and shout out in frustration. What the fuck am I doing with my life? Caleigh is giving me permanent whiplash. She loves me, she hates me, she kisses me, she comes to meet me, and we make love, then she tells me it's a mistake and walks away. Goddamn it, it hurts so fucking much. I feel the pain carve a hollow in my heart, my soul.

Caleigh made me feel for the first time in my life. I actually cared about a woman instead of just discarding her like others that came before her. I let myself fall in love. With her, with the life I could have with her by my side. I did it all for love, something I didn't know anything about until I met Caleigh Rae Flynn. She's extraordinary. She has her flaws, like I have mine. But she's perfectly imperfect and she made me a better man just for knowing her. That's why I know I'll never get over her. There will never be another that signs their name across my soul, owning me the way she does.

Chapter Nineteen

Caleigh

I pull up outside Rhiannon's house and take a few deep breaths before walking to the front door. I let myself in and creep quietly down the hall to the guest bedroom.

Hardin is fast asleep as I lean down and kiss his forehead. He stirs a little but rolls over in his sleep and cuddles up to his favourite Mickey Mouse plush toy. I sit on the bed next to him and kick off my shoes. With a weary sigh, I begin to change into my pyjamas. My heart feels heavy, like it's weighed down with a million emotions. Probably because it is. I can't believe I slept with him. Of course, I wanted to, but that's not the point. The point is, I was weak. I let my love for Brent eclipse anything else I was feeling.

Walking into the en suite, I turn on the light and grab my toothbrush from the sink. I look in the mirror and see sadness reflected back at me. I don't want it to have been a mistake, I want to let myself love Brent. But something is stopping me.

I can't believe he's quitting the band and moving to Brookhaven. He's in for a culture shock, for sure, when he realises that this town is just like any other. Places he's visited, things he's seen, he won't find any of that here.

He's used to the fame, the fortune, living life on the open road. He's never been tied down, never put down roots anywhere. He's never stayed anywhere long enough for that to happen. So, now that he's about to put down roots, he'll probably end up aching for the life he led before.

I know that, in time, he'll find someone else to love. He says I am his first love, but I won't be his last. Now that he knows how love works, he'll find someone special and build a life with her. I just wish it didn't hurt so goddamn much when I think about him being happy with someone who isn't me.

I wish I could borrow somebody else's heart, one that isn't filled with as much sorrow as mine. Then maybe I'd stand a chance of being open to love again. But Brent showed me what it was like to love someone other than Angelo. He showed me how to live again, really *live*, not just exist. He is the keeper of my heart, and I will never be able to give it to another man. I might not be Brent's last love, but he'll be mine.

With a sigh, I rinse my mouth out with mouthwash before heading back into the bedroom. I sit down in the space next to Hardin on the double bed we're sharing for the night.

Lying down, I pull the covers over me and close my eyes, visions of Brent dancing behind my eyelids. Images of his taut, muscular body, his soft lips and his soulful eyes plague me. No matter how hard I try not to let it, my mind wanders back to how it felt to be pressed up against him, how it felt to have him buried deep inside me, how my body ached deliciously after the orgasms I experienced tonight. Who am I kidding? My body *still* aches with the memory of the orgasms that rocked me to the core.

Sleep takes its time, claiming me as my mind is stuck in an endless loop. Why did I agree to meet him tonight? Did I know what would happen? Did I hope for it? If I didn't, why did I dress provocatively? Was it to show him what he'd been missing? Was it to make it impossible for him to resist me? All I know is that I wanted what happened as much as he did. It's why I allowed him to kiss me when he asked permission. It's why I let him strip me and make love to me one last time.

Did I know it was going to be the last time before it happened? Was it some form of closure? Of goodbye? If it was, then how am I still feeling so confused? I'm more confused now than before. I love him, I want him—and not just in a sexual way. I need him. Yet I reject him and break his heart, shattering my own in the process. Man, I really am screwed up.

Why does love have to hurt so much? I'm broken, but I can't seem to walk away and sever ties completely. I need a clean break. That's what moving to Brookhaven was meant to do. But now I know he's moving here too, that I could see him in the street, in the supermarket, holding hands with another woman ... that thought cleaves my heart clean in two.

***

After a restless night, I wake and grab my dressing gown. Hardin isn't in bed, so he's probably playing with Luna somewhere.

I walk into the kitchen and see Rhiannon making the batter for pancakes. My stomach rumbles, and it's only now that I remember I didn't have anything to eat last night.

"Morning, beautiful," Rhi says, sounding positively effervescent.

Her positivity is too much for me this morning, so I reply with a flat tone.

"Hey."

Just one word, that's all I can manage.

"Did you sleep okay?"

"No."

"Honey, what's up?" she asks as a frown mars her beautiful face.

"Nothing."

"Nothing or the Brent kind of nothing?"

I mutter something unintelligible, and she huffs at me like an annoyed mum.

"Sorry, Rhi."

"Honey, Lewis has already left for work, and the kids are in the garden. It's just you and me. You can tell me anything, I won't judge, I swear."

"W-we ... we slept together."

"Oh, honey," she sighs as she puts the bowl down and rounds the breakfast bar to wrap me in a hug.

I rest my head on her shoulder and she strokes my hair, whispering that it will be alright. "Nothing will ever be alright again."

"Yes, it will. It might take time, but it will get better, I swear."

"I love him, Rhi. I can't help it. I want to be mad at him for lying. I want to hold that against him as some kind of barrier to keep up between us. But any time I see him, I feel my resolve melt away. My fragile strength evaporates, and all I can see is love."

"Then why fight it, honey? Who says you have to stay mad at him? Who says you can't just let go of the past and look to the future?"

"I am looking to the future. A future without him. And it scares me."

"Oh, Caleigh." She sighs and sits on the stool next to me before taking my hand in hers. "You deserve to be happy. And who's to tell you that he isn't the one to make you happy?"

"I don't need a man to make me happy, Rhi. I'm perfectly capable of finding happiness of my own making."

"I know, honey. That's not what I meant. I just meant that if he makes you happy, if your heart races just from hearing his name, if looking at him makes you weak at the knees … if what you two have is special, then why not just stop preventing yourself from allowing it? I'm sorry to say this, Caleigh, but you're kind of standing in your own way here. You need to stop and just go with your heart."

"That's not going to happen," I say as I shrug out of her grasp and walk to the back door.

I look out and see the children running around, laughing and squealing. Their happiness makes me smile. My heart is full of love for my little boy, my family, my friends. I don't have room in my heart for Brent. Not after everything that's gone on, anyway.

Once upon a time, I thought we could carve out a life together. Instead, he carved a hollow in my heart. A deep black chasm that I don't think anything will ever heal.

"Honey, don't let anger cloud your judgment," she says as she places a hand on my shoulder.

"I'm not. Am I?"

Am I? God, I'm so confused. All I really know for sure is that I'm looking to move and start my business. I'm looking out for me and Hardin. Anyone else isn't a priority.

"Caleigh, I know it's none of my business really, but you want to move here, right? And you want to work in the area. What would you think about finding a house to rent privately instead of buying?"

"What? Why would I do that?"

"Well, partly because Brent bought your dream home out from under you—which I admit, was totally a dick move—and partly because you want somewhere to live sooner rather than later. You'd be able to find a house for *rent* quicker. Then you could look for somewhere to buy, once you're already here."

"That's not such a bad idea. And yes, it was totally a dick move. The jerk did it because he knew I wanted it."

"Did he really? You can't really know someone else's motivations."

"Well," I say with a sigh as I turn to face her, "actually, he said it was because he fell in love with the house. Turns out he'd been looking to move here for longer than I could possibly have known."

"Oh." Her face suddenly brightens. "Then that's one less reason for hating him."

"Would you stop with the pros and cons list already? I know you're keeping a tally in that beautiful mind of yours," I say as I give her a playful shove.

"Maybe I am. Is that really such a bad thing? I mean, it kind of seems like you can't keep track, so I thought I'd do it for you. Want me to list some of the pros?"

"I most certainly do not. I want to spend the day with my best friend, my goddaughter, and my son before returning home. I want no more mention of Brent *fucking* Ryder."

"Then I shall not mention him again. Today, anyway."

***

After a lovely day with my bestie and the kids, Hardin and I made the long-ass drive home. I'm so shattered. A long soak in a hot bubble bath with a glass of rosé sounds perfect about now.

Tucking my little man in bed, I get ready to tell him a bedtime story.

"So, what's your choice tonight then, baby?"

"I want to hear a story about Brent. He said he was playing a game, like hide and seek. Will you tell me about it, Mummy?"

So much for not having to talk about him again today. But I should have told him about Brent when he left, and Hardin was asking a bunch of questions I couldn't answer.

"Well, I'll tell you if you promise to go to sleep straight after."

"I promise, Mummy."

"Good boy. Now, lie down and I'll begin."

He snuggles down underneath his duvet and I begin to tell him about Brent being a famous singer and wanting to hide out for a while. He asks a couple of questions, so I answer him as honestly as possible, without telling him the details too big for little ears.

"Do you love him, Mummy?" he asks sleepily.

His question should shock me, but he's always been sharper than a tack, and kids have a way of asking things so bluntly.

"I—" I pause to swallow around a lump in my throat. "I do, baby."

"And does he love you?"

"You'd have to ask him that, sweetheart."

"But I can't, because he's not here."

He might never be here again either.

"All I know is that he says he loves me, and I think he means it."

"Are you going to marry him?"

"What? No. Baby, I think that's enough questions for tonight."

"But why, Mummy?"

"Sometimes people love each other, but they can't be together."

"Why?"

"Hardin Flynn, stop asking so many questions and go to sleep," I reply playfully.

"I just think if you love him, you should tell him."

"Goodnight, baby. I love you. Sweet dreams," I say as I kiss his forehead and turn off the bedside lamp.

"Night, Mummy. Love you to the moon and stars."

"I love you to the moon, the stars and the milky way."

I close the door quietly and choke back a sob as I go to run myself a bath. As the water fills up, I brush my teeth before stripping out of my clothes and putting them in the hamper. Stepping into the bubbles, I slowly submerge myself. It instantly begins to soothe my aching muscles. If only it could ease my aching heart too.

Why the hell does everything have to be so difficult?

Tilting my head back, I close my eyes. I concentrate on breathing deeply and totally relaxing. I am in need of some 'me time'.

The glass of rosé I brought in before tucking Hardin in is calling my name. I answer its siren call and sigh in appreciation as the subtle hint of strawberries and cherries hits my taste buds.

Thinking back on what Rhiannon said earlier, I realise she's right about one thing. Finding somewhere to privately rent would be faster. And better for my bank balance until I get clients.

I rang the estate agent about the studio for rent for the yoga studio and told them I'd take the place, in the hopes of actually securing the house I looked at. Yet another reason why I'm so mad at Brent. I guess I shouldn't have been so hopeful about the house, but I was, and now I have to find somewhere else to live fast, before my money is wasted on the deposit for the studio.

As I stand and grab my towel, I pull the plug out of the bath and step out. I don't feel tired enough to sleep, so I pull on my pyjamas and pad downstairs to find my MacBook. I pull up a list of properties to rent in Brookhaven and make a list of phone numbers to ring tomorrow.

I admit defeat, accepting that nothing more can be done about it at this time of night, so I head up to bed. With my mind running through a million different things, I'm not sure how easily sleep will come tonight.

Sliding under the covers, I get myself comfortable and close my eyes. Images of a solid wall of muscle come to haunt me. Memories of how it felt to touch him again, how electric it felt when his hands brushed over my skin, how alive he made me feel … it's like I was walking around in a daze all the time he was gone.

Am I doing the right thing in trying to move on without him? There isn't an easy answer, whichever way I look at it.

Chapter Twenty

Brent

I guess now is as good a time as any. Or not. That's the age-old question—when is the right time to tell people bad news? Well, it's not bad news for me, but the boys will see it that way, and Gordon will burst a blood vessel or two. Although, I have a feeling he knows something like this is coming, because he's been nothing but nice to me since I came back from River's Edge all those weeks ago. He's been buttering me up for something, I just know it. I guess it's possible he just realised his mistake, but it's doubtful. Highly suspicious, actually.

The boys and I are gathered at the studio, having just recorded the last song for the album. As promised when I agreed to it, "The One That Got Away" is a bonus track for iTunes only, so it's not being released as a single. It's my last goodbye to the fans, and to the boys really.

I've been sitting here nervously wringing my hands, trying to work it into conversation, but it just isn't happening.

"What do you boys say we open a bottle of the good stuff to celebrate?" Gordon asks with a big cheesy grin.

"Hell yeah," the boys all chorus together.

"What say you, Brent, my boy?" Gordon asks as he sidles over to me. "Your enthusiasm is noticeably absent."

"Sorry, Gordo," I reply with a shrug.

He looks at me in disdain. He hates being called anything except for his full name. Gordo is my way of getting under his skin—in a harmless way, of course.

"I was actually hoping for a glass of the good stuff myself, so sure, let's go."

"That's my boy," he says as he ruffles my hair, making it messy.

I hate when he does that. I guess it's his payback.

We pile into the minivan and head for Gordon's house. Once we arrive, the boys all sit around the poker table in his man cave as they wait for him to pour the whiskey and deal the cards.

"Actually, guys, I, umm … I have something I'd like to talk to you about."

Their heads all whip round to me.

"I–it's, umm …" I scrub a hand over my face and wring my hands nervously in my lap. "Sorry, I'll start again. The truth is, there's something I have to do. I've been thinking about it for a while, and before you ask, yes, I've thought this through."

"Spit it out then, boy," Gordon says as he looks at me expectantly.

"Well, I, umm … I'm done. It's been one hell of a journey, but for me it's come to an end."

"Stop speaking in riddles, dude. The end of what?" Ash says as he swigs his whiskey.

"This. Us," I say as I wave my hands around, as though that will help them see what I mean, even though I know it won't. "My days as lead singer."

They take a collective breath, and their eyes go as round as saucers.

"You're stepping down for Ash to step up permanently?" Jude asks.

"If that's what he wants. But that's not why I'm doing it. Look, I haven't explained this the best way, because it's not an easy task. I'm leaving. Permanently."

"What?" they all ask in unison.

I say ask, it's more like they scream at me.

"Your contract isn't up, son," Gordon says with a smile, one that says "I've got you over a barrel."

"Do you remember the clause we put in those contracts, Gordon? You know, the one that says we can buy our way out? Well, here," I say as I hand him a cheque. "This is me buying my freedom. I always knew it would come with a price, but it's a price I pay willingly."

"Why are you doing this, Brent?" Jude asks as he comes to stand next to me, pouring himself another whiskey, and me a double.

"Is it because of her?" Ash asks.

"Who? The girl back in the Podunk backwater town?" Gordon chimes in.

"Don't," I warn. "This isn't about her. Well, not entirely. She was the catalyst, yeah, but I realised that it was something I'd been considering for a lot longer than I cared to remember."

"You've been in a funk—for want of a better way of putting it—for a while now. I've seen you when you think nobody's looking. And then Caleigh came into your life and made you realise that you really did want to go back to being a regular guy."

"Something like that, Ev."

I can't help the long sigh that leaves me. I can feel my heart breaking at the thought of not being in the band, not being with my best friends every day. But that's only a piece of my heart. The majority of it lies with Caleigh, and what little piece I have left to myself is ready to move on from this.

I want peace and quiet, solitude, anonymity. I want the house in Brookhaven. I guess I want the normal life I got a taste of in Caleigh's hometown, in her arms. The normal life I never got to have of my own, what with being in the limelight for so long.

"I-I umm ... I bought a house."

My confession silences the room.

"In River's Edge?" Ev is the first one to speak.

"No, a town a couple of hours away from there, actually."

"Really? But what about Caleigh?" he asks, concern etched on his face.

"Well, I didn't want to move to such a small town and have her in a constant state of worry that she'd bump into me. But fate laughed at me that day," I say with a wry chuckle and a slight shrug. "Fate threw her in my path again. It turns out she's looking for a house in the same town."

"Of all the places in all the world, Caleigh and you end up thrown in each other's paths again. It might be funny if it wasn't so tragic."

"Tragic how, Ev? He gets to woo her all over again," Ash jumps in.

"He's trying to get over her, and this ain't gonna help," Jude says before I can.

"Jude's right. I'm trying to move on, but then she gets thrown back into my life and it's crazy. We ended up wanting to buy the same house. I paid over market value because I'm a selfish asshole who didn't want her to have the house. Then we meet up and end up sleeping together, then she tells me it was a mistake and breaks my heart all over again. So, I'm fucked either way."

The words just tumble out. I'm unable to stop them, much as I'd like to.

"Oh man, I'm sorry," Evan says as he comes to stand beside me.

He rests a heavy hand on my shoulder and offers me a small smile.

"Then wouldn't you be better off here, surrounded by friends?" Gordon asks.

His words would have you believing he cares, but the tone he uses implies otherwise.

"I've made up my mind guys. I'm sorry, but it's settled. I signed the paperwork for the house; the money cleared. It's mine. All I have to do is pack my stuff and move in. What's done is done."

"I can't believe you're leaving us in the lurch—again. Only this time it's *permanent.*"

"I'm sorry you feel that way, Gordon," Evan says. "But it's what he wants to do, and I support him in that. Brent is a human being, with feelings, emotions. He needs to be treated as such." There's a slight hint of bitterness in his tone.

"So what? We just let him go play happy families or whatever the fuck, and meanwhile we're a band member down?"

"Shut the fuck up, Gordon, okay? Ash stepped up before and maybe he can do it on a more permanent basis. But the point here is that Brent is a free man. He's entitled to do whatever pleases him, as are we all. You've got your quarter of a million buyout. So, shut the fuck up," Evan seethes.

It isn't like him to get so worked up. I've only seen him like this less than a handful of times.

"Don't talk to me like that, Winslow, or you'll be next."

"Oh, what, really? You want me to quit the band too? If that's what you want, Gordon, then just fucking watch me. I don't know what the hell happened to you, man. You used to be like another father to us. Now you treat us like the money-makers we are. And that's *all* we are to you. Money, money, money."

"Watch your tone, son."

I watch as the rage bubbles inside both of them. They're standing and staring at each other, and I'm not sure who will be the first to cave.

"Don't push me, Gordon."

The anger rolls off Evan in waves, in a way I've never seen. He's never gone toe to toe with Gordon before.

I mean, sure, we've all had our disagreements, reasons to be disgruntled with each other, but never like this.

"Settle down, guys, please," I implore as I come to stand between them, placing a hand on both their chests. "This won't get us anywhere. I'm leaving, but that doesn't mean the band has to fold. Ash, you're a good frontman. Jude, Evan, you guys are awesome at what you do, and the three of you love being in the spotlight. I've fallen out of love with it, but that's not the end for the three of you."

"And how do you expect us to spin this to the press?" Gordon asks through gritted teeth.

"Really, Gordon, that's what bothers you?" Ash asks as he pulls a chair from the table and sits on it backwards. "Do you really want Brent to stay when it no longer makes him happy? Do you want to work him to the bone until there's nothing of him left?"

There's a beat or two of deathly silence.

"No. I just … Look," he sighs. "I just … I wish this wasn't happening. I don't want Brent to leave, but you're right, he deserves to be happy. I just don't want it to be the end of the band."

"Then stop pushing us," Jude says as he stands and paces the room. "The rest of us are staying, aren't we? Evan? Asher? Any plans to leave?"

"Nope," Ash says with a grin.

"Not unless Gordon keeps pushing my buttons," Evan replies coolly.

"I'm sorry, son," Gordon says as he places a hand on his shoulder. "I didn't mean to … I just … I'm sorry, okay?"

"Fine," Ev huffs as he pours himself another large drink. "Top up, boys? We should be toasting Brent's last day and wishing him well on his journey, wherever that may take him," he says as he holds the crystal decanter in the air.

We all hold our glasses aloft, even Gordon. Evan walks around and tops us all up.

"To Brent, wherever his journey may lead."

They all repeat the sentiment, bringing a tear to my eye.

"I'm sorry, Brent," Gordon says as he comes to sit next to me. "I just saw all our hard work coming apart at the seams. I shouldn't have lost my temper. We okay?"

I nod and take the cigar he hands me. He gives one to the rest of the boys, and we sit smoking cigars and drinking whiskey for the rest of the day.

***

Sure, quarter of a million was a steep buyout price when we first had the clause put in the contracts, but handing that cheque to Gordon,

I couldn't have been surer that it was what I wanted. It's not like it put too big a dent in my bank balance, and it's worth every penny if I can forge my own path, have a life free of the fame.

After talking it out all night, we took the private jet this morning and flew out so the boys can see the house. I gave them a tour and even Gordon was impressed. It's a beautiful place, and they can see why I want to live here quietly.

"This little terrace right here, this was worth every penny you paid for the place," Ash says as he sits sipping his beer in the bright afternoon sunlight.

"Beautiful, isn't it? It's a sun trap. I can see myself sitting out here often."

I run a hand through my hair as I tilt my chin upwards towards the sun.

"You look so much better as a dirty blond than that nasty brown hair dye, bro," Jude says from beside me.

"Thanks, I think."

"Sorry, I mean, I guess it suited you. But it wasn't *you*, you know?"

"I know what you mean dude, hence why I went back to my normal colour."

"Do you have any plans now that you're *retired?*" Evan asks, air-quoting the word.

"I don't know. Renovating this place a little. After that, who knows?"

Scrubbing a hand over my face, I realise that I really don't have any plans for after the band. I never thought that far ahead. It's not like I need the money, but I don't like sitting around idly either.

"You could always build your own soundproof studio at the end of the garden. It's definitely big enough."

"I'm trying to leave all that behind."

"I mean for pleasure, not business. You know music is in your blood and you'll never fully cut it out."

"I know, Ev, but I don't need a soundproof studio to tinker with Bess and Jeri-Lynn."

"True, true. Pass another bottle, dude?"

I hand him a beer and flip the cap off another for myself.

"You could always develop a green thumb and tend to the roses in this gorgeous garden," Ash says.

"Screw that. I'm hiring a gardener. You know that any living thing

I touch dies."

"Well, that's true. I've seen you kill off more houseplants than I've had hot dinners."

Everyone laughs, and I can't help but love the way it feels to have the boys around. I'll miss them, for sure. The camaraderie we have, the family we've built together—I'll have none of that when I'm here alone.

But everyone has to grow up and fly the nest at some point. Now is my time. It's not like I'll never see them again, I just won't live within walking distance anymore. That really will be weird.

The sun begins to set, and we head inside as a chill begins to settle in the air.

"Everyone for a pizza? Where's good around here?" Jude asks as we settle in the living room.

"Umm, good question. Haven't really been around long enough to find out, you know?"

"Then pull up the takeaway app, dude, I'm Hank Marvin over here."

The boys get rowdy, so I do as I'm told and take their order.

***

Packing my bags feels somewhat bittersweet. My mum and dad were surprised as hell when I told them I'd quit the band, but even more so when I said I was moving away. Of course, my mum was her usual fussy self. She didn't want me to be alone, she wondered how I'd feel living so far from home, who'd cook and clean … I told her I'd do it all myself. It's a good job Caleigh taught me to cook a couple of basic staples, as they'll likely become a large part of my "cooking for myself for the first time" diet.

As for the cleaning, there'll only be me to tidy up after, so it's not like it'll be hard. And I've done it since I left home…well, when I've been home long enough to need to. The truth is, you don't have to do much for yourself when you're crammed into a tour bus with everyone else. But it's not that big of a deal, even though she made out like it is.

I have boxes labelled for the kitchen, living room, bedroom etc. My clothes are packed into holdalls, and everything is done. The last box has been taped shut, and the boys are on their way to help with the move.

It's not like I actually own that much stuff. I've never really needed to. But there's enough that I can't do it all by myself.

Standing in the living room, I look out at the front garden. The *For Sale* sign signifies the end of a chapter in my life, but also the beginning of another.

I watch the boys pull up outside, then I open the door and stand aside as they walk in. They all seem to be smiling this morning, which I take as a good sign, a sign that they've come to accept my choice—or at least very nearly, if not fully quite yet.

"Hey, bro, wanna give us a hand loading stuff into the van?"

"Sorry, Ash, my head was elsewhere."

I grab a box and follow suit as they all take stuff out to the waiting van.

"Have you got the essential stuff packed to take with you?" Evan asks.

"Yeah, I think I have everything."

"Well if you don't, you know it's stuck on the van until we get there, right?"

"I know, I know. I *think* I have everything, but if I don't, it's too late now."

"You have a few bits back at the new house anyway, don't you? You know, tea, coffee, sugar, bread, butter … oh, and milk?"

"Yeah, I did that the morning we flew back here, before we left Brookhaven."

"Good, good. You'll probably have to do a full food shop, unless you want takeaways every night."

"I will once I'm a bit more settled in. I'm not daft, Ev."

"I know, you just … well, you've always been like a brother to me, to *us*, and it's hard to believe you'll be miles away from us."

"It's not like we'll never talk again, Ev. You make it sound like I'm leaving your lives, not just the neighbourhood."

"It's not just the neighbourhood though, is it, bro? It's hundreds of miles away, not five minutes' walk from my house."

I put down the bag I'm holding and wrap an arm around his shoulders.

"You, Julia and Jessa can come visit me any time you like. It's an open invitation. And I'll be back to visit when the new baby comes. Plus, you know Mum and Dad would never let me disappear."

"I know, man, I'll just miss you."

He wraps me in a hug and doesn't let go until I make a choking sound, and he breaks away laughing.

We pack up the last of my things and everyone waits outside while I take a last look around the house.

I open the back door and take in deep breaths of fresh air. Closing my eyes, I feel the sun's warmth on my face and bask in it for a few moments.

Locking the door, I leave the key on the side. The place will be locked up tight and the estate agent has viewings lined up already, so I'm sure it won't be long until it gets sold. With one last look around the living room on my way out, I sigh deeply before making my way out of the front door and locking up.

I hand the key to Jude, and he promises to get it to the estate agent as soon as he's seen me off.

I can't believe I'm really doing this. It's really happening. I'm actually leaving this place and starting afresh. A myriad of emotions washes through me as I walk to the van. Evan is dropping me at the airport before driving with the rest of my belongings.

***

Two weeks later

This last couple of weeks have been a rollercoaster. I'm fully settled in my new home, all my belongings safe and sound with me, thanks to Evan.

I've spoken to my mum every day. She and Dad will be visiting in a couple of weeks when Dad can get time off work. He's still not keen on the fact that I've moved away or that I won't be going into the family business now that I've—and I quote—quit playing around with my guitar and become a grown-up.

He accepted me being in the band, accepted I made good money from it, but when it came to the crunch, he still always believed it was just a hobby and that I'd grow up eventually and follow in his footsteps.

I didn't know that until Mum told me during one of our nightly conversations. I mean, I knew he hadn't liked me not having the same passion for his career as he does, but I thought he'd begrudgingly accepted my choice. Obviously, I was wrong.

I should feel happier than this. I do feel happy, I just feel empty at the same time. I've never needed anyone else to make me feel whole, I've always been happiest alone. But then I met Caleigh, and everything changed in the blink of an eye. Of course, I'm not reliant on her to be able to find happiness, but now that I've tasted what life can be like when you're in love ... well, now I know that there's a part of me missing, the best part. Caleigh Rae Flynn. She's the final piece of the jigsaw that would make me feel complete.

I never knew real love until I met her. Never knew that love was something I even wanted. But now that it's missing, it feels like there's this huge hole in my life, in my heart: a deep, dark, gaping black void.

I should also be happy that the last album I recorded with the boys is about to be released. The iTunes version of the album will contain a previously unreleased song, a song that will be unavailable anywhere else: "The One That Got Away". I don't know how to feel about that. I should be happy it's on the album, but there's this niggling thought that it was something personal. I wrote about someone I loved and lost, and I'm still not one hundred per cent sure I want the world at large to hear it.

Why do thoughts of Caleigh consume me so? I should know by now that she doesn't want me. The last time we were together, she made it abundantly clear it was a mistake, one not to be repeated. I don't agree in the slightest, but it takes two people to make a relationship work and only one to break it.

I'm not stupid. I know I was the one that broke it, but it's Caleigh that's keeping me at arm's length now. She won't allow me the opportunity to repent for my mistake, to make it up to her for as long as it takes. But even knowing she doesn't want me doesn't shake my love for her. I fear nothing will, and that any relationship I subsequently end up in will pale in comparison.

Lying on the oversized, luxurious couch I felt the need to splurge on—after all, who wants to be uncomfortable sitting there day after day—I cradle Bess to me and strum a few chords. The boys were right. Music is in my veins, and it will never fully leave me.

Before I realise it, I'm playing Caleigh's song. My heart pangs with longing as a tear falls down my cheek.

Chapter Twenty-One

Caleigh

To say this last couple of weeks have been hectic would be an understatement. I was lucky in my search for a house to rent, so it's been madness trying to get everything moved in before Hardin starts at his new school.

Rhiannon and Lewis helped us out with the move, as did Mum and Dad. It was a wrench saying goodbye to my parents, knowing they won't be just a couple of doors away anymore, but we have weekends and school holidays for visits.

It's Hardin's first day at school, and all I can say is I'm glad he has Luna with him. It's only natural as a parent to worry, but I'm sitting here biting my nails, waiting on edge until it's time to go and fetch him.

I'm sure he's okay, but I can't help but wonder if I did the wrong thing, tearing him away from all his old friends, his teachers, his grandparents. Will he get used to the way of life out here? Will he make new friends at school or feel like an outsider?

The radio plays in the background and I hear the DJ announce the release date of Whiskey Lullaby's new album. It's due out next week.

I can't help the pain I feel in my chest, knowing he's out there, possibly quitting the band after this album is released.

Knowing he'll be in town soon after that hurts more though. So close, yet so far. How will I react if I bump into him in the street? My new house isn't exactly that far away from his; he lives between me and Rhiannon, close to Hardin's school. So, it isn't implausible that I might bump into him somewhere along the way. Whether it's in the street, at the supermarket or the farmer's market—though from what I remember he can barely cook, so he might not be there—or if I'm out with Rhiannon one evening. Will I even be able to look him in the eye?

My watch beeps, alerting me that it's time to fetch Hardin. I grab a light cardigan and my handbag before locking up and making the short walk to the school.

As I pass what's now Brent's house, I realise I'll need to find another route to and from school so that I don't have to pass by this place four times a day.

"Caleigh," a familiar voice calls from up ahead.

My head snaps up and I meet the gaze of the very person I wished to avoid, the one I thought I'd have more time before seeing. I didn't even think he was here yet. What's he doing here so soon?

"Caleigh, please?" he calls as I cross to the other side of the street.

I almost break my neck as I go over on my ankle as I try to walk faster, but I embrace the pain and keep moving. He calls out once more, but I increase my speed and turn the corner at the end of the road. As I slow down, the pain in my ankle begins to really throb, but nevertheless, I can't be late to fetch Hardin, so I forge onwards.

As I arrive at the school gates, the bell rings and a sea of children spill from their classrooms. I see Hardin standing by Mrs. Buckle's classroom, waiting for the teacher to spot me before letting him go. Once she sees me, she waves and lets Hardin go. He runs over to me, chattering so excitedly I can barely keep up.

We hold hands and Hardin skips happily along beside me. It isn't until I get to the corner of the road that I realise I intended to find a new way home, and now that Brent appears to already be here, I need to find it sooner rather than later. But I don't have time to explore, so I take a few deep breaths and stand tall. I can walk past his house without breaking into a sweat, or worse, bursting into tears. Though the pain in my ankle makes me want to shed a few tears.

I try to walk quickly past his house, but the best I manage is hobbling. Hardin asks why I'm walking so funny, so I tell him I hurt my foot on the way to the school, but I don't tell him why.

"Hey, Mummy, look. It's Brent."

Oh shit. As if my afternoon isn't bad enough as it is.

"Hi, Brent."

"Hello, Hardin," he replies as he comes to a stop in front of us.

He's so close I can smell his aftershave. Damn, he smells so good.

"Hello, Caleigh, it's nice to see you both."

"I've just been to school. It was my first day. I had Mrs. Buckle. She's very nice."

"Come now, Hardin, we don't want to take up too much of Brent's time," I say as I go to walk away.

"Oh no, not at all. I'm free as a bird. So, Hardin, your first day, hey? What did you do?"

"Well, Mrs. Buckle made me stand up and tell everyone my name. They were all very nice, and we played games at break time."

"That's good. You're making friends already."

"Yeah, there's one boy who wasn't very nice, but Mummy always said if anyone is mean, kill them with kindness."

"Oh, did she? And how do you do that?"

"Even when they're mean to you, you be nice to them. Eventually, they'll stop being so mean."

"Well that does work, you know. I once had a boy bully me, and I was nothing but nice back. He got bored of picking on me and you know what? Now he's one of my best friends."

"Really?" Hardin asks excitedly.

"Oh yes. Evan is one of my closest friends and plays in the band that I was in."

"You mean Evan Winslow? Mummy told me about the band. Well, a bit anyway. The story she told me was mainly—"

I glare down at Hardin and he closes his mouth.

"Was mainly what?" Brent asks, a quizzical look on his face.

"We really should be going. Lots to do. Come on, Hardin."

"Okay, Mummy. Bye, Brent."

"Bye, Hardin, I'm sure I'll see you again. See that house just there?" He points ahead of him, making Hardin look round. "That's my house."

"You live here now? I thought you moved around lots with the band?"

"I did, but I'm no longer part of the band anymore. I left a couple of weeks ago."

"Really? Why?"

"Hardin Flynn, you ask too many questions."

"It's fine, Caleigh. I, umm … I wanted to settle down somewhere. I wanted a place to call home."

"Won't you miss your friends?"

"I will, but I'll still see them. They'll visit me here and I'll visit them sometimes."

"So, the whole band will come to your house?" Hardin asks, barely able to contain his excitement.

"Oh yes."

Hardin bounces on the balls of his feet and claps his hands. "Can I meet them?"

Brent must see the hard look in my eyes, because his next words are chosen carefully.

"Maybe. We'll have to see what your mummy says when they come round next."

"I'm sorry, Brent, but we really must be going."

I tug on Hardin's hand, and his face falls as he waves goodbye.

***

"I'm telling you, Rhi, it was planned. He was in the street when we came home. I can't see a reason to bump into him accidentally twice. Once is just coincidental timing; twice is a careful plan. And he kept talking to Hardin, knowing how excitable he is."

"Honey, you're going to see him around. You'll have to get used to it. Perhaps you can learn to be polite while escaping too much conversation."

"Hell, no, I'm looking up a new route to school."

"Caleigh Rae Flynn, since when were you such a coward?"

"Since he broke my goddamn heart."

"Honey, we all have exes. We're all destined to bump into one every now and then."

"Every now and then? Rhi, he lives a stone's throw from me. I should have looked for another house, but I didn't have long enough, I had to get the studio up and running instead of paying dead rent on it."

"And you've done that. But you can't look for somewhere else to live if you don't have gainful employment. When your studio is bursting at the seams, then you can look to buy a place further away from Brent, but within walking distance of the school."

"You have too much confidence in me."

"No, I have just enough. Maybe even not enough. But you're distracting me from the point at hand."

"Am not," I reply defiantly, with a hand on my cocked hip, as if she can see me.

"Caleigh, honey, it's really quite simple, all you have to do is grow up."

"Rude."

"Rude, but true, nonetheless. You're acting like a teenager whose boyfriend dumped her, but you live in the neighbourhood, so you have no choice but to see him."

"Maybe I am being petulant, but my point is still valid. He staked it out, waited until we returned. I can't pass his house four times a day."

"How could he have known you'd be back so soon? Do you think he followed you to the school and hid in the bushes? Then he sprang out at you on your way home because he's a stalker?"

"That's not what I'm saying."

"Then how did he know to wait outside until you returned? Do you think he put a tracker on your phone last time he saw you?"

"Now you're just being stupid. That's not what I think at all. But it's a bit too big of a coincidence. How do you not think the same?"

"Because coincidences don't arouse my suspicion. He could have been walking back from the shop for all you know."

I sigh loudly enough for her to hear. "This conversation is getting me nowhere."

"You thought I'd be on your side and add to your theory, say he was obviously stalking you. But you were wrong, and now you're acting like a stroppy pre-pubescent brat."

"Gee, thanks for the support, Rhi."

"Oh, honey, I support you. You know I do. I just believe it was all a coincidence and you should just brush it off."

"I think I'm going to go and have a long soak and a glass of rosé."

"Okay, honey, but listen. I love you. You're my best friend. I don't want to see you hurting, but I just think you need to pull up your big girl panties and get on with life. Show him his proximity doesn't affect you. So far, all you're doing is the opposite."

"I just can't help it, Rhi."

"Because you still love him, honey."

"I know."

I bite back unshed tears, unwilling to shed another tear over the man I loved. *Love. Present tense*, I think to myself.

"Go and have that soak in the bath, honey. Then go to bed and wake up tomorrow with a new mindset."

"I promise to try."

We say our goodbyes and I pour myself a glass of wine before I head upstairs to run a bath. I add in lavender bubble bath in the hopes of it having the soothing effect it always had on Hardin as a baby. Lavender always calmed him enough to fall asleep, even when he was teething.

Stripping off, I dip my toes in to test the water before submerging myself up to my chin. The scent is gorgeous. I inhale deeply and sigh as my muscles begin to relax.

I didn't mean to be so snippy with Rhiannon. I know she was just trying to talk some sense into me. But she struck a chord. She actually did make sense, annoying me because I knew I was in the wrong and was too stubborn to admit it.

Why did Brent have to turn up earlier than I expected? Why did the only house with decent rent have to be a stone's throw from him? Why did seeing him give me butterflies? Those butterflies might as well have been bats with how they were beating their wings.

I thought I had longer to prepare myself for his arrival. Oh, who the hell am I kidding? I was never going to be prepared, no matter what I did or didn't do.

Sipping my wine, I try to relax my mind as well as my muscles. I wish it would stop racing with thoughts of Brent.

Brent standing before me looking like a wall of solid, taut muscle, eclipsing the sun from my view. Brent's smile and how it lights even the darkest of nights. Brent standing naked and wet in my shower. Brent worshipping my body and making me tingle all over. When did my thoughts end up in the gutter?

Chapter Twenty-Two

Brent

It's been a week since I saw Caleigh, and what a painful week it's been. Having nothing to do with my time, I've sat by the bay window, hoping to catch a glimpse of her. I've gone to the shop so much that I have a fridge full of milk, just because I hoped I might see her in the street. But it's all been to no avail.

Today is release day for the new album, and yet I can't find it in me to be excited. Asher texted me earlier to say I should listen to the radio—which I did—because they were hyping up the album and talking about it possibly being our best yet. But then they mentioned the one thing I wish they hadn't: my departure from the band. That doused any excitement I might have felt.

With that news being broken, it was only an hour before articles popped up online from trashy magazines speculating over my reasons for leaving. Did I have a falling out with the others? Did I get fired by Gordon over leaving mid-tour?

I pull Google alerts up on my phone and delete them. I was stupid enough to have one for any time my name was mentioned, and my phone has been going haywire since the announcement on Country FM. They aren't the only radio station to be broadcasting about it either. It's now mainstream. Bloody typical. One station gets the jump on announcing it and the others jump on the bandwagon.

I don't even know how they found out. Ash promised that the boys hadn't said a word to anyone. And we might have had our differences recently, but I can't believe it would be Gordon. Can I?

Gordon called and promised to quash the speculation, but then he asked me if I'd give an interview to the press, saying it would likely be the best way to pour water on the flames. I declined, but when my phone started blowing up with notifications, I texted him and said I'd consider it, but I wanted to sleep on it. I asked if he knew who told them, and he promised to call me back when he found out.

An hour later and he told me it was one of the guys at the recording studio. *Not very professional of them*, I thought as I listened to him ranting.

He asked if I wanted to sue, but I told him not to be stupid. What's done is done now. They were bound to find out at some point, I just wish it has been when Gordon was meant to have told them. He was going to tell them that I just felt the draw of home and there was no falling out with anyone involved. But if he says that now, it just looks like he's trying to cover something up.

Maybe I should give an interview. That way, people might think I'm telling the truth. However, there's always the chance that they would believe me as much as they'd believe a statement from anyone *after* the fact. It looks like we're trying to cover our asses. Hell, I don't know!

Deciding I need some fresh air, I lock up and take a walk.

My phone rings and I frown as I see Gordon's name on the screen. What does he want now?

"Hey, Gordon, what's up?"

"Hey, Brent. So, this might sound a bit weird, but would you be open to coming back as a one-night-only thing to perform 'The One That Got Away'?"

"What? When? I didn't think the guys were touring again so soon."

"They're not; we were just spit-balling ideas for promo of the new album, and I threw out the idea of a one-night-only reunion of all band members."

"Gordon, I'm not being funny, but I only left a few weeks ago, and you know why I left, so I really don't want to do something that thrusts me back into the limelight I was so desperate to escape in the first place."

"Fair enough, son. I just thought you might want her to hear you sing it."

"She wouldn't come to one of our gigs. Not now, anyway. She hates me."

"And how would you know that, boy? Women are hard to figure out sometimes. You never know how she feels unless she tells you direct."

Or she avoids you in the street, knowing full well you live somewhere between her and her son's school, I think to myself.

"I just know, Gordon. Now, I'm sorry, but I'm actually on my way out somewhere."

"Okay, son, don't forget to give me an answer with regards to an interview."

"I will. I'm just getting in the car, so I have to go. Sorry," I rush to say, in a bid to get rid of him sooner.

"Speak soon, kid."

I get in the car with no fixed destination in mind. Driving around, I finally spot a small café and stop for a coffee. The barista recognises me, so I sign an autograph for her and pose for a selfie. She's so excited that she gives me my coffee and a muffin on the house. She refuses my money when I try to hand it over, saying she'd like to buy Brent Ryder a coffee. Probably something she'll tell her friends about later.

Sitting in a booth at the back of the café, I pull my hood up and turn my back to the window. Maybe today wasn't the best day to come out. What do I do if I'm asked why I left the band? Jeez, I hope not many people in Brookhaven even know who I am. Maybe it would have been better if I'd moved to an even smaller town.

As the evening settles in, I find myself parking the car randomly and getting out to walk about, just to see what's around. I hear music and it's like my feet take me to the source of it on autopilot. It's a relatively decent sized place from the looks of it. The sign in the window reads *Open Mic Night.*

I walk in, order a whiskey sour and sit at the bar. The bartender smiles at me and asks if I'm new around here. At least one person doesn't know who I am. I think. I just smile and say yes before turning to watch the singer on stage. She's belting out the lyrics to a hauntingly beautiful song by the amazing Evanescence, a song that brings tears to my eyes: "My Immortal".

This woman has some serious balls taking on a song sung by Amy Lee of all people, but she's goddamn talented, I'll give her that.

The room erupts into applause as the song comes to an end, and the pretty brunette smiles shyly, as if she doesn't know her own talent.

Talent scouts would eat her up. She'd be offered recording contracts left, right and centre. But of all people, I know that everything that glitters isn't gold. And if she really is as shy as she looks, then fame and fortune would eat her alive, chew her up and spit out only her bones. They don't give you fair warning before you sign your name on the dotted line. And if you're young, all you see is the money and the women, the partying, the booze, and drugs if that's your scene, which it isn't mine. You don't see it ever getting old. You think you'll always want the same things. But one day, you'll find fame and fortune isn't all it's cracked up to be.

Maybe that day will come when you first fall from grace, for example you get caught snorting blow and get arrested, and that makes front page news. Oh, not of the newspapers maybe, but the place where it counts most for "celebrities": trashy magazines and online outlets. Or maybe you cheat and get someone else pregnant—again, front pages of those magazines. Perhaps it's a "kiss and tell all" kind of situation: you sleep with someone and they sell their story to those magazines. It's not like any of those things will break you, but the sparkle of fame will begin to wear off. The more you do, the duller the shine becomes, until one day there's none left at all.

Nobody tells you that life in the limelight brings its share of problems, even if you are squeaky clean. I'm talking anxiety, depression, suicidal thoughts and more besides. I should know, after all the doctor Gordon brought in told me it was anxiety at first, then it was depression, for which he stuck me on some happy slappy pills that I didn't think I needed. Turns out I was wrong though, not about the depression, but the anxiety. Yeah, that sucked. Having panic attacks and having to hide them from my bandmates, my *brothers*, because I thought they'd be disappointed in me, maybe look for a replacement.

Of course, when I actually told them, they weren't disappointed in me at all. They helped me overcome it—yet another reason I stuck with them for as long as I did; I didn't want to leave them after all they'd done for me to get me to overcome my fears, some rational, some not so.

I listen as the next person up, a good-looking young lad that reminds me of a younger Evan, sings his heart out to a song I love: "Where Your Road Leads".

Hearing the lyrics, I'm struck with the kind of pain I only thought possible for other people, the kind that makes you feel like you've been eviscerated. It's not that it's a sad song; it's actually a beautiful song. It's more that the words remind me of all I would have done for Caleigh.

As if that didn't pour enough salt in the wound, the next singer gives his rendition of "The Only One Who Gets Me". Man, Charles Kelley has more talent in his little finger than I do my whole body. And he's a damn cool guy, too. I've met him, Dave and Hillary several times now, and they've always been so cool, so open, so friendly.

The love that man has for his wife is written there in song. So honest, raw, real. The guy on stage must have as much heart as Charles, must love someone the same way, because his version is enough to bring him to his knees.

I watch as he kneels down, and a woman from the audience brings her hands to her face, covering her mouth, as he holds out a hand. In that palm is a box, an open ring box. The stage lights glint off whatever stone is at the centre of it and the woman furiously nods her head.

That's the kind of love I want. Honest, real, full of raw emotion. I want passion, I want laughter, tears—the happy kind. I want it all. Even the arguments over silly things, the hot, angry, make-up sex. I want to experience every aspect of an all-consuming love.

An idea comes to mind, so I finish my drink and make my way outside to my car. I only had the one drink, so I'm not over the legal limit to drive. Thank goodness for that, too, because I have somewhere to be, some planning to do.

Shit, Caleigh might hate me, especially as she told me last time we slept together that it was a mistake. But maybe that was just her pride talking. Maybe there's some sliver of hope, even if it's only a tiny one. And that's a chance I'll have to take.

***

I've been back and forth between planning. I have nothing but time on my hands, so I am giving this plan my all. It's coming together slowly, I think.

I've been back to the open mic night, hearing more people give it their all, but no more proposals. Not yet, at least.

It got me to thinking, though. If Charles Kelley could lay his heart on the line and have a song recorded about the love of his life, then why can't I?

Gordon sent me the full version of the album, including my song, as Vox Records decided to have enough copies made for the band and a few to give away to fans. I have yet to listen to it, but knowing that Caleigh's song is out there for the world to hear doesn't scare me as much as it did at first.

Last time I was at open mic night, I met a girl. Her name was Rhiannon. She was shocked to see Brent Ryder in the flesh, and she stared daggers at me for a while before approaching me. We ended up exchanging numbers, and she's told me exactly where Caleigh lives. For part of my plan, I needed to know her address, so stumbling across a friend of hers was really very convenient. I would have probably been seen as a stalker if I'd found out my own way.

"Do you want to pick a card for the flowers, sir?" the lady arranging the flowers for me asks.

Caleigh loves flowers. She says they make the world a brighter place. But the one time I bought her flowers when we were together, she said that she doesn't like that they die.

I remember telling her they die in the wild, just as often as they do in vases. That memory is what sparked my idea.

I choose a card and she offers me a pen. I write my message before tucking it neatly into an envelope and paying for the flowers.

"And these are for delivery today, sir?"

"If you think you can manage it, yes."

"You're lucky; it's a quiet day. Wednesdays always are, for some reason. And the house is close by, so I can deliver and be back relatively quickly."

"Well, thank you, I appreciate it."

"Let me get this right. I'm to deliver the flowers, and if asked, I am to say they were paid for in cash and I have no idea who sent them?"

"She'll know it's me anyway, unless she has more than one admirer. But, yes, that's what I need you to say. I know it's a little white lie, but you wouldn't let that stand between a man and the woman he loves, would you?"

"No sir. Call me a hopeless romantic. I just love love."

"Thank you," I reply as I hand over the money and a tip for her helping me with phase one of the plan.

After I leave, I head into town and hit the gym. I've been getting myself more in shape recently. Not that I was in bad shape exactly, but because I want to be more toned. Plus, the gym helps me burn off the nagging doubts about the plan.

I've been past the building that Caleigh rents for her studio. I know it's hers, because I've seen her in passing as I head to the gym. After that, I found a new route to the gym so that I wouldn't run in there and profess my love for her, and because I know she's avoiding me, so I don't want to piss her off.

The name of her studio made me do a double take. I literally had no idea what it meant, so I googled it on the way to the gym that day.

If I'd walked past it when Caleigh wasn't around, I would have had no clue what they did there, but I get it now. Savasana is a yoga term. Now it makes sense. And I'm guessing that any potential clients would be familiar with the meaning of the word.

My phone chimes as I get to the front door of the gym, so I pull it out of my pocket.

>Any ideas what you're going to do to try and win Caleigh back?

I type out a reply to Ash.

>Who said I wanted her back?.

>Umm…everyone. You, Jude, Gordon … And Evan in particular is under the impression you are going to try.

>You're a bunch of nosy fuckers, aren't you? I have an idea. It's a 3-step plan.

>What's step one?

>Well, I'm having a bouquet of flowers delivered today.

>Flowers? Man, let me tell you. I know nothing about love, but you better be upping your game after flowers. After what you did … yeah, flowers aren't winning her back anytime soon.

>Alright you nosy little shit. I've been talking to a friend of hers, who helped me plan steps 2 and 3. But the card with the flowers is more important than the flowers themselves. Look, please don't be telling anyone I'm a sentimental little sap, but there is one artificial flower. It looks as real as the others, so it won't stick out like a sore thumb. The card reads: I will keep loving you until the last petal falls. It's a play on her love of Disney, and the fact that artificial petals don't fall.

>What's the Disney reference? I don't get it.

>Neither did I until she made me watch the live action *Beauty and The Beast* with her. That's where it's from.

>Oh, cool. Well, it sounds sappy to me, but if that's her favourite film or whatever, she'll be touched by the reference. Sounds like a better first step than I thought.

>Oh, I'm so glad I get your seal of approval :P Anyway, heading into the gym now. Catch you later.

>Later dude.

With that, I finish pulling my top on and head into the gym, ready to bust some serious ass in this workout.

***

I can't help but wonder if Caleigh threw the flowers out. I didn't sign my name, but I'm certain she knows they're from me. If she threw them out, she won't understand the reference on the card. She's meant to watch all the other flowers die and then realise that there's still one too-perfectly healthy one left.

Pacing the floor will only burn a hole in the carpet and drive me crazy, so I sit down and try to absorb myself in the book I've been reading.

What I've learned so far is that George R. R. Martin is the one author I've read that's capable and comfortable enough to kill off his main characters without batting an eyelid.

I saw the show and didn't like the ending much. It's like it was a bit too rushed, but that's a controversial opinion. I've had plenty of time on my hands to get caught up with all the popular shows people are raving about. But if you ask me, *The Witcher* was better than *Game of Thrones*. Not the earlier seasons, maybe, but certainly the latter. I have a love-hate relationship with *The Walking Dead*, to the point I quit watching around season seven.

I watched *Stranger Things* for the first time. I don't know why I waited so long. Maybe because I was too busy and maybe because there was so much hype about it that I thought it couldn't all be true. But much to my delight, it's as amazing as people say. I binged the whole three seasons over the weekend. Now I'm on tenterhooks for season four.

The truth is, it appealed to me because of its whole eighties vibe as well as the inexplicable things that were happening. The Duffer Brothers have hit the jackpot there, that's for sure.

As I finish the end of the book, I hear my doorbell ring. I use my phone to access the camera to see who it is. The last thing I need is someone trying to sell me something and I can't get them off the doorstep for half an hour.

I see Jessa stood at the door, and as I look further beyond her, I see Evan and Julia at the car.

Scrambling to get up and to my door as fast as my feet will carry me, I almost trip over the rug, but manage to right my balance and rush to the door.

"Jessa, baby, hi."

I pick her up and swing her around, which makes her giggle.

"Hi, Uncle Brent," she replies as she peppers my face with kisses.

"Hey, man," Evan calls from the kerb.

I put Jessa down and tell her to wait on the doorstep while I help her mummy and daddy with the bags.

"What are you guys doing here?" I ask as I pull Julia in for a hug.

"A little birdie told us you had a three-step plan to win back the girl of your dreams," Ev replies.

"And that involves you dragging your wife and daughter on a plane why?"

"Because if she knocks you back and you have nobody to lean on, Ev thought you might eat your body weight in ice cream and start watching chick flicks," Julia says with a grin.

"I could get used to eating Ben and Jerry's for breakfast, lunch, tea and supper, I guess."

That earns me a chuckle from both of them. Ev comes up and slings an arm round me as he hands me a bag.

"Here, take this."

Neither of us lets Julia do any heavy lifting.

"Don't worry; if all goes well and you two have some kissing and making up to do, we'll skedaddle faster than you can say boo. Nobody needs to have to bleach their eyeballs."

"Gee, thanks Ev," I reply with a wry chuckle and an elbow to his ribs.

"Hey, don't touch what you can't afford."

"Can't afford, man? You're cheaper than"—I catch myself and look around—"a happy meal at McDonalds."

We both know I was going to say two-bit whore, but not while little ears are present.

"A happy meal," Jessa squeals as she claps her hands together.

"Oh, gee, now look what you started. Thanks *bro.*"

"What do you say Uncle Brent makes his own version of nuggets and chips? It's way better than McDonalds," I say as I pick Jessa up and twirl her around.

"Nuh-uh. Nuffing better than 'Donalds," she answers in that sweet child-like way.

"Would you like to place a bet? If you don't like Uncle Brent's nuggets better, I'll take you to McDonalds tomorrow."

"Deal."

She squeals as I put her down, and Ev gives me a look that says "You cook?". That cocked eyebrow and cocky smirk say it all.

Jessa follows me into the kitchen, so I grab her one of my t-shirts off the washing line, so she doesn't get her clothes dirty.

"You going to help me mix things together, Jessa?"

"Can I?" she asks excitedly.

Julia walks into the kitchen and tries to smother her laugh as she sees me with an apron tied around me. She fails epically, of course.

"Let me tie your hair back, Jessa."

After tying her hair in a bobble, Julia sits at the breakfast bar and watches us, while Ev leans in the doorway, almost filling the damn thing.

I let Jessa squish the turkey mince in between her fingers while I add seasoning. I crack an egg into a small bowl so no shell lands in the meat, then pour it in and watch as Jessa squeezes the yolk and it pours all over her tiny fingers. She giggles in delight and I sigh contentedly. I could really get used to having a family to do this kind of thing with.

Since being here, I've bought an Echo and asked Alexa for recipes and cooking instructions. It's been so nice to eat fresh, homemade food, instead of takeaway. I even learned how to cook my mum's lasagne. She gave me the recipe over the phone, and I was pleased with the outcome, even if it didn't taste exactly like Mum's. She told me afterwards that the missing ingredient is love. She said if you cook with love, everything tastes that much better.

I can't wait for her to come and visit at the end of the week. Dad coming, well, I can take it or leave it. I love the old man, but he sure does like to needle me over not doing things the way he always thought I should. We rub along for Mum's sake, but really, I doubt he's even looking forward to the visit himself.

After grating the courgette and carrot, I add them to Jessa's big bowl, and she pulls a face at me.

"What's dis, Uncle Brent?"

"Special ingredients that make them taste better than McDonalds," I reply in a whisper, like it's our little secret.

Her eyes light up and she mixes everything in with her messy hands.

"Wonders will never cease," Ev says as he watches Jessa and me.

"And what's that meant to mean?"

"Just that I never thought I'd see you don a pinny and start cooking. Well, actually, it looks like my daughter is doing the grunt work, but I'll give you a pass on that."

"Never doubt the powers of Alexa and my mum."

"Another woman? I thought you wanted Caleigh back?"

Confusion etched on his face, he's a picture right now.

"Darling, do you really know nothing? Alexa is the Amazon Echo. She's a bit like Siri on your phone."

"Oh," he sighs as he smacks himself in the face with his palm.

I chuckle and shake my head at him whilst scooping out the mixture to form into nugget shapes. Jessa sees what I'm doing and tries to give it a go herself. She doesn't make them perfect, but then neither do I and I'm a thirty-odd-year-old man.

So, I try to make mine a little bit more like hers, in case she feels self-conscious. Would she, at her age? Is she too young? Well, never mind now, because mine are perfectly imperfect, just like hers.

***

After agreeing that my nuggets and homemade chips were better than McDonalds, Jessa had a bath and Julia put her to bed in the guest room.

It's just the three of us now, and it's nice to chill out with my best friend and his wife. There's a bottle of wine open and we're sitting on my oversized couch, a fire roaring in the beautiful inglenook fireplace. The house is probably a tad big for one person, but with the three of them here, it feels more homely.

Truth is, I didn't buy it with just me in mind. I wanted space for a family, but the only person I see that family with is Caleigh.

Thinking about her, I pull out my phone and check it, like I've done periodically all day. Still no texts. Maybe she's too angry. Maybe she just doesn't care. But I have to believe that when all is said and done, there is still hope. No matter how tiny that spark might be, it *has* to be there. Without hope, I have nothing.

"...yeah, and Ash said that this one here was pulling out all the stops."

I look at Evan and realise I missed half of what he said. I pocket my phone and pay more attention to the here and now.

"But what did you have in mind, Brent?" Julia asks.

"Well, step one was flowers."

"Dude, really? Flowers are your big move?" Evan cuts in.

"No, they're step one."

I tell them about steps two and three. They both grin like loons when I finish explaining.

"I hope to god you pull this off, bro."

"I would melt if someone did all that for me," Julia says with a sigh.

"Oh, someone, huh? Just *someone?*" Evan asks as he tickles her ribs until she laughs almost loud enough to wake their sleeping daughter.

"Okay, okay, you win. I meant you and *only* you," she replies breathlessly as she bats away his hands.

He leans in to kiss her, and a twinge of jealousy shoots straight to my heart. I want what they have so damn badly.

"Have you listened to the new album yet?" Julia asks and Evan tries to hush her.

"It's fine, Ev. Yeah, I've listened. It might even be the best album yet."

"Shame it's your last, but I understand," she replies sweetly.

"Can I tell you the truth, Julia?"

"Of course."

"I never played for the attention of fans, for the limelight or the money. I played because music runs through my bloodstream, like it's needed to keep me alive. Don't get me wrong, the money was a nice bonus, and for so many fans to love us and our music, that was amazing. But I grew tired of it, wished for the good old days at open mic nights and smaller locations. I wished I could play just because I wanted to, not because I *had* to."

"I can understand that. Plus, the saying goes 'all that glitters isn't gold' and there's a lot of truth in that."

She echoes my own thoughts, and it's nice to hear someone else say those words.

"That's so true, Julia. Some things in life are more important than money or fame. I found one of those things on my little sojourn to the quiet little town when I disappeared. It was so nice not to have anyone recognise me, not to be mobbed for my autograph or a bunch of selfies. Don't get me wrong, I'd do anything for our fans, it's just that it felt nice to drop off the grid."

"And you liked the feeling so much, you decided you wanted to feel more of it. There's nothing wrong with that, Brent. Nothing at all. Plus, I know that you've never been in love until Caleigh, but I can tell you, love is a wonderful thing to have in your life. If you find it, you need to hold onto it."

"I found it, and I lost it. I'm not blaming *any*one or *any*thing else. It was all on me. But if there's one thing I've learned, it's that I can't give up on her. I asked her to tell me she didn't love me, and if she did, I'd leave her alone. But she didn't, so I'm like a dog with a bone. I won't let go without a fight."

"It may be an uphill battle," Julia says as she reaches for her wine, "but nothing in life worth having is ever easy."

"I've never felt like this before, Julia. Never had to fight for what I want. In all honesty, everything came too easily. Now that I have something to fight for, I'm woefully underprepared, but I won't give up. God knows Caleigh's worth it."

I sigh as I think of her. Is she thinking of me? What's she doing right now? What's she wearing? I picture her wearing nothing but a smile, which makes my cock twitch, so I switch to thoughts of my dad and the possibility he'll be a douche all weekend.

That's as good a way as any to get rid of a budding erection. Hell, it's enough to make my balls shrivel back up inside me.

Chapter Twenty-Three

Caleigh

If he thinks he's winning me over with flowers, no matter how stunning an arrangement it is—which it really is—and a Disney reference, that boy has another thing coming.

Nice job on referencing my second favourite film, but no. Just no. I am not caving in *that* easily.

Rhiannon has helped make one thing clear—I still love him. But she also said that I ought to make him *earn* my forgiveness, and as nice as it is to have flowers delivered, it doesn't even scratch the surface.

To be honest, I don't know what it will take for him to earn back my trust. I can't figure that out. I don't believe there's any *one* thing on its own that will do it. All I do know is that I need to remain strong, not show any outward sign of weakness, not give in to him as easily as my heart wants me to.

With Hardin settling in nicely at school, and the studio getting noticed more thanks to paid advertising and word of mouth, things are beginning to feel a lot more like home right now.

Mum and Dad came to visit, which was nice. I showed them the studio and mum even stayed for a class.

I've decided to stop avoiding Brent's house on the school run. The other way adds ten minutes to our route, and it's hard enough getting a five-year-old ready and out of the door for eight o'clock as it is. It's time I did what Rhiannon said and pull up my big girl panties, suck it up like an adult.

Life isn't all about Brent, even if love is a wonderful thing to have in your life. I have much more important things to focus on, like Hardin, like my new career. It's so nice to have a stable routine, one where I can be around for Hardin more. Where I can walk him to school and back, be around to help with his homework. It's nice to work during school hours but have weekends off. During the school holidays, Rhiannon has offered to look after him while I go to Savasana. I said I'd hire a sitter, but she wouldn't hear a word of it. In her words, she's a lady of leisure. With Lewis being a tad old-fashioned, he doesn't want her to have to work while Luna is young. So, she said it makes no difference if she has just Luna or Hardin too, and it would be nice for them to play together.

Maybe one day, when the studio is full to bursting, I might be able to afford to hire help and take some time off during his school holidays so that we can take a little holiday for a week, somewhere nice like Devon or something.

"Mummy, can I go to Billy's for a sleepover?" Hardin asks as Mrs. Buckle lets him leave.

"Not tonight, darling, not on a school night. But maybe over the weekend, okay baby?"

"Okay, Mummy. Can I just go and tell Billy? He's waiting for me just there," he says as he points at a cute little blond boy.

"Okay, honey, but make it quick. We're making something special for tea tonight."

He runs off and stops next to Billy. He waves his arms around, a habit he has when he's talking. He obviously inherited my mannerisms.

We skip along the road home, and Hardin chatters excitedly when he sees Brent outside his house.

"Hey, Brent," he calls.

"Hey, little man," Brent calls with a wave. "Hey, Caleigh."

I offer a small smile and wave as we pass, but then I see a gorgeous woman coming out of his front door. My heart feels as though it might come up out of my mouth. I put my head down and speed up. Hardin questions why we're going so fast, but I just tug his hand and he walks faster to fall in step with me.

We hang our coats up and Hardin asks for his normal snack. I make it for him, and he sits down in front of the telly to eat. Not something I allow him to do often, but I need a few moments of peace to collect my thoughts.

Who was she? A friend? A neighbour? *Something more?* If it's more, then why did he send me the flowers?

Maybe he thought I'd call or text to thank him, and then felt like

I'd blanked him. Truth is, I picked up my phone to thank him, but then I couldn't send the text. I hovered over the button, but when it came to it, I just deleted the words and put my phone away, and gave Hardin a bath to distract myself. Sure, I'd had a chance to text him when Hardin wasn't here, but I got the flowers just as I got home from work and then had to shower and change ready to collect Hardin. I was too busy, or at least that's what I tell myself to quiet the nagging thoughts.

Turning my iPod dock on, I find a playlist on YouTube and let it play while I gather the ingredients needed to cook our tea. We're making courgetti bolognese, a healthier alternative to spaghetti. I even bought a weird new spiralizer thingy to help make the courgette into long strands like spaghetti. I haven't used it yet, so we're going to give it a whirl this evening. Even though right now, all I feel like doing is having a bath and going to bed.

"Want to Want Me" by Jason Derulo and Luke Bryan begins to play, and I can't help but dance around the kitchen, looking oh so elegant in my slippers and apron. This song just makes me happy, and this version in particular makes me smile, probably because Luke admits he can't hit the notes that Jason does. I like his modesty.

Hardin comes in and puts his plate in the sink before washing the chocolate off his hands.

"Can Brent come for tea, Mummy?" he asks with a smile.

And just like that, my good mood evaporates. An ache in my chest replaces it.

"Not tonight, baby. Another night, maybe," I reply around the lump in my throat.

"Okay."

He skips off back to the living room, no doubt to watch more telly. Skipping the end of the song, I try to clamour back some of my good mood.

***

After bathing Hardin and reading him a bedtime story, I change into my pyjamas and head back downstairs. I load the dishwasher, turn it on and make myself a coffee before heading back to the living room to watch a DVD.

I put *10 Things I Hate About You* on, one of my all-time favourites—not just because Heath Ledger is a total hottie, but it helps.

When my favourite scene comes on, I can't help but swoon as Patrick belts out the lyrics to "Can't Take My Eyes Off You" and the marching band starts up on the football field. Totally cheesy, but a win in my book. I always only had eyes for Patrick.

As the film ends, I notice the time and am shocked by how late it is. Guess I'll have to forego the long hot soak in a bath and opt for a shower instead.

I let my head fall back against the tiles and the hot water wash over me. Closing my eyes, I picture Brent. His smile flickers behind my eyelids and I feel my own lips stretch in response to the image in my mind. How I miss those soft, pink lips, his soft hands with calloused fingertips from playing guitar, his perfect abs, his tight ass …

My eyes fly open, my brain unwilling to picture more of him, lest I just give into my heart and let down my defences. I *have* to be strong. I've come this far without him and I'll go on further. Won't I?

What did Rhiannon say? She said to open my mind and my heart to the idea of loving and being loved by Brent. That if we were meant to be, then somehow, we would. She also said something about being "master of your own destiny"—or in my case, should that be mistress? She said that sometimes fate needs a helping hand. I'm not sure whether I believe in fate or making your own destiny, and Rhi was talking at crossed purposes about them both, probably due to the wine.

***

"The class was great, thank you, Caleigh. You know, you're just what we need around here."

"Aw, thank you, Ali. You're too kind." I take a long gulp from my water bottle.

"No, really. I mean, there's a group of us who go to a local Weight Watchers together. I'll certainly be telling them all about it and seeing if I can persuade a few of them to try yoga with you. There used to be a class around here, but the instructor was rather abrasive. So much so, that people stopped coming and she closed up eventually."

"Well I'm sure we can fit you all in; this is a decent-sized studio after all. Maybe we could even think about doing a special class just for you. As you know, it's unisex classes at the moment, but if, for example, your Weight Watchers group was all female and a little self-conscious of having males in the class, we could accommodate that."

I begin to pack away my things, ready to fetch Hardin.

"That's so thoughtful, Caleigh. And I'm sure my class would thank you for it. We come in all shapes and sizes, and some are more self-conscious than others. I think some of them think that yoga is only for super skinny women, because that's mostly what they saw passing by the old studio. In fairness, that's probably why more didn't join."

"Well, we come in all shapes and sizes, and there are exercises for all. Nobody should feel too self-conscious to come. Everybody is welcome here, and if the abrasive instructor put them off, then no offence meant, but she shouldn't be in the business."

"Well, I heard that she used to be quite sweet and caring, then one day, her partner left her for a younger woman. Rumour is he married her and had kids with her, even though he'd never wanted kids with Karen."

"Gosh. Well, I think that would make me terribly sad, but I don't think it's something you should take out on other people."

"Oh, I totally agree. Some of her older students stayed with her through it because they knew what Karen was like before, but newer students like me could only hack it for a short time."

"I don't blame you, Ali. I think I would have been the same. My instructor before I moved here, she was a lovely woman, had the gentlest nature of anyone I've ever known. She helped me heal a little after my husband passed away, but then I didn't have a class to go to when I moved back to be close to my parents in River's Edge. That's one of the reasons I started my own class."

"I'm so sorry about your husband," Ali says with a sad look in her eyes.

"Thank you. It's been a few years now, and I'm in a better place than I was. Largely because I have good people around me."

My watch beeps, reminding me it's time to pick Hardin up.

"Sorry, Ali, that's my warning that it's time to go and fetch my son from school."

"Oh, right. Sorry to have kept you."

"No, no. Honestly, it's been lovely talking to you."

"It's been lovely talking to you too. You know, you seem like you'll really fit in around here. A nice, warm and welcoming atmosphere with a lovely, compassionate instructor. You'll do really well."

"Well, take some of these," I say as I hand her some flyers, "and just let any of your friends know that we can do an all-female class, and I'm sure we can figure out a discount rate for a large number of you."

"You're really too sweet. Thanks, Caleigh. I'll see you on Friday."

"It'll be nice to see a familiar face," I reply as I walk her to the door. "If the class keeps growing, I'll have to assign myself a mnemonic to remember everyone's names."

Ali giggles as we walk out, and I lock the door. She really is a pleasant woman, someone I could see myself becoming firm friends with.

After fetching Hardin from school, it's time to do my least favourite kind of shopping—food shopping. If only there was someone to do it all for me. I mean, seriously, I'd rather watch paint dry.

As I'm walking down the aisle, I see a familiar face. At least I think that's her; I didn't get the best look the other day. Saw enough to know how beautiful she was though.

"The photo doesn't do him justice," the woman says.

"He's extremely handsome, isn't he?" says the woman she's with.

I walk down the aisle and push my trolley into a gap in the row down the middle of the aisle so I can't be seen. Hardin's harder to hide, but thankfully he's busy deciding what to pick for the treat I promised him.

"You're telling me, honey. I'm married to the man, and I have to keep pinching myself to make sure he's real."

The woman she's with laughs, and I can't help but feel sucker-punched at the word "married." When did he get married? Tears sting as I try to bite them back. I don't want Hardin to see me cry, don't want to be seen crying in the supermarket either.

I ought to make a run for it, but it's like my feet are welded to the floor.

"I'm holding out hope that I can get meet and greet tickets next time they're on tour. I think I'd die of a heart attack if I got to see Whiskey Lullaby in the flesh, an arm's reach from me."

I watch as the woman quite literally swoons, and I can't help but roll my eyes at her. There are two flaws in her thinking. One: Brent is no longer with the band, so she won't meet him. And two: he's already married, so it's not like he's going to look at her in that way.

"I'll see if the hubby can have a word with the boys and get you backstage passes, if you leave me your number. And once again, thank you for coming to my rescue."

"You'd do that for me?" the woman squeals, nearly bursting my eardrums.

"It's the least I can do. You saved my bacon after all."

"I only did what anyone would have done."

"Trust me, there are plenty of people around who wouldn't," she replies as she places a hand on the other woman's arm.

"Honestly, there are some ignorant people in the world, but I believe in paying things forward. Be the good you want to see in the world, that's what I say."

Seriously? Could she be any more like a Hallmark greeting card?

"Well, I appreciate your kindness. My hubby will too. I don't know what we would have done if Jessa couldn't have the turkey nuggets his best friend helped her cook the other day. She's been nagging since then to have them every single evening."

"Well, it sure beats kids wanting nothing more than fast food, honey."

"Oh, it sure does. I just kind of believe my daughter has been replaced by an alien."

They both chuckle as my heart plummets to my boots. I think I'm going to throw up. Brent not only got married, but he married a single mum? It didn't take him long to move on, did it? Are single mums his type? Like an insta-family kind of thing without any of the groundwork? Seems like I got out just in time. Hardin and I aren't anyone's insta-family. We're a package deal, but not for a man who sniffs out single mums a mile off so that he doesn't actually have to conceive the child and do all the usual stuff like changing nappies, feeding, bathing. Shit. I have to get out of here.

"Mummy, can I choose a magazine instead? I can't find anything I want," Hardin says as he runs off towards the magazines—which happen to be right next to the two women—before I can stop him.

"Hardin, wait," I call after him.

I take a couple of deep breaths and try to swallow around the lump in my throat. I feel sick to the pit of my stomach.

Taking off after him, I see him accidentally bump into Miss Stunning Blonde with Long Legs.

"Sorry, it was an accident. My shoes are slippery on this floor." He apologises profusely to her.

"Don't worry, young man," she says as she looks down at him with a smile. "Are you okay? Did you bump yourself on that shelf?"

He looks at his arm, and that's when I see it bleeding as he holds it in the air.

"Oh my, let me go and fetch someone with a first aid kit," the other lady says as she disappears around the corner.

"Hardin, honey. How many times do I need to remind you not to run on this floor in your slippery school shoes, huh baby? Are you okay? Does it hurt?" I abandon my trolley and kneel down beside him.

"Sorry, Mummy," he cries as he wraps his arms around my neck.

"Woah, careful little man. Let's get you cleaned up before you get blood all over your mummy."

She smiles down at me, all pearly white teeth and dimples. Damn, she's so gorgeous. I don't blame Brent for making a move. If I swung that way, I would have done too. Probably wouldn't have married her after two minutes, but hey, that's his lookout.

"Sorry, Mummy," Hardin says as he pulls away.

"It's okay, baby. I can always wash my clothes. But the nice lady is right, we need to get you cleaned up."

The other lady comes back with a first aider who's carrying a box.

"Are you the handsome little fella this nice lady was telling me about?" she asks.

"Me, handsome?"

"Oh yes, she definitely means you. She said to look for the most handsome boy in the store. Said he had the brightest smile it could light the whole world."

Kneeling down next to him, she asks to see his arm and he shows her without fuss.

"Ouch, this looks painful. Were your shoes a bit too slippery?"

"It's my fault. I ran when Mummy told me not too. She always says my school shoes are too slippery on the tiles."

"And she's right, by the looks of things," she says as she cleans his arm up.

"Am I going to have to go to hospital?" he asks with a pout and a wobbly bottom lip.

The first aider looks up at me with sad eyes.

"I think so, young man. But I'm sure they'll give you a lollipop if you're a brave boy. They do that with my Thomas."

"Do they? I promise I'll be brave. Where does Thomas go to school? How old is he?"

Ever the chatterbox, even when he's in pain.

"He goes to Brookhaven Primary. He's five."

"FIVE?" He yells loud enough to pierce her eardrum. "I'm five and I go to that school. What's his last name? Mine's Flynn."

"Really? Golly, what a coincidence. Do you know a boy called Thomas

Grey?"

"I do. He's my best friend. He was the first one to be nice to me when I started there."

"Really? What's your name? Let me guess. It's Hardin, right?"

"YES!" he squeals. "How do you know?"

"Well, Thomas came home the day you started school and started chattering about his new friend, Hardin. He's talked about you every day since, too."

"He has? I love Thomas, because when this boy wasn't very nice, he stood up for me. When the boy spilled my juice on the table, Thomas gave me twenty pence to buy a new one."

"Aw, that's not very nice is it? Was that boy called Lucas, by any chance?" she asks as she puts a bandage on Hardin's arm until we can get to hospital.

"He is, yeah."

"He's not very nice to a lot of people, or so Thomas tells me."

"He's always getting his name put in park."

"Well, the teachers must know he's not very nice if that's the case."

"What does putting someone's name in park mean?" Miss Gorgeous with Long Legs asks me.

I briefly explain as best I can. "Oh, there's this chart on the wall, and all the students' names are on cards. If you misbehave, you get your name moved down the colour chart or something and being put in park makes you lose your breaktimes."

"Hey, you're Caleigh, right?"

"I am. How did you know?"

"Brent talks about you and Hardin all the time. I saw you across the road the other day. I only got a brief glimpse, but a gorgeous woman with pink hair and a son called Hardin—it's not hard to connect the dots."

So, he talks about me to his wife? How odd.

"All done here, Mum," the first aider says as she stands.

"Oh, thank you so much. Sorry, I didn't get your name."

"Anita. Anita Grey."

"Thank you, Anita."

"It's my pleasure."

She sneakily shows me a lollipop and I nod, allowing her to give it to him.

"Would you like this, for being such a brave boy?" she asks him.

"Can I, Mummy?"

"Of course, baby. You've been so brave allowing Anita to clean and bandage you up."

"Thank you, Anita," he says as he wraps her in a hug.

"You're very welcome, Hardin. You're a very brave little soldier. You'll have to tell Thomas that you might have a cool little scar."

"Let me take you to hospital," Miss Gorgeous with Long Legs offers.

"It's okay, I have my car here. Thank you though."

"Please, I insist. Your hands are shaking; you're in no fit state to drive."

Are they? I look down at my hands and realise she's right.

"Let her take you, miss," Anita says warmly.

"Okay, thank you."

"I'll get your shopping packed into bags. Do you have anything frozen? I can take it back home with me and drop it round once you get home if you give me your number."

"I do have a few frozen bits, but that hardly matters in the circumstances. Plus, I haven't even paid yet, and I don't have cash, only my card."

"That's no problem. Just give me your number."

I reel off my mobile number as she types it into her phone.

"It's Caleigh, right?"

"Uh, yeah. Sorry, my brain's a bit scrambled," I say as we begin to walk towards the double doors to exit.

"Don't worry, Caleigh, you have people who can help you, so just let us. All you need to worry about is Hardin."

"I don't think it's a very deep cut, if that helps," Anita says. "He may get stitches or it may just be glue, but either way, he's a little warrior so he'll be fine."

"Thank you so much for helping, Anita. I remember you from Mrs. Buckle's class now."

"Yes, I've seen you waiting for Hardin. I didn't really pay much attention, even though I should have known by your gorgeous hair. I was too focused on this little man."

She ruffles his hair and he looks up at her with a smile.

"You be good for Mummy now, won't you, Hardin?"

"I will. I promise."

"You're a good boy. No wonder my Thomas likes you."

We say our goodbyes and get in the car with the woman whose name I still haven't caught.

As we make our way to the hospital, she tells me her name is Julia and her daughter is a little younger than Hardin, at only three. She'll be starting nursery this year.

Julia seems nice; it's no wonder Brent set his sights on her. I really need to get over this shit with him. He's taken now, and I'm fine alone. Well, maybe not fine yet, but I will be once I shake him from my system.

Julia sits with us as we wait to get Hardin into triage. I try telling her that she should get home, but she says it's fine because she's texted her husband and let him know, so he's taking care of Jessa.

I feel a pang of jealousy as she speaks about Brent. She really is a very nice person though, and I'm just hoping she makes him as happy as he deserves.

I send Rhiannon a text but tell her we're okay, and she doesn't need to drop everything and rush over like she wants to. She says it must be weird for me when I tell her I'm with Brent's new partner. I can't bring myself to say wife, not right now, anyway. Hardin needs me, and I don't want to waste time explaining it all to Rhi. I'll chat with her later when I call her to update her on my brave little soldier.

We get called through to triage by a pretty brunette, and Hardin shows her his war wound.

"Hi, Hardin, my name is Louise. How did you manage to do this?" she asks as she unwraps the bandage and takes away the blood-soaked gauze.

"I hit my arm on a shelf when Mummy was shopping."

"Oh no, that must have been a very sharp shelf. That's not good, is it?"

"It was the edge of a magazine shelf. If you hit that, it can come quite sharp," Julia says.

"Ouch, maybe the supermarket should be told, and they could make changes, so this doesn't happen to anyone else."

"I think that's a good idea you know, Caleigh," Julia says as she looks at me. "I know his shoes were slippery, but that's no excuse really. They ought to think of changing to plastic shelving or putting something on the edges of the current shelves."

"Am I getting stitches?" Hardin asks Louise as she cleans up the blood.

"Well, I think this just requires a little glue. I can get a nurse in cubicles to do that for you."

"Will it take long to heal? Does he need to take time off school?" I ask.

"Well, the nurse will give you an aftercare leaflet, but try not to get it wet for the first five days, and if it does get wet, *pat* it dry, don't rub. He might be best not going to school tomorrow because he'll be a bit sore and may need some painkillers. He should be okay to go back in a day or so, depending on how sore it is. The last thing we want is for it to get bumped and split back open and then you end up coming back here for it to be glued again."

"Okay, thank you."

"Right, Hardin, I've put a new gauze over it until the nurse calls you through. Mum, if you want to go back into the waiting room, someone will be with you shortly."

"Thank you, Louise."

"You're most welcome."

We walk back into the waiting room, and a few minutes later, another nurse calls us through. She shows us into the cubicle and Julia holds my hand as Hardin sits up on the bed and allows the nurse to look at his arm.

"You've been in the wars, young man," she says with a warm smile.

"I fell when we were food shopping," he replies in his ever-chipper way.

Kids are so resilient, and I am thankful for that right now. I can't say the same for me. I feel sick as I look at the cut and can't help but blame myself for his fall.

"He'll be okay, Caleigh," Julia whispers as she squeezes my hand.

I'm glad she can be so strong, because I feel like a nervous wreck. Hardin's never had stitches or had a cut glued. He's never broken a bone, never done anything to end up in hospital. I know it's almost inevitable, but I feel like the worst mum in the world right now.

"Okay, now Hardin, I'm going to need you to be very still. Can you do that for me?"

"Uh-huh," he confirms with a vigorous nod.

"Good boy. If you're brave while I glue this, you can pick a lolly from my jar over there, if it's okay with your mum."

"It's okay, Anita gave me a lollipop when she cleaned my arm up. You can keep the lolly for the next boy or girl who comes in. They need it more than me."

He really is the sweetest, most thoughtful little boy. His words make me smile.

"Aw, Hardin, that's such a lovely thing to do. How about I give you a sticker instead?" she asks as she gets the things ready to glue the cut.

He nods his head but sits upright and keeps the rest of his body still.

"Okay, now this might sting a little as I close the cut, Hardin. Do you want to hold Mummy's hand with the other one?"

Holding out his uninjured arm, he takes my offered hand. I squeeze his hand and smile at him.

"I'll be brave, Mummy."

"I know you will; you're my little soldier."

He winces a little as the nurse presses the two sides of the cut together for a few seconds, but other than that, he's braver than I thought he might be.

The nurse gives us an aftercare leaflet, and once we get back into Julia's car, I read it:

General Advice:
- avoid touching the glue for 24 hours
- try to keep the wound dry for the first 5 days
- showers are preferable to baths to avoid soaking the wound
- use a shower cap if the wound is on the head
- pat the wound dry if it gets wet – don't rub it

Things to avoid during the first 5 days:
- don't stick a plaster on the skin glue
- don't put creams or lotions on the glue
- don't wear clothing that could rub against the glue
- don't pick at the glued area
- don't brush hair around the glued area

I guess that's easy enough, except we'll have to be careful in the shower. The nurse was kind enough to give us a few waterproof dressings; I just hope they work.

Julia pulls up outside my house and gives me the number for Sandra, the lady who was with us earlier. I didn't even think to get her number to let her know when I'd be home.

"Thank you for everything, Julia. You really didn't have to help."

"Oh, my goodness. You'll have to go and fetch your car first. You don't want to get clamped on the supermarket carpark."

"I hadn't even thought of that."

"Let me take you to get it."

"Oh, it'll have to wait. It's time for Hardin to eat, and he probably has homework."

"You only get three hours free parking, honey. Don't worry, let me sort something, hang on."

She pulls out her phone and taps away.

"Right, that's sorted," she says as her phone chimes in response. "Have you still got your seatbelt on, Hardin?"

"Yeah."

"Okay, good boy. Right, let's get you two sorted out, shall we?"

She pulls back onto the road and when we pull up, I look up at Brent's house. There's a knot in my stomach as he comes to the front door and waves.

"Right, Hardin, Brent is going to look after you while I take your mummy to get her car. We'll be back soon, okay?"

"Cool."

He claps his hands together in glee as I walk around to unbuckle his belt.

"Bye, Mummy," he says as he kisses my cheek.

"Bye, baby, be good."

"Brent," he shouts as he heads up the steps, "I hurt my arm, but it's glued back together now."

"Oh no, buddy. Were you brave at hospital?" he asks as he ruffles his hair.

"Uh-huh. The nurse gave me a sticker, look," he replies as he shows off his shiny sticker.

"That's awesome, buddy. What do you say to a nice fruit smoothie? You can come and meet Jessa too."

"Do you have strawberries?"

"I sure do. Want some in your smoothie?"

"Yes please."

Hardin bounces on the balls of his feet as I watch from the end of the path.

"Is that okay with Mummy?" Brent asks, looking at me with a warm smile.

"Sure. Are you sure you'll be okay with him? We can take him instead of imposing."

"Of course. He'll be fine here. He can play with Jessa until you girls get back."

"Thank you, Brent."

"Bye, Mummy," Hardin say with a wave as a little blonde-haired girl comes to stand in the open doorway.

"Bye, baby. See you soon. Be good."

"I promise."

With a wave, he dashes off with Jessa. Brent chuckles and follows them inside.

I'm not sure it's good to have him get attached to Brent, given the circumstances. But what's done is done now.

Julia turns the radio on quietly. A song plays and my breath catches in my throat as I realise it's Brent.

I did it all for love,
Something I knew nothing of,
Until the day I met you,
And you showed me the way.
But now I'm here without you,
Lost in a sea of despair.

The lyrics are beautiful, but make my heart constrict. Before I can stop them, tears start to fall. I move to wipe them away and Julia notices.

"He wrote it for you, you know?"

My head whips around so fast I'm not sure I haven't given myself whiplash.

"You didn't know?" she asks, shock evident on her face.

"I-I've n-never heard this song before," I whisper as more tears fall.

"It's only available on the iTunes album. Or it will be once that version is released. They're holding it off until—well, I guess until you've had a chance to hear it on the radio."

"I-I'm n-not sure what you mean."

We pull up in the car park and Julia turns to me, her eyes soft and full of compassion. She's a stronger woman than I would be if my husband wrote a song about someone else.

"Honey, it's not really my place to speak for him, but Brent loves you."

I see the sun shining on her wedding ring and my heart hurts more than I ever thought possible.

"B-but h-he can't. He m-married y-you."

"Married me? Oh, honey, I'm not married to Brent. I'm married to one of his best friends, Evan. What made you think I was with Brent?"

"I-I o-overheard you in the s-store earlier, talking about how handsome he was in the picture in the magazine. Sandra said you were lucky to be married to him, or y-you did, I-I can't quite remember."

"Oh, honey, I was talking about Evan Winslow."

"A-and I-I jumped t-to c-conclusions."

God, I wish I could stop stuttering, but I feel like I'm stumbling over my words thanks to how hard my heart is beating.

"Brent only has eyes for you, Caleigh."

Julia takes my hand in hers and softly squeezes it. The radio still plays in the background. As I take a few deep breaths, I feel tears racing down my face.

"What If I Never Get Over You" by Lady Antebellum plays, reminding me how many times I've listened to it these last few weeks. I cried every time, because I wondered what would happen if I never got over Brent.

"Don't cry, sweetie. You can't cry pretty, as Carrie Underwood would say. And you don't want to end up with panda eyes."

I manage a small chuckle at her words.

Julia turns the radio off, probably for fear I won't stop crying. It feels like a dam has finally burst and now I can't do anything to stop it as the tears cascade down my face.

She reaches into the glove box and hands me a pack of tissues. I sniffle and thank her as I wipe my cheeks and blow my nose in a rather unladylike way.

"You should talk to him. Or if you can't talk, at least listen," she softly urges.

"Did he really write that song about me?"

"He sure did. It was the last thing he did before leaving the band."

"I-I don't know what to say."

"That's why you should hear him out."

"I-I—"

"As I said, it's not my place to speak on his behalf, but I would urge you to hear him out."

"We haven't seen each other for a while."

"Are you scared of what he has to say?"

Her bluntness shocks me but urges me to confess the truth.

"Yes," I whisper.

Julia squeezes my hand and looks at me with compassion written across her face.

"Oh, Caleigh," she replies softly. "Honey, there's nothing to be scared of, unless you don't feel the same way. But—and please correct me if I'm wrong in my assumption here—it seems like you might. After all, if we're over someone, we don't sit and ugly cry, do we?!"

"I-I g-guess not, no."

I wipe away fresh tears and sigh.

"Can I ask ... do you still love him?"

Taking a deep, steadying breath, I dry my eyes and make eye contact, so she knows I'm speaking the truth.

"I really do."

"Then, darling, you need to go to him. Or, if you can't or *won't* do the running, let him come to you. Be open to communicating with him."

"I will."

I mentally pull up my big girl panties.

"Thank you, Julia. Not only for your help today, but for your honesty and helping set me straight."

"You're most welcome. Good luck. Although, I don't think you'll actually need it."

I open the door and thank her again before walking to my car, feeling lighter than I have all day, maybe more than I have in weeks.

Chapter Twenty-Four

Brent

Somebody knocks on the door, so I pause the DVD and go to answer it.

"Hi, Jules, everything okay?"

"Well, her car wasn't clamped, so that's a start."

"I want to ask how you even ended up bumping into her, but little ears in the living room … you know?!"

We walk into the living room and see the children sat in front of the telly. *The Princess and The Frog* is paused, and Evan is sitting with a beer in his hand.

"Mummy," Jessa squeals as she turns and sees Julia.

Julia bends down and wraps her daughter in a hug. I go to sit down, but another knock at the door stops me.

"Hi," Caleigh whispers as I open the door.

"Hi, come on in. The kids are watching a film."

"What are they watching?"

I tell her as I lead her into my living room.

"This place is beautiful."

"Thank you. I mean, you know the layout of the place already, but I've added my own touches here and there."

"And it looks gorgeous."

"Mummy," Hardin shouts as he runs up to her.

"Hey, baby, how's your arm?"

"A bit sore. Jessa and I were playing carefully until Brent said he could put a film on."

"Have you been a good boy?" she asks, although she knows the answer. I know she knows, because she's a good mum, she's intuitive, and she's taught him well.

"I have, haven't I, Brent?" he asks, looking up at me.

I smile at him as I reply that he's been as good as gold.

"Brent's so funny, Mummy. He had us laughing at him doing other people's voices."

"Is that so? And who were you impersonating?" she asks with a large smile on her face.

"Doctor Fa-silly—"

"Oh, Doctor Facilier, the bad guy?"

"Yeah, him. I can never say his name."

"Well, I'm glad you had fun, baby, but we should get going so we can have something to eat. I don't know about you, but I'm starving."

"Oh," he says, his face falling.

"What's the matter, baby?"

"Nothing."

"No, come on, tell me what's bothering you."

"We haven't finished the film."

"Oh," she says with a sigh. "Well …"

"Caleigh, can I talk to you for one quick second?" I butt in.

"Sure."

I pull her to one side and whisper so that we aren't overheard by little ears.

"You could stay, let him watch the rest of the film. We could get a takeaway or something."

"Oh."

I watch as her bottom lip trembles slightly.

"I could, umm … I could always cook something for everyone … i-if y-you don't mind me using your kitchen, that is."

"Sure."

I can practically feel myself smiling from ear to ear. This might be a one-off. It might not lead to her talking to me. But I'll take it. For now.

"Great. What do you have that I can make for us?"

"There's plenty of fresh vegetables and some chicken breasts, or there's turkey mince. I'm sure there's probably something else too. Depends what you want to make. Shall we go and take a look?"

"Yeah, sure."

She smiles, and it warms me from the inside out.

"Hardin, we're going to stay and watch the film, okay?"

"YAY! Thanks, Mummy."

"Go back into the living room and ask Evan or Julia to put the film back on, okay baby? Brent and I are going to go and see what there is for me to cook for us all."

"Okay, Mummy."

He skips off and I lead Caleigh into the kitchen. She rummages through my fridge and pulls out ingredients.

"I don't suppose you have any herbs and spices, do you?"

"Actually, I do. They're over there in the spice rack."

"A spice rack? For a guy that told me he couldn't cook?" She sounds amused.

"Yeah, I actually learned to cook some healthy basic staples, along with my mum's lasagne."

"Ooh, get you. Brent Ryder, country music star extraordinaire turned master chef overnight."

"Are you sassing me?"

She cocks her hip, placing a hand on it and gives me a hard stare.

"Don't make me beat you with a wooden spoon, Mr. Ryder."

My cock twitches at her words.

"Kinky!"

She reddens, and my heart squeezes as I realise that I've never seen her looking more beautiful than in this moment. She's stunning, to put it simply.

I don't want to push her too far, so I show her the spice rack as well as where I keep the pots and pans. Pulling out my wok, she gets to work. She chops and dices, showing serious knife skills.

I turn on my iPod and set it to shuffle. "Country Girl" by Luke Bryan starts to play and Caleigh's eyes light up as she begins to shake her hips to the rhythm.

It's nice to see her seem so carefree around me once more, but I'm not a fool. I know she hasn't forgiven me. She might have got part way there if I'm lucky, but she isn't all the way over the finish line yet.

"What are you cooking, good looking?"

"Ah, it's a surprise. Just wait and see."

She smiles at me, and damn if my heart doesn't kick into gear, thundering against my rib cage all because she threw a smile my way.

"Can I do anything to help?"

"You can wash the veggies."

She points to the pile of vegetables she needs washing and goes back to singing. I daren't tell her she was right about not being able to carry a tune; it might earn me a slap. But honestly, I don't care that she's a little off-key. She'll always be perfect to me.

Once I'm done, I hand her the pile of carrots, broccoli florets and other bits and pieces she managed to locate in my kitchen. She hands me a knife and I start peeling and chopping. The aromas in the kitchen, coming from what must be a sauce of some kind, smell amazing.

"Do you have any mozzarella?"

"I'm not sure. Did you check the fridge?"

"I wasn't looking for it at first. Give me a sec."

She leaves her pan on the heat and I find it odd that she's cooking it all just in the wok. She's neat and tidy, even when cooking. Me? I have a million pots and pans out and the kitchen looks like a bombsite until I load the dishwasher.

Emerging triumphant, Caleigh smiles as she slices the mozzarella. I still don't know what it is she's cooking, but damn it smells and looks great.

"Next time, you need to try my chicken lasagne."

Next time? Maybe she's coming around to me after all.

"Chicken lasagne? I'm sorry, but that sound all kinds of wrong," I say as I pull a funny face.

"I'll have you know," she says with a hand on one hip and the other waving a wooden spoon at me, "that it's actually really goddamn tasty. Don't knock it until you've tried it."

"But come on, Caleigh, lasagne is meant to be beef."

"I'm telling you, Brent, it's not as bad as it sounds. I didn't like the sound of it at first either, but then Rhi cooked it for me and totally changed my mind."

"Who's Rhi?"

"My best friend, Rhiannon. I've told you about her, I'm sure."

"Oh, you probably did."

"Well, she lives here in Brookhaven. Her daughter Luna goes to the same school as Hardin. You'd like her, she's good people, so is her husband Lewis. Although he's a workaholic solicitor, he's a good guy."

I like to see her so open and willing to talk to me again. There was a time I thought she'd never speak to me for as long as we both lived. And me buying what could have been her house can't have helped.

***

We're sitting in the living room, having eaten the delicious meal cooked by Caleigh's fair hands. Everyone is stuffed, including me and I have a big appetite. It was the best home-cooked meal I've had in ages. Probably because it was cooked by the woman I love.

The film is over, and the kids are playing quietly while the adults sit around drinking wine. I won't deny it feels good. More than good, actually. It feels amazing. But is it only temporary? I can't become complacent about trying to win her back. My plan still needs to go full steam ahead.

"… he was so blind drunk that he thought the wardrobe was the en suite bathroom and peed in his shoes which we on the bottom shelf."

I tune in to the tail end of what was said and realise they're telling stories about me.

"Hey, jerk, you're meant to be my best friend!"

"Hey, don't look at me. Caleigh asked, and I answered. Would have been rude to leave the lady hanging," Evan says with his hands in the air.

"Daddy, what's a jerk?"

Suddenly all our heads whip around to find Jessa with a puzzled look on her face. Shit! That's all my fault.

"It's a bad word that Uncle Brent shouldn't have said," Jules says, giving me a murderous look.

"I'm so sorry, Jessa. I shouldn't have said a cuss word. Don't you ever say it, okay?"

"Okay, Uncle Bwent."

She's so damn cute when she talks. She's so clever, smarter than her daddy, so she must get it all from Jules.

"I'm sorry, Jules, Ev. I wasn't thinking."

"I've said worse, trust me," Ev replies.

"You have and you shouldn't. *Think* before you open your mouth in future," Jules says, giving him a stern look.

"Sorry, Jules."

At least he has the grace to look contrite.

"So, that wardrobe story was quite tame. I'm imagining he's done worse," Caleigh says, cutting the tension.

"Oh, he has. Plenty worse. But not a conversation for around little ears," Ev says with a chuckle.

"I could tell you some stories about Evan," I chime in. "But I can tell you all about that when they've gone home, so he can't kill me for it."

"I bet you boys got up to no good pretty often, huh?"

"When we were younger, we could get away with a lot more. But trust me, we were never rock stars who threw TVs out of windows or whatever."

"That's too cliché for you, huh?" she asks with a wry smile.

"Very. We try to avoid stereotypes. Plus, we were *country* stars, not rock."

"Oh, and that makes all the difference does it?"

"It sure does," I reply with a wink.

"Well, you can tell me all about it another day. For now," she says, looking at her watch, "it's time I got Hardin home for bed."

"I'll walk you home," I blurt without thinking.

I wait as she seems to think it over, rather than giving me a straight no.

"Okay. That would be nice."

Hardin doesn't want to leave Jessa, but Caleigh says that she's sure he'll see her again soon.

"Don't forget what I said about peppermint tea, raw ginger or acidophilus tablets, Jules," Caleigh says as she grabs their coats.

"I think ginger might make me feel sicker as I really don't enjoy the taste."

"Trust me, the peppermint tea tastes awful too. Put one sweetener or one spoonful of sugar in it and it tastes better. Honestly, it helps with the morning sickness."

"Thanks, Caleigh. And once again, I'm sorry about Hardin."

"Hey, he could just as easily have bumped into someone else or just slid into the shelf. Seriously, it's not on you. Don't worry about him; he'll be fine."

"I just feel so bad."

"Well, don't. Just put it to the back of your mind."

Julia gets up and hugs Caleigh, and as they stand there holding each other, I think about what kind of friendship they could have if we did this more often. If she and I were together, they could become very good friends, very easily. The two of them have this natural ease around each other. It's nice to see because they both mean a lot to me.

As we walk out of the door, Hardin takes Caleigh's hand and then mine. It surprises me a little, but I don't want to let go and make him think I don't like him, because I do. Caleigh doesn't say anything about it, so I just let go of my worries and hold his hand as he skips down the street.

I look at the house she's renting. It's bigger than her place back in River's Edge, and it has character, just like her. I can imagine her living somewhere like this, but I would prefer to imagine her living in my house, with me.

"Thank you for walking us home, and thank you for allowing us the pleasure of your company tonight. I really enjoyed it. I'll pick my car up on my way to work after dropping Hardin at school, if that's okay?"

She'd been worried about having a glass or two of wine with her meal, but I said her car would be safe outside my place until morning.

"Can you give this to Luna, please, Brent?" Hardin asks as he fishes something out of his pocket.

"Sure thing, buddy. What have you got there?"

"Just something we were playing with and she liked it."

He hands me a toy car and smiles a big toothy grin.

"Aw, that's a nice one, buddy. You sure you don't want to keep it?"

"Nah, I have lots of them and Jessa said she didn't have any cars."

"Well, I'm sure she'll really appreciate it, little man. It's a very kind gesture."

I ruffle his hair, and he looks at me with a cheesy grin.

"I like Jessa. She's fun to play with."

"She sure is."

I can't help but smile as Caleigh unlocks the door and tells Hardin to go and brush his teeth. He says goodbye and crushes me in a hug before doing as he's told.

"They'd make a cute couple," I say with a smirk.

"Don't go marrying them off just yet, mister."

"Oh, I won't. But they are awful cute together."

"Jessa's a sweet kid. Gets it from her mum, by the sounds of things. They're nice, your friends."

"They are. They're the grown-ups. Asher and Jude are a pair of teenagers trapped in men's bodies. But they're cool all the same."

"I bet they'd have a few more stories to tell about you."

"Oh, they would, and they wouldn't be pretty ones."

"I'll have to ask them then."

"Don't worry, ragging on me is one of their favourite pastimes, so you ask, and they'll provide all the gory details."

She smiles at me, and unlike recently, it's a genuine smile that lights her eyes.

"Well, I won't keep you any longer. You have a good night now," I say as I walk a couple of steps backwards.

I don't want to push my luck with her, not when she's actually starting to come around to being in the same room as me. Baby steps.

Caleigh steps up to me and ghosts a kiss across my lips. I feel a tingling sensation from her soft lips against mine.

All too soon, she pulls away from me. She offers me a small smile and walks a couple of steps back towards her door.

"Goodnight, Brent."

"Goodnight, Caleigh. Sleep well."

Chapter Twenty-Five

Caleigh

I don't know what made me kiss him goodnight. Maybe it was because I felt giddy being in such close proximity to him. Maybe it was the wine. Maybe it was just the fact that I'm learning to accept that I do still love him.

After everything, my heart still beats faster when he's near. I know that I can be a strong, independent woman. But I also know that it doesn't make me less independent if I love somebody. I've said it before, but I really mean it this time. Being in a relationship doesn't make you co-dependent for everything. It means a lot more than that. It means loving someone and being loved by them. It doesn't mean giving up on everything you had before them, it just means letting them into your life, opening up to them and being together against all odds.

When I think about what happened with Brent, the lies he told … he had no choice but to tell them. He wasn't doing it because he *wanted* to lie to me, he was doing it to keep his cover. Do I wish he'd told me and trusted me to keep his secret? Of course, I do. But he didn't, and what's done is done. There's nothing he or I can do to go back and change it. But we can move forward. The question is, can we move on together? Does he still love me the way I love him? I guess there's only one way to find out.

Hanging out with Brent and his friends last night was fun. I don't know many people around here except for Rhiannon and my clients, so I don't get to hang out like that often.

I know I feared the worst with Julia when I first met her, but I should have trusted that Brent really meant it when he said he loved me, and that he wouldn't have moved on so quickly.

I look at the flowers he bought me, still in the vase, even though most of them are dead. I just can't bring myself to throw them away when one of them is still vibrant and full of life. He said he'd love me until the last petal fell, so why did I let my head mislead me into thinking the worst about him and Julia?

Picking up the card that came with the flowers, I read it over and over, even though I have it committed to memory.

The sheer vibrancy of the last flower left alive piques my interest. Why is that one so full of life when the others are all but dead? Plucking it from the vase, I feel an artificial stem. I trace a finger along the petals and realise that it's not real, that's why it looks different to the others.

The penny drops. He'll love me until the last petal falls, but the last petal will never fall, because the flower isn't even alive. He'll *always* love me. My god, I feel so stupid.

I pick up my phone and send Rhiannon a text as I place the flower on the worktop and finish getting ready to take Hardin to school.

"I'm ready, Mummy," he says as he walks into the kitchen with his buttons done up incorrectly.

"Come here, baby, it looks like you missed a hole."

I button up his shirt and help him do his tie. Since when do primary school children even need to wear ties? I know I didn't when I was his age. It's not like a five-year-old can tie one.

My phone chimes and I read Rhiannon's reply. She thinks it's cute that he did that with the flowers. I guess I'd be inclined to agree. Seems Brent's a sweetheart after all. He might have been Britain's sweetheart of country before, but now I selfishly don't want to share him. I want to make him mine and mine alone. But how do I tell him that now?

Another text comes through from Rhiannon.

>Hey, how do you fancy a girl's night out tonight? Lew will watch the kids.

>Where you thinking of going?

>There's an open mic night in town at Busby's.

>Oh man, really? You know the way to a girl's heart. I reply sarcastically.

>Pretty please? I'll even buy the first round.

>Ugh. Make it two rounds and you're on.

>Deal. Want to meet at mine to get ready?

>Sure. Around 6?

>Sounds good. Catch you later, alligator.

I smile to myself, regardless of not really fancying going to hear people sing. It's going to be a long night.

I drop Hardin off at school and walk back to Brent's to fetch my car. I should go up and knock to tell him I'm taking it, but it's so early in the morning and I don't want to wake him.

"Morning, gorgeous," a voice calls, making me look up.

I swear I'm almost drooling at the sight of Brent in nothing but a pair of faded blue jeans. His taut, muscular torso is on show and it looks like he's either been in the shower or working out, as his skin looks slick with something wet.

"Good morning, Brent."

He waves and offers me the most gorgeous smile.

"Got time for a coffee?"

Looking at my watch, I see I have about another hour before my first class of the day.

"Sure."

I walk up the path and he stands aside to let me in.

"Good morning, Caleigh," Julia says as she notices me.

"Hey, Julia. Hi, Jessa," I say softly as she toddles over to me and puts her arms in the air. I pick her up and sit her on my hip. She twirls my hair around her fingers, and I sigh happily. It reminds me so much of when Hardin was younger.

"Have you eaten?" Brent asks as he comes up behind me.

He's almost close enough to be touching me; I can feel an air of electricity around us.

"Umm, no. I was going to grab a bagel or something before work."

"Sit. I'll bring you some blueberry pancakes."

"This from the man who can't cook? I'm impressed."

"Don't be until you try them," he replies with a chuckle.

"Come, sit down," Julia says as she moves some toys from the couch.

"Bwent gived me a car fwom Hardin," Jessa says as I put her down.

"I know. Hardin said you didn't have any cars and you really liked it. So he wanted you to have it."

"Can you tell him fank you pwease?"

My heart melts a little at the way she talks. She's so goddam sweet.

"Of course I will, sweetie."

Brent brings me pancakes and I tuck in. The smell alone is delicious and makes my stomach rumble.

"Something smells good," Evan says as he enters the living room.

"It's these pancakes; they're delicious," I reply as I swallow a bite.

"Where's mine?"

"In the kitchen. Haven't made them yet because you were in the shower," Brent replies as he walks away towards the kitchen.

Evan sits down on the floor, playing with Jessa, until Brent brings him his breakfast.

We sit around and talk about everything and nothing until it's time for me to go to work. It's been nice getting to know Brent's friends better. I could see Julia being a good friend in time.

***

It's been a heck of a day. Ali brought a group of people along for the afternoon session. It was fun, but man, I am exhausted now. Almost too exhausted to go out with Rhiannon, but I won't back out now. I could use a piña colada or something expensive, as it's her round. Whatever it is, I need to unwind.

I pull clothes out of my wardrobe but can't decide what to wear. Busby's isn't anything fancy, but every girl needs an excuse to dress up and look nice.

Finally, I settle on my favourite oversized purple cashmere jumper and a pair of black skinny jeans that Brent once said looked painted on. He said they make my ass look great. I pull out my black Louboutins and my favourite pair of Iron Fist shoes which are purple with black skulls on, trying to decide which would look better. The Louboutins are hot as hell, but the others match the colour of my jumper.

Decision made, I grab the Iron Fist heels and pack them in my bag to get ready at Rhiannon's. Grabbing my makeup bag, I pack that too before heading into Hardin's room to see if he's ready to go.

He has his favourite Mickey Mouse plush in his hands and is dressed in the jeans and t-shirt I laid out for him. He looks so cute just sitting there on his bed.

"You ready to go and stay at Auntie Rhi's house?"

"Yes, Mummy. I'm dressed, see," he says as he points at his George of The Jungle t-shirt and blue jeans.

"Good boy. Now, you've got some clothes in this bag," I say as I hold it out, "and you have your Mickey to sleep with. Do you want to take anything else?"

"No, Mummy. As long as I have Mickey."

We head downstairs and I call a taxi, knowing I won't be able to drink if I drive.

Hardin sits in the window until he sees the taxi pull up. He jumps down and grabs his coat before rushing to the door.

***

"I'm telling you; you look hot as. You need to stop messing with your hair, else it'll come loose."

I stop fidgeting with my hair, like a child scorned. Rhiannon decided to style my hair in a fishtail braid over my left shoulder, and she took my makeup and gave me smoky eyes. What can I say? She does it better than I do. I normally only apply minimal makeup in nude tones. But Rhi said that for one night, I should try something new.

"Do we really have to go to Busby's? Can't we go elsewhere like a cocktail bar or something?"

"Nope," she says, popping the P.

"Damn, you're so bossy, Rhi."

"You should know better than to argue with me," she says with a wink as she finishes curling her hair.

"Yes, Mum," I quip as I poke my tongue out at her.

We finish getting ready, then we head downstairs and see the kids in their pyjamas. Hardin looks up at me with a big toothy grin.

"You look so pretty, Mummy."

"Why, thank you, darling. Now, you'll be a good boy and go to bed when Uncle Lewis says so, won't you?"

"I promise, Mummy."

"Good boy. I love you lots like jelly tots," I say as I crouch down and pull him in for a hug. "I'll see you in the morning, okay?"

"Okay."

He gives me a kiss and then wipes his lips in case he got lipstick on them. I can't help but laugh when he sees the smear of red on his hand.

Our taxi arrives and the kids come to the door to wave us off.

"I don't know about you, but I can't wait for that first drink," Rhi sighs as she sits back in the taxi.

"I already can't wait until we leave."

"You're such a buzzkill, girl. You need to let your hair down and have fun. Not literally, because that braid took me ages."

As we pull up outside Busby's, Rhiannon claps her hands together and lets out a little squeal. I swear to god, she's like a hyperactive kid sometimes. How she can be so excited for an open mic night, lord only knows.

"I'll have a porn star martini and, what are you having, babe?" she asks as she looks over her shoulder at me.

"Umm, I'll take a New York sour, please."

I survey the room. It's not packed yet, but it will be by about nine o'clock.

"Sorry, I'm not familiar with that one," the bartender says.

"It's bourbon, red wine, lemon juice and syrup."

"Coming right up."

When he's fixed our drinks, we take them and slip into a booth. It's a wonder that any of them are free, being the most comfortable seats in the place, but you won't find me complaining.

A few singers get up and do their thing, and I find it's not as bad as karaoke back at The Lock. Back then, we had some good singers and some that sang more than a little off-key. But here they have all been pretty good so far. They have the crowd warmed up too.

Rhi and I talk about whether or not she should get up and sing once she's had another drink or two. She's got a great voice, but also gets stage fright, so she needs a couple of drinks for liquid luck.

If only I was Harry Potter and could pretend to slip some *Felix Felicis* into her glass and get her up there without feeling so nervous.

"What would I even sing?" she asks as she sips her drink slowly.

"Umm ... how about 'Cry Pretty'?"

"I'm no Carrie. I can't sing that."

"Yes, you can. I hear you sing it all the time."

"But not so bloody public."

"Maybe not, but you have the voice for it."

"How about something a little more ... I don't know ..."

"No, decision made. You are getting up there and singing that song."

"Damn, look at you being the bossy one," she says with a pout.

"Yeah, well, someone has to be when you're dithering."

"Thanks, babe, you're such a good friend."

"Hey, less of the sarcasm. I *am* a good friend," I reply with a nudge to her ribs.

"Woah, careful woman, you'll spill my drink."

I get up to fetch the next round and put her name down to sing while I'm up.

As I slide back into the booth, I see her surreptitiously slide her phone back into her clutch bag. I open my mouth to ask about it, but she shuts me down with a hard stare. She's up to something; I just need to figure out what.

Chapter Twenty-Six

Brent

I am more nervous than when I used to get up on the stage with the boys. But along with nerves, I feel a rush of adrenaline. I'm a mixed bag of emotions right now. I have no idea how she'll react.

I reach for Jeri-Lynn, pull her strap over my head and cradle her to me. I feel my heart beating a staccato rhythm in my chest. I breathe in a deep breath, hold it for a moment, then release it. Holding out my hand, I see it tremble slightly.

"You'll do fine, dude. You just have to sing from your heart," Evan says as he claps me on the back.

"Are the boys here yet?"

"Five minutes out. They'll be here in time, don't worry. When have we ever let you down?"

"Never," I confirm with a sigh.

He's right, they've never let me down and they aren't looking to start now. When I told them both about my plan and that Evan was already here, they were only too happy to catch the next flight out.

I strum the first few chords of the song softly, giving me something to do with my hands and channel this nervous energy.

"Yo, Brent!" Asher calls as he enters the room the manager kindly allowed us to use.

"Bro," Jude says as he pulls me in for an awkward hug around my guitar.

"Glad you made it, boys."

"Glad to be asked, man. It's going to be epic."

"Yeah, maybe. I'm not sure."

"Stop doubting yourself, man," Jude says as he pulls his guitar from its case.

"I can't help it. I just feel so fucking nervous. What if she rejects me?"

Evan cuffs me around the back of the head and the boys laugh it up.

"Will you stop it? I saw the way she looked at you back at your house. She still feels something for you. You just have to *show* her you love her instead of telling her."

"And now, ladies and gentlemen, we have special guests joining us on stage," I hear the emcee announce. "Please give a loud round of applause for the one, the only, Whiskey Lullaby."

There's raucous applause as we file out of the side room onto the stage. People are cheering as we take our places, but I tune it all out as I survey the room, wanting to see one person and one person only.

I spot her in a side booth with Rhiannon. The look on her face is one of incredulity. I'm guessing Rhiannon kept her word and didn't tell her why they were coming tonight.

She looks stunning. A purple jumper that hangs off one shoulder, her pink hair trailing down one side of her neck. I bet if I was close enough, I'd smell her strawberry shampoo.

I take a seat behind the microphone set at the front of the stage, and the boys take their places behind me. One last show as the four of us. This should feel incredible, but I feel butterflies in my stomach, or maybe they're moths considering how hard their wings seem to be beating. I have to get a grip on myself.

"Good evening, ladies and gentlemen," I say into the microphone, and the crowd applaud loudly. "This isn't exactly a first for us, seeing as we started off at open mic nights just like this one. But it will be our last as the four of us."

I take a gulp from the water bottle that's at my feet before continuing.

"You may have heard that I left the band, but for one night only, we are back together again to perform a song I wrote for a very special lady. I don't mind telling you all, she means the absolute world to me, and I want her to know just how deeply in love with her I am. So, ladies and gentlemen, this is 'The One That Got Away'. "

I softly strum the intro with my eyes closed. Looking up, I open my mouth and feel like I'm pouring my heart out of it.

As I'm playing, the boys join in, and so do the members of the audience that we had strategically placed around the room to join in. It's like that scene in one of her favourite films where Heath Ledger gets up and starts singing "Can't Take My Eyes Off You" and the brass band strikes up and start to play. Only this time, it's a lady with a violin, a man with a cello and another man with a guitar.

Okay, so it's not a whole band ensemble like the film, but it's as close to it as I could get.

"I wonder, does she think of me at all? I miss her love; I miss it all."

Looking directly at her as I end the song, my heart flutters in my chest as I see the raw look in her eyes. She takes my breath away and I can't help the lone tear that falls.

Wiping my eyes discreetly—I hope—I swig back some more water as the crowd applauds.

Caleigh stands up and hesitates before pushing past people in the opposite direction of me. My god, I blew it. What the hell do I do now?

I look at the boys and they look at me. They look as bewildered as I feel. My eyes pick out Rhiannon in the crowd as she follows in Caleigh's wake.

Was I wrong? Did she feel nothing when we were all together at my place? Are we supposed to be friends or nothing at all? What the hell do I do now?

I want to leap down off the stage and follow her, but it's as plain as the nose on my face that she doesn't want me to.

Jude claps me on the shoulder and guides me back to the side room. I sit on the stool and put my head in my hands. My heart feels like it's been cleaved in two. Not neatly either; it's a goddamn mess and I don't know if it will ever heal.

The boys remain silent as the tears begin to fall and I tug at my hair, wishing I could tear it all out by the roots.

"What the fucking hell do I do now?" I shout.

"Chase after her," Evan says bluntly.

"Why? It's clear how she feels now I've poured my heart out and she's rejected me."

"Boy, for a smart guy, you really are dumb sometimes. I saw how she looked at you back at the house, and there was nothing but pure love in her eyes."

"Ev, she loved me once and I screwed it up. Then I thought we were getting somewhere recently. I had it all planned out to *show* her I loved her instead of just keep repeating the words. But now she's run off to god knows where and I-I just c-can't..."

I trail off as more tears fall. Unscrewing the bottle cap, I chug the remaining water.

"I can't keep chasing after a woman who doesn't want me."

"Has she told you she doesn't love you? You asked her to tell you that and she never did, did she? She can't say those words because they aren't true. Pull yourself together, get out there and find her. Look in every corner of the bar, call her mobile, call Rhiannon. Do *something!*"

"Gee, thanks Ev, call a spade a spade, why don't you?"

"I will until you get it through your thick head. Give me your damn phone and I'll call her. You have to do something; you can't just sit here and mope."

I pull out my phone and see two missed calls and a text from Rhiannon.

>We're in the back car park, come and get her.

I don't have time to explain to the boys as I take off running. The message was sent five minutes ago, and every second I waste sitting with the boys is a second closer to the girls leaving.

Pushing through the crowd, I don't have time to stop for selfies or to sign autographs, I just shout my apologies to everyone I pass.

At last I find the rear exit and push the door open so hard it bounces off the wall.

"Caleigh," I call as I look around for any sign of her.

"We're over here," Rhiannon calls with a wave.

I can just about see them with the dim light of the hallway and the blinking lights on the car park. Of course, it would be too much to ask for them to actually work. Sprinting over to them, I stop and put my hands on my knees, trying to catch my breath.

"I'll, umm, I'll leave you guys to it. Caleigh, I'll be back inside if you need me, okay?"

I smile gratefully at her before she disappears.

"Caleigh?"

She looks up at me, and even in this dim light, I can see she's been crying.

"Caleigh, please talk to me."

"I-I d-don't know what t-to say."

"Look, I've asked you this once before, but I'm going to ask you again. Tell me you don't love me, and I'll leave you alone."

"I c-can't say that, Brent."

"Then tell me what's going on in that pretty little head of yours. Please, Caleigh, I'm not above begging. I'll get down on my knees if that's what it takes."

"I w-was overwhelmed."

"Did I royally screw up?"

"No. No, it wasn't you. I just … I felt awkward with people looking around to see if they could spot who you were singing about. It was a beautiful gesture, so romantic and sweet … I was just a little overwhelmed by it all. You on stage, singing to me as if I was the only woman in the room …"

"You were the only woman in the room, Caleigh."

I kneel down in front of her, not giving a damn if my clothes get dirty.

"When you're around, the whole world fades into oblivion."

"That's part of what scares me, Brent."

Her words are so quiet I barely hear them.

"What, that I love you so much?"

"Yes … and that I love you just as much."

"You do?"

The fact that she loves me makes my heart start to beat again.

"I do, Brent. I really do. And that's scary to me, because I haven't felt this way since Angelo."

I put my arm around her, and when she doesn't flinch, I pull her closer to me. As she snuggles into my chest, I inhale her strawberry shampoo.

"Loving you makes me feel alive again, Brent. After Angelo, I was so broken. There was an empty void in my life where he had once been. Then for so long it was just me and Hardin, nobody else mattered. But then you came along," she says as she looks at me, taking a deep breath before continuing, "and with you, you brought laughter, happiness, love. I hadn't imagined myself with someone else until you."

"I've never been in love," I say as I cup her face with my hand, "until you. You're it for me, Caleigh. I know I messed up. I messed up *bad*. But if you'll let me, I'll spend the rest of my life showing you just how much you mean to me."

"I want to. I'm just scared."

"But you want to try?"

I stare into her beautiful eyes, the dim light of the car park making it hard for me to see the gorgeous green gems that they are.

"I do."

That's all I needed to hear, and I'm sure my heart skips a beat.

Leaning in, I slant my lips over hers, using my tongue to seek entry to her mouth. She submits to me and I kiss her deeply. It's fiery, passionate and hot enough to scorch the earth.

"Come home with me?" I ask as I break the kiss.

"I-I c-can't. I'm meant to be staying with Rhi."

"Please, Caleigh? I need you. You can get a taxi back to hers later."

"Let me text her and see if it's okay."

She pulls out her phone, and as though Rhiannon had been waiting for her to ask, Caleigh smiles and puts her phone back in her pocket before leaning in to kiss me.

"She said yes," she whispers.

"Then what are we waiting for?"

I take her by the hand, and it's like little sparks of electricity travel along my skin. I've missed this so much.

***

I almost drop my keys as I try and unlock the front door. I'm nervous like a teenager all over again. Caleigh giggles and takes the keys from me, slotting the key in and opening it first time. God, I'm making myself look incompetent. But better she knows that now, I think to myself as she waits for me.

As she closes the front door, I push her up against it, my mouth crashing down over hers. She kisses me back with just as much fervour as she reaches to push my leather jacket down my shoulders. I slide it off and drop it on the floor. Then I cage her up against the door with an arm on either side of her head.

It's been too long since we did this, not counting the time she branded a mistake. I've yearned for the soft touch of her lips, the taste of her strawberry lip gloss—which is missing tonight, which is a pity—the intoxicating scent of her and the feeling of her body pressed against mine.

Soft hands explore my torso and my breathing hitches. She reaches for the hem of my t-shirt and lifts it up torturously slowly as she slides her hands over my chest. I slide my arms out of the sleeves and she drops the material along with my jacket. I shiver as she kisses down my neck and to my Adam's apple. All the hairs on my arms are standing on end, goosebumps evident on my skin.

"I've ... missed you ... Caleigh," I say, but it comes out in little gasps as she continues to kiss across my collarbones and up the other side of my neck.

"And I've missed you," she says as she traces a path of kisses along my stubbly jawline.

Pulling back slightly, I cup her face in my hand and stare deeply into her eyes. They're afire with lust and I'm sure are a reflection of how my own must look right now.

"Let's not do this here," I whisper into her ear as I kiss down to the hollow of her throat.

She shivers as I kiss her as delicately as a butterfly's wings.

I take her hand in mine and walk to the bottom of the staircase. I don't want her to change her mind, but I'm giving her time to back out, just in case.

"Why are you going so damn slowly? Get your sweet ass up those stairs," she says as she smacks said sweet ass.

"I love it when you're so demanding," I reply with a wink over my shoulder, before pulling her upstairs as fast as I can go without stumbling.

Kicking my bedroom door open, I turn around and sweep her off her feet. She squeals and giggles as I pepper her face with kisses before lowering her reverently to my bed.

When I moved in, I obviously bought all new furniture. This bed is brand new and ready to be christened with this stunning pink-haired goddess.

I kick off my shoes and lean down to undo the zip of Caleigh's jeans. She's wearing the ones she wore last time, the ones that look painted on. I peel them down her legs to reveal a purple lacy thong. As if my heart couldn't race any faster. I reach her feet, and her purple heels are so sexy that I put them back on once I've pulled off her jeans.

Tracing my hands up her silky skin, I watch as she shudders underneath my gentle touch. She's so perfect, it should be illegal. I could stand and look at her all day long. No, not a day, that wouldn't be long enough.

"I could get impatient, you know," Caleigh says, snapping my attention back to her beautiful face.

"Sorry, baby, I was just admiring the view."

"Admire it from a little closer up then, huh?"

"Happily."

I strip down to my boxers and sit beside Caleigh as she sits up and pulls her jumper off, exposing a matching lacy bra. She really is stunning, especially naked—or nearly naked.

Lying back, she pulls me with her. I lie beside her and wrap her in my arms. Her lips meet mine in a frenzy. I've never known such a passionate woman. She's incredible, but what's more incredible is that she's *mine*.

I kiss my way down to the swell of her breasts, down the valley between them and unhook her bra as I go. She drops it to the floor and exposes her perfect breasts. Reaching out, I brush my thumbs over her nipples and they instantly pucker.

Tracing a line down her stomach, I kiss all the way to the edge of her thong, earning me little moans as I go. I position myself between her legs, nudge them wider open and put my hands behind her knees, raising them from the bed.

Slowly, very deliberately, I kiss my way down one thigh and then the other. Her knees tremble as I take my time. Caleigh grips the sheets beneath her, but when I don't go to directly where she needs me to be, she grabs my hair and tugs me closer.

I kiss her over her lace thong, making her whimper and writhe beneath me.

"Brent, please ..." she pants.

"Please what?"

"I need you."

"Where?"

"You're going to make me say it?" she asks, her voice an octave higher.

"No baby, I want you to show me."

I look up and see her cheeks flush pink as she uses her fingertips to push down the sides of her thong. Her ass comes off the bed as she shimmies them down to her knees, where I slide them off the rest of the way.

Caleigh stills for a moment and I just wait to see what she'll do next.

Reaching down, she toys with her clit. My eyes zero in on even the smallest of movements. She writhes on the bed and I just continue to watch for a moment, mesmerised, unable to move.

"Brent ..."

My eyes snap up to hers and I see the hunger in them.

"Please ... I need you."

I lower myself to the floor at the foot of the bed and reach up to pull Caleigh down so that her ass is on the edge of the bed.

That first taste of her is exquisite. It reminds me of how much I've been missing.

She gasps and arches her back as I slip one finger inside her. I use my tongue to tease her clit and Caleigh makes little mewling noises. She raises herself up on her elbows to watch what I'm doing, so I deliberately slow my movements.

I lick and suck, increasing the tempo to match the rhythm of my heartbeat. Unable to take it any longer, she falls back to the bed with a soft thud.

There's part of me that wants to draw this out forever, but I'm far too impatient to be inside her, where I belong.

"Brent, I-I'm g-going to—"

She cries out, unable to finish her sentence as her climax takes over.

Unable to wait any longer, I stand and tell her to move her sweet ass up the bed, before crawling up onto the bed between her legs.

"Fuck, I love you," I say as I look down at her perfect body.

She's so hot it should be illegal. With her hair splayed out on the pillow, like a shiny pink halo, she's the image of perfection. Beauty personified. I just want to absorb this moment, to remember how she looks, how she feels. I want her to be the woman I wake up next to for the rest of my life.

I brace my arms either side of her head and lean down to suck her nipple into my mouth. A moan escapes her as I lean over to do the same to the other.

Wrapping her arms around my neck, she brings me in for a kiss. It's hot, it's messy, but it's perfect. She reaches between us and takes my cock in her soft hand, making me groan. She aligns me with her, and I take it slowly, relishing the feeling of her once more.

Caleigh wraps her legs around me, and I feel a sting as her heels dig into my ass. As I ease further into her, she moans and drags her fingernails down my back.

She tugs my hair back and kisses up the side of my neck, delicate little kisses along my jawline as I sink into her until I fill her. It really is the little things in life that make my heart swell.

I build a steady rhythm and Caleigh bucks her hips from the bed to meet me thrust for thrust. Leaning down, I kiss her. It's white-hot and sears its way across my heart.

"Brent, stop."

I still, and for a moment I'm confused, until I see her smile as she places her hands on my chest, pushing me sideways. She straddles my waist but wastes no time aligning the two of us and sliding down over me. Clenching her walls around me, she elicits a guttural growl from somewhere deep inside of me.

Gripping her hips, I hold on tight as she rocks against me. In all my life, I never knew sex could feel this good.

Sex has always been nothing more than that, just sex. But meeting Caleigh changed everything. Making love to her is the most euphoric experience. And I think at least part of that can be attributed to the feelings and emotions that go along with it. She isn't some random hook-up, some groupie that's only too willing to be used. Those chicks know what they're signing themselves up for in order to have one night with one of us. But Caleigh? She's different in every way. She owns my heart and soul.

Her breasts bounce, and her hair falls over them, so I sweep the strands back over her shoulders. I brush my thumbs across her nipples, making them pebble. She arches her back and reaches down to tease her clit with her middle finger as she keeps rocking back and forth.

"I ... love ... you ... Brent," she pants out.

Her head falls back, exposing her throat, so I trace the line of it with one hand, letting it slide to the swell of her breasts and down the valley between them.

Taking her hand in mine, I lean up and suck her finger into my mouth. Her head snaps up to watch what I'm doing. There's something about tasting her on her own hand that really turns me on. And by the look in her eyes, it affects her the same way.

"You're so beautiful."

"And you're incredible," she replies as she leans down to kiss me. It's a soft, sensual kiss. Her tongue dances gently with mine and it's like my heart takes flight.

Caleigh places her hands on my chest and uses that as leverage to move herself up and down, agonisingly slowly. Her nails dig into me and I relish the sting. She ups her pace and I buck my hips to meet hers. Building a punishing rhythm, she moans loudly as she gets closer and closer to the orgasm she's chasing.

Finally, she shouts out my name loud enough to wake the neighbours.

I waste no time as I roll her over and chase my own climax. It doesn't take long before I'm crying out her name.

As we relax, we lie next to each other in a tangle of limbs. My heart races faster than a galloping horse.

I breathe deeply and inhale the sweet scent of strawberries. I release a sigh and Caleigh looks up at me.

"Something wrong?" she asks quietly.

"No, baby, just the opposite."

I pull her closer and close my eyes. This is as close to heaven as a man can get on earth.

Epilogue

Caleigh

It's a beautiful day and Brent and Hardin are waiting for me to finish packing the hamper. We're going for a picnic in the park with Rhiannon, Lewis and Luna.

"Hey, Mummy, don't forget to pack the strawberries and cream," Hardin says as he runs in from the back garden.

"I won't, baby. I promise."

He goes back to play football with Brent, and I hear triumphant yelling—he must have scored a goal.

These are the days I live for. After Brent and I got together properly, Hardin and I moved in with him—after Hardin got to know him better, that is. The house that I wanted is finally my home, but more than that, it's *our* home. There's so much joy here, so much love. I can feel it all around me, all the time.

Brent and Lewis became good friends, much to the happiness of both me and Rhiannon. Now the six of us go on days out and take the children to theme parks. We've even got a holiday booked for all of us. Of course, it had to be somewhere pet-friendly, seeing as though Brent bought Hardin a border terrier that he called Tramp. All we need now is another dog to call Lady.

It took a lot of convincing for me to allow him to get Tramp. I've always said no pets, but we fell in love with his picture on the shelter's website and Brent wore me down until I finally caved.

"Are we nearly ready to go, boys?" I call from the back door.

"It's three-all mummy. Can I just score one more goal?"

"Okay, baby, just the one, otherwise Auntie Rhi will be on the phone nagging me for being late."

He tackles Brent for the ball and Brent trips, leaving the goal open. Hardin scores one last triumphant goal and squeals as he runs around, shouting that he's the winner and Brent's a loser.

I can't help but giggle as Brent gets up and pretends to limp to the door.

"Oh, you think that's funny, do you?" he asks as he picks me up and twirls me around.

I laugh louder until my phone rings and he has to put me down.

"See what you've done now?" I ask as I flash the screen at him, showing him Rhiannon's smiling face.

"Hey, babe," I answer.

"Where are you? We're already on our way and I haven't heard from you."

"Sorry, Rhi, the boys were playing football and I couldn't drag them away. We'll be leaving in five minutes."

"Okay, just hurry. I'm hungry."

"Well, you are eating for two now."

***

After a long drive, we pull up somewhere all too familiar. I thought we were going to the local park, but after driving past it, I questioned Brent about where we were heading. He wouldn't give me any clue and now I know why.

The river looks beautiful in the daylight. It's been too long since I've been here. Of course, I've visited my mum and dad, but we haven't exactly had a picnic on the riverbank.

I see Luna running around chasing Lewis before he picks her up and spins her around. I can't wait to meet the new baby. I know I'll love him or her just as much as I do Luna.

"Hey, you finally made it then," Rhi says as I place the hamper down before shaking the blanket out.

"Well, to be fair, I would have made sure we were ready sooner if I'd known we were going to drive for two hours."

"At least you're here now. Come on, sit down."

Brent helps me lower to the ground. Being fair, my bump is so big that I can't get up and down without help these days. I can't wait until the baby's here so I can move without looking and feeling like a penguin waddling around.

I unpack the hamper and Hardin comes to sit down beside Luna ready to eat. The two are as thick as thieves, and I can't help but wonder whether our daughter and Rhiannon's new baby will be as close.

"Hey, those strawberries are for after dinner," I say as Brent swipes one from the punnet and bites into it.

"I can't help it; strawberries are delicious. The scent, the taste, the juices …"

I feel myself blush as I take in the meaning of his words. I only ever use my strawberry shampoo now as he loves it so much. To be honest, I'd do just about anything for him.

***

Hardin and Luna are flying kites with Lewis and Brent while Rhi and I relax on the riverbank, soaking up the sun. It's pure bliss.

"Mummy, come fly a kite with me," Hardin says as he comes to stand next to me.

"Okay, baby."

Brent comes up from behind and helps me to my feet. He takes my hand as we walk over to where the kite is resting. I take the string that Brent hands me, while Hardin takes the kite and walks away, ready to let go as soon as I'm ready.

"Ready, Hardin?" I call.

"Okay, Mummy."

"Three … two … *one.*"

He lets go and the kite soars across the sky. I look up as something about the pattern catches my eye.

"Oh my god."

It's not a pattern after all. It says, "Marry Me?"

I turn to look at Brent and he's down on one knee. All of a sudden, Rhiannon takes the string from my hands and reels the kite in.

"Caleigh Rae Flynn, this last year with you has been the best year of my entire life. I've learned a lot about myself, because you have taught me to open my heart. I've never loved anyone until I found you. Together, our wounded hearts began to heal. While there may still be scars, we live and love in spite of them—or maybe *because* of them." He pauses to swallow as his eyes brim with unshed tears.

His hand is shaking as he holds the box aloft.

"Together we have everything we could ever want—*except* for one thing. There's one thing I want more than anything; I want to make you my wife. Caleigh, would you do me the greatest honour you could ever do me and become my wife?"

I feel tears streaming down my cheeks, but I don't care.

"Yes!" I squeal.

Brent takes the ring from the box and slips it onto my finger. I look at it for a moment and it's absolutely breathtaking.

In an instant, I'm wrapped in Brent's arms as his lips come crashing down over mine. His kiss is soft and sweet, just like him. My knees feel weak and my heart feels so light it could grow wings and fly away.

Mrs. Caleigh Rae Ryder. Why does that sound like the best thing I've ever heard?

"We have somewhere to be," Brent says as he breaks the kiss.

"We do?"

He takes me by the hand, and we leave the hampers and kites behind as we walk up the dirt path to the main road. We walk down towards The Lock and I see a banner hanging outside that says *Congratulations Caleigh and Brent.*

As we walk inside, I look around and see all my family and friends gathered around. I've never felt so happy that I could burst … until now.

My mum and dad are wearing matching smiles, as are Ash, Evan, Julia, Deb and Damien. They all applaud as we walk around the room to greet everyone.

"Let's see the ring," Julia says as she hugs me.

Holding out my hand, I show her the solitaire cut diamond. It's so big and clear and absolutely beautiful.

I still can't get over it. I'm engaged. It may be the second time in my life, but you can be damn well sure it's the *last.*

***

I said my story didn't begin with once upon a time. That I didn't meet Prince Charming, fall madly in love and live happily ever after.

Well, now you know that's … well, it's not a complete lie, because we had our hiccups along the way.

But one thing I know for sure—my story does come with a *happily ever after.*

The End

About the author

Keren is a bookworm whose bookshelves groan under the weight of her obsession, but she believes there's always room for "one more book." She lives in the UK with her son and when she isn't reading or writing, she's nurturing the reader and writer in him as he's currently writing his own book. Keren loves to connect with her readers. You can reach out to her on social media. She loves to talk anything books, movies and TV. Her other obsessions include Disney, Marvel, and she's a Potterhead for life.

Also by Keren Hughes

Safe
First of The Jagged Scars Duet series

In every way Elise is a survivor.

As a child, she was abused by the first man she trusted completely.

As a teenager, she was manipulated mentally and physically by a man, to the point that she could not see just how bad their relationship was. She ended up too scared to stay, but even more scared to leave.

Having suffered for years at the hands of men she trusted, she met Jensen. Finally, she felt that she had someone good in her life. Their relationship was all too brief, and when it ended she built a wall around her heart. How could she ever trust a man again?

Elise; a single, disabled mum. It was all too clear that men could not see past her disability. Forsaking the love of men, she concentrated on her son, Caleb. It was the one thing she knew she could do right. Her love for Caleb was beyond measure. He was her whole world. However, Elise's best friend Sam had other ideas, and set her up on a blind date with an extremely hot paramedic.

With so much hurt in the past, she was not sure if she was strong enough to face rejection again. Could she truly open her heart again to another? Could Elise finally find her safe haven in his arms, or would he just add another scar to her soul?

Home
Second of The Jagged Scars Duet series

~Home isn't a physical place, it's the place where your heart beats.~

Drew Wright always said he had the "reverse Midas touch"; everything he touched turned to shit instead of gold.

As a child, he was beaten, neglected, and abused by drug addicted parents whose next fix was more important than having food in the cupboard. Plagued by flashbacks of a past that haunts him, he's worked hard to become a paramedic and help others often caught in the grip of the same trauma he experienced.

After being set up on a blind date with the love of his life he thought he'd lost, it seemed his luck was turning and fate was giving him a second chance. Happily married with two children, he has everything he ever dreamed of.

But then one tragic moment throws his world into upheaval and lands Drew in the middle of a battle to hang on to the life he loves.

Can he separate the past from the present and save his future?

Or will the demons that have stalked him his whole life finally devour him?

Secret Santa

Being born and raised in the town of Snowflake has its perks for Aneurin Mackenzie, she's seen it all; businesses booming and the town flourishing. Sadly, she's also seen it torn to shreds by a previous mayor.

Then, in comes cocky, arrogant, filthy rich Preston Wolfric III with his "fresh ideas" to bring business back to this small town. He wants to turn Snowflake around, bringing it to the 21st century.

However, Nye will not let her town be changed without a fight.

He's a big city alpha male, she's a small town girl with no desire to change. She plans to run him out of town but what she doesn't count on is that cocky jerk making his way under her skin, seeping into her veins.

She didn't realise how devastatingly handsome he is. He didn't realise what he needed was right in front of him.

What will happen when Preston and Nye's worlds collide? Will there be sparks or will it become a fire that lays waste to everything they thought they knew?

Do opposites really attract?

Out of the Ashes

After the divorce from hell, Jenna Morgan swears off men. But could the town "bad boy" Nate, be the one to make her break that oath?

Freeing herself from the constraints of her ex, she decides to do the one thing she always wanted to but was never allowed; get a tattoo.

Nate Peterson is the town bad boy and owner of the Blank Canvas tattoo parlour. Walking into his shop could change her life forever.

At a speed-dating event, Jenna meets the business-savvy lawyer, Levi. Surely it couldn't hurt to go on one date, with both men?

Conflicted by the choice, she sees and feels herself falling for the boy from the wrong side of the tracks.

After a couple of crazy months together, a tragedy tears them apart. Nate finds himself pushing everyone away, including Jenna.

Realising his momentous mistake, Nate wants to win her back. But can he earn her trust again? Did he destroy everything he wanted but never knew he needed?

Will fate help push the pair back together or will it tear them asunder?

Husband Material

When you're alone over the holidays, with overbearing parents, what else are you meant to do except ask a random person you meet in the airport to be your fake spouse? Joss and Stone hatch a plan to be each other's plus-one to family events, then when it's all over, they'll go their separate ways. They're not hurting anybody, right? When they arrive at Stone's family home, Joss builds a pillow wall between them in bed. But what can Stone do to bring down her walls, emotional and physical? Neither can deny the burning attraction, but they barely know each other from Adam. They can never be anything other than fake husband and wife... can they?

Paper Hearts

Winter and Devlyn are polar opposites, but they do say opposites attract. As their eyes meet across a crowded room, there are sparks, but will those sparks become a flame? And if there is a fire, is there anything anyone can do to extinguish it?

Winter's ex thinks he can. He has plans for the pair and one goal in mind; win back Winter's heart. With Simon's games, will the pair be able to overcome the insurmountable?

An undeniable chemistry lures Winter and Devlyn together, but when tragedy strikes, will it tear them apart or will it only make their bond stronger?

More Than Words

Evie

Taking my daughter with me, I moved far away from my

hometown. I wanted to leave my past behind. I was not looking for a relationship. Love had got me nowhere, just pain and darkness, heartbreak and disappointment.

Suddenly a shard of light brightened my world. Trey showed me compassion, love, and had broken down the walls I had tried so hard to build. My worry is, will the darkness I have been trying to hide from come back to haunt us.

Trey

Abused, neglected, broken and rejected; this was my life in foster care with my younger sister Leah. I had been trying to protect her all my teenage years, but she took her own life. I was devastated by the loss and determined to make something of myself. After school, I studies law, and as a solicitor I helped survivors of domestic abuse.

I never thought I'd find love and then I met Evie. Her strength amazed me; she juggled her life as a single mom and owning a business. We were drawn together, but Evie had her secrets and I had mine. Together we are strong. But are we strong enough?

More Black Velvet Seductions titles

Their Lady Gloriana by Starla Kaye
Cowboys in Charge by Starla Kaye
Her Cowboy's Way by Starla Kaye
Punished by Richard Savage, Nadia Nautalia & Starla Kaye
Accidental Affair by Leslie McKelvey
Right Place, Right Time by Leslie McKelvey
Her Sister's Keeper by Leslie McKelvey
Playing for Keeps by Glenda Horsfall
Playing By His Rules by Glenda Horsfall
The Stir of Echo by Susan Gabriel
Rally Fever by Crea Jones
Behind The Clouds by Jan Selbourne
Trusting Love Again by Starla Kaye
Runaway Heart by Leslie McKelvey
The Otherling by Heather M. Walker
First Submission - Anthology
These Eyes So Green by Deborah Kelsey
Dark Awakening by Karlene Cameron
The Reclaiming of Charlotte Moss by Heather M. Walker
Ryann's Revenge by Rai Karr & Breanna Hayse
The Postman's Daughter by Sally Anne Palmer
Final Kill by Leslie McKelvey
Killer Secrets by Zia Westfield
Crossover, Texas by Freia Hooper-Bradford
The Caretaker by Carol Schoenig
The King's Blade by L.J. Dare
Uniform Desire - Anthology
Safe by Keren Hughes
Finishing the Game by M.K. Smith
Out of the Shadows by Gabriella Hewitt
A Woman's Secret by C.L. Koch
Her Lover's Face by Patricia Elliott
Naval Maneuvers by Dee S. Knight
Perilous Love by Jan Selbourne
Patrick by Callie Carmen
The Brute and I by Suzanne Smith

Home by Keren Hughes
Only A Good Man Will Do by Dee S. Knight
Secret Santa by Keren Hughes
Killer Lies by Zia Westfield
A Merman's Choice by Alice Renaud
All She Ever Needed by Lora Logan
Nicolas by Callie Carmen
Paging Dr. Turov by Gibby Campbell
Out of the Ashes by Keren Hughes
A Thread of Sand by Alan Souter
Stolen Beauty by Piper St. James
Mystic Desire - Anthology
Killer Deceptions by Zia Westfield
Edgeplay by Annabel Allan
Music for a Merman by Alice Renaud
Joseph by Callie Carmen
Not You Again! by Patricia Elliott
The Unveiling of Amber by Viola Russell
Husband Material by Keren Hughes
Never Have I Ever by Julia McBryant
Hard Limits by Annabel Allan
Anthony by Callie Carmen
Paper Hearts by Keren Hughes
The King's Spy by L.J. Dare
More Than Words by Keren Hughes & Jodie Harrold
Lessons on Seduction by Estelle Pettersen
Rigged by Annabel Allan
Desire Me Again - Anthology
Mermaids Marry in Green by Alice Renaud
Holy Matchmaker by Nancy Golinski
Joshua by Callie Carmen

Our back catalog is being released on Kindle Unlimited
You can find us on:
Twitter: BVSBooks
Facebook: Black Velvet Seductions
See our bookshelf on Amazon now! Search "BVS Black Velvet
Seductions Publishing Company"

www.ingramcontent.com/pod-product-compliance
Lightning Source LLC
Chambersburg PA
CBHW050722180626
46814CB00002B/564

* 9 781912 768974 *